She

"Wh[...] over Will's lips, "nothing could make the pain go away."

He breathed against her, as if he also couldn't believe she was with him. "I'm not about to leave you, Kat," he said, voice low and tortured. "Not when we could finally get what we deserve out of life."

She was beyond wondering exactly what he meant by that, if he was talking about the money she stood to inherit or if he was genuinely wishing they could be together again. Who cared right now? *Why* care?

But what if all this emotion had only been brought on by the terror of the boat wreck, the island....

The killer.

Kat locked her arms around him, rocking in cadence to a faint alarm signal that was growing louder, louder....

Danger. Danger. Danger....

Dear Reader,

Believe it or not, I turned in a blurb for a "deserted island" story months before *Lost* became a TV hit. I wanted to write about a Japanese pearl diver because, when I was just a tyke, I used to love this exhibit at Sea World—an attraction that, sadly, was shut down years ago. But I never forgot the female divers (or the pearls!). On a visit to Japan, I took a minitrip to Mikimoto's Pearl Island, where I was lucky enough to see an ama exhibition (and buy pearls, natch). But something was missing from my ama-gets-shipwrecked story…and my editor, Susan Litman, provided the extra kick: Why not make this a mystery? I loved that, and this book was born.

So get ready to play a very deadly game of *Survivor* with Katsu Espinoza, an Everygirl Bombshell. Thank you so much for reading about her adventures!

Crystal Green

Crystal Green

BAITED

Published by Silhouette Books

America's Publisher of Contemporary Romance

 SILHOUETTE BOOKS

ISBN-13: 978-0-373-51426-7
ISBN-10:   0-373-51426-3

BAITED

www.SilhouetteBombshell.com

Printed in U.S.A.

CRYSTAL GREEN

lives near Las Vegas, Nevada, where she writes for the Silhouette Special Edition, Silhouette Bombshell and Harlequin Blaze lines. She loves to read, overanalyze movies, do yoga and write about her travels and obsessions on her Web site, www.crystal-green.com. There, you can read about her trips on Route 66, as well as her visits to Japan and Italy.

She'd love to hear from her readers by e-mail through the "Contact Crystal" feature on her Web page.

To Pamela Harty.
Thank heavens for the day you and Deidre took
me into the family of your agency.
I appreciate all you do.

Prologue

As another scream tore through the island forest, Katsu Espinoza stopped in her tracks, trying to get a lock on where the sound was coming from.

The pulse in her head kicked to a deafening beat while she lifted her face to the gray sky, panting, blinking as a drop of rain bled from a palm frond and splashed onto her forehead. She tightened her grip on the long screwdriver in her hand—the best weapon she'd been able to scrounge from their meager store of supplies back at the cave.

Please, Kat thought, *prayed*, please give me another sign to follow.

Even if the sign was another tortured yell that would let her find the next victim—whoever it was—before it was too late.

At the same time, she wished for silence. God knew what the killer was doing to the screamer. From what she and the other survivors had seen of the previous victims, she didn't want to guess.

Blood running to the ground from the mutilations…
Eyes staring in dead terror at nothing…
Mouths open in silent cries…

Kat shut her eyes against a surge of nausea, but the vivid red images of flesh kept stabbing into her.

One victim.

Two.

Three…

Murder. A killer in the midst of a group of people she'd set out on a boat tour with only days ago. It'd started off so innocently, just like any other morning where you got out of bed, brushed your teeth, ate your breakfast and did your thing.

But then the storm. The wreckage. This island.

Even now, she couldn't believe what a nightmare the harmless little cage-diving expedition had turned out to be. Couldn't believe a person like her—a normal girl whose biggest problems included endlessly paying off old credit-card debt and navigating a hapless love life—was actually chasing down a killer.

But all that was behind her, a hazy dream that was just as out of reach as the thought of being rescued from whatever nameless piece of land they now existed on.

As Kat waited, a flash of lightning flickered, whitening the sky and the forest around her. A rumble of thunder shook the air, then the chop of her own labored breathing. Tiny explosions of raindrops on leaves echoed her crazy heartbeat while she stood braced, ready to run toward…

Another shriek: *Nooooo…aaaahhhhh!*

Startled, adrenaline sparked her forward, toward the sound.

Ohgod, ohgod, ohgod…

Kat took hold of the screwdriver as if it were an ice pick and charged forward, parting the vegetation, dodging leaves, tripping over vines and sloshing through the mud.

The cry ripped her in two, because part of her wanted to help but the very average I'm-not-a-super-hero part only wanted to stay alive.

Before she could really think about what she was doing, she stumbled into a clearing, screwdriver poised.

Opposite her, the newest victim sat slumped against the trunk of a tree, blood and raindrops mingling on a terrified face. His mouth, gaped open, still held a frozen yawp for mercy. His hands were wrenched behind the tree—obviously tied. When the victim spotted her, he leaned forward, eyes widening.

Lips forming a soundless word.

Help.

Kat hitched in a breath as she took a sharp look around. Dark foliage. Quickening raindrops. A body…*two* bodies…sprawled in the high grass to her right.

Legs turning to slush, she dragged her gaze away and fought to walk to the victim. Still, she couldn't help eyeing the bodies, trying to see who they were.

Or who they used to be.

Careful, she told herself. What if this newest sacrifice is hiding something behind his back? What if he's the killer, and he's tricking you, luring you into something you won't be able to handle?

Don't trust anybody.

"Who did this to you?" Kat whispered, crouching. She still had the screwdriver ready, just in case.

The victim's eyes weren't focusing, and she could tell he was struggling to stay conscious. Could she get him back to the caves in time so they could be saved?

The next blinding second, the victim's gaze fixed on something behind Kat, mouth falling open again... But it wasn't to answer Kat's question.

His blood-rimmed mouth was starting to scream.

Dread flew up Kat's spine. Blinded by panic, she instinctively grabbed a handful of mud, preparing to whip around to throw it in the face of whoever was at her back, then follow up with the screwdriver. She'd fought in too many brawls back home to lose her street sense. It was second nature to strike first.

But she never had the chance.

Chapter 1

Kat knew it was going to be a long day the second Yoko Nakamura muttered, "scum" and tripped her as they entered the Neptune Point Pearl-Diving Show boat.

Kat decided to ignore her self-appointed rival, instead taking position at the back of the small, open-sided vessel. Once there, she adjusted the sexed-up *ama* uniform—an *isogi*—that Neptune Point made her wear for the entertainment of the tourists who visited the San Diego theme park. The garb featured an almost-puritanical white hood, but when the isogi's long-sleeved white shirt and extended wraparound skirt got wet, the costume turned transparent. Anything for the sake of entertainment, right? But the effect was a far cry from what a traditional Japanese pearl diver would have looked like back in the heyday of the trade.

Yet it wasn't like Kat was here to sell *truth*. Hell, she wasn't even a full-blooded, one hundred percent natural Japanese girl herself—not with all her dad's Mexican-American genes running willy-nilly all over her facial features and under her skin. Nope. Her job was to present a fantasy, to whet appetites so the crowds would shuffle from the observation bleachers and into the cultured-pearl shop after the show, spending their hard-earned cash on things she could never even dream of affording. Things like blue seed-pearl necklaces, creamy bracelets, exquisite rings.

Tracy Ito, wonder-roomie and best friend, took her spot in between Kat and Yoko, and their driver took off from the prep dock toward the entrance of the Pearl Lagoon. Tracy was also fully garbed in *ama* finery.

"Think you can chill out today, Yoko?" Tracy asked.

The other diver ignored Tracy, concentrating on smoothing out her own *isogi* instead. Kat had been enduring problems with Yoko ever since her rival had joined the shift a couple of weeks ago. She hated Kat for a hundred reasons: mostly because Kat had beat Yoko out for the lead diver position—and the slight raise that went with it. A prideful Yoko had taken this to heart. She was constantly messing with Kat under-water, snatching oysters from under her grasp to make sure she had a higher count in the unofficial, normally playful daily competition to see who could bring up the most booty. No bones about it—Yoko was determined to position herself to take over Kat's job when the time came.

A meaningless rivalry, Kat thought. But Yoko's dislike was also more personal.

Light-skinned and so very Japanese on the calm surface, Yoko had reportedly lived in the U.S. for about six years—it'd been enough time for her to develop a Yankee-style habit of "keeping it real" and expressing her true opinions, unlike a more tempered girl from her old country would. Back home she would've been encouraged to hide her racial disgust of Kat in public. But here, in this country? Nah.

Yoko finished fussing with her uniform then shot Kat a cool sidelong glance. Three guesses as to what was coming next.

"*Eta*," Yoko mouthed without giving voice to the insult.

Finally past her limit, Kat made a move toward the other woman, only to be held back by the levelheaded Tracy.

Good thing, because anyone familiar with Japan knew what *eta* meant. In spite of Kat's limited knowledge of her Japanese mother's culture, she knew it was a slur for a social underclass known as *burakumin*, a taboo subject no one dared discuss in polite company. *Burakumin* were considered unclean in part because of their blood-related professions: leatherworkers, slaughterhouse workers, and the like.

Scum of the earth, Kat thought. That's what her mother's family had been. And that's why Mom had jumped at the chance to marry Lieutenant Joe Espinoza, who'd whisked her out of Japan and into the golden country of Disney and Levi's jeans—the culture Mariko Okamoto had worshipped.

Little had she known that, after she died, her own mixed-blood daughter would suffer in America just as Mariko had in Japan, nicked by slurs that were just as hurtful.

Not that Katsu would *ever* let anyone know that.

"*Eta*," Kat said, testing the word and calming down only because she knew it would nettle Yoko. Their boat glided nearer the lagoon. "I don't know, Tracy. I kind of prefer what the kids in middle school used to call me."

Tracy, ever the willing straight man, didn't miss her cue. "And what *did* they call you?"

"Spic-anese." Kat nodded proudly. "Has a more clever ring to it, don't you think?"

"Definitely a keeper."

Predictably, a flustered Yoko quickly flipped both of them off, and, as they rounded the corner into the lagoon, slid her hands into a graceful two-handed wave aimed at the audience.

"What a pill," Tracy whispered, also morphing into super *ama*, speaking through her smile and waving at the crowd while keeping her head slightly lowered in an act of submission and shyness.

Kat followed suit, liking her job—and the decent paycheck—too much to play Yoko's destructive game right now. "Water off my back—that's all she is."

They circled the rim of the small arena, making sure to push the stereotype of the adorable Asian doll to its fullest. Hey, it was in their job descriptions and it paid the bills. If they'd been real *ama*, they would've presented a different picture: Their bodies would've been muscular and maybe even chubby, the better to keep warm against the water. Their hair would've been shorter and their skin tanned by the open elements. Actually, the Neptune Point Pearl Divers looked more like geisha than laborers; they were made up to be slender, petite, quiet, pale.

At least from a distance.

Under the *isogi*, Kat was anything but the cliché. Even if she applied waterproof cosmetics to lighten her complexion, in her off hours she proudly wore the slight rosy-tan skin she'd gotten from her dad. Her almond-shaped brown eyes were just a little wider than the other *amas*', but she'd inherited her mother's delicate chin, gently shaped cheekbones and tea-brown hair, which Kat wore to her shoulders. The white costume hid a streamlined body, chiseled by hobbies such as surfing and skin-diving.

A twenty-four-year-old water baby and good ol' American melting pot. A mixture of everything life had thrown at her.

Tracy chatted as the boat putted by the audience. "Hey, look, your boyfriend's here."

Kat scanned the front row, finding an older, too-thin man wearing a baseball cap, a tiki-print shirt and sunglasses. He was hunched over, leaning his forearms on his khakied thighs.

"Boyfriend?" Kat asked. "Duke?"

"You've spent enough time with him these past

months. I don't know, Kat, I'd totally go for your new pal, if I were you, even if he *is* old. The guy's loaded and a sugar daddy could pay off those debts of yours. Know what I mean?"

"Nice, Tracy." Kat didn't know what else to say. Her quick friendship with Duke Harrington couldn't be debated under a modest smile or even in the few seconds they had before the lagoon show really began.

He was someone to hang with. A mentor. And Duke liked to drop into the pearl-diving scene every once in a while to watch her work and take slow walks through the park. Just enjoying life while he could.

Kat offered him a welcoming wave, but he responded a little stiffly. Her heart jolted.

Was it a bad day, like the ones she'd seen him suffer through before he'd had stomach surgery and gone on the new medication? And here she'd thought that this round of treatment was supposed to be helping.

The smell of gasoline and ocean wind accompanied the gurgle of the boat's cut engine. As the show's announcer began her presentation—a spiel aimed at convincing the masses to buy pearls—the *amas* dipped into the murky lagoon constructed for the exhibition. Before each diving session, technicians transferred oysters from a pearl farm to the water, making Kat's job a smooth one.

Four times a day and then home to check the surf report. She had a beautiful life.

She swam to the side of the boat and grabbed a small, open barrel-shaped basket and tied it to herself. It would float next to her, a receptacle for oysters. After fixing a mask over her face, she sliced forward, pushing the basket in front of her as the emcee's happy voice filled the arena.

"The *ama,* who dive for everything from seaweed, abalone, shellfish, lobster, sea urchins and octopus to oysters, are usually female in Japan. It's said that perhaps women can withstand the stress of the cold water better than men, or perhaps they're more capable of conserving heat."

Kat took one last look at Duke, glad for every day he could be here. Glad that his stomach cancer hadn't physically barred him from coming to her shows...*yet*.

Just before Kat dove, Yoko swam to the spot next to her.

"*Eta,*" she said again, diving under.

Frustration singed through Kat's chest, but she quelled it. Dammit, she'd spent most of her life here in the States blowing off the comments of prejudiced ignoramuses, so why was one stupid word from a jealous cow like Yoko bothering her?

She wouldn't let it.

Kat hesitated only a moment, staring at the water, just like she did with every dive, building her confidence.

Every time you go under, you win, she thought.

No fear. No problem.

After a deep breath, she dove headfirst, heart in her throat, caught in a silken web of excitement and wariness.

Silence enveloped her as she darted down, propelled by well-worked muscles. She was at home now, cradled by liquid comfort, suspended in a hushed womb where nothing could touch her. Here, she could feel her dad's presence again, his own love of the ocean all around her. It was the only place she could channel him now, the only place that cushioned the pain of losing him…and the failure of their relationship.

As she floated farther downward, Kat was alert enough to realize that the deep was also a dark place, hiding danger behind every shift of light. A foreign world where she didn't really belong, no matter what she told herself.

It was a capsule of contradiction, mixed emotion.

Unfathomable.

The blue-green depths were beautifully eerie, lending to the welcome uneasiness. She loved everything about the water—the sounds, the legends, the freedom. Diving was a chance for tranquility, a chance to prove that she could beat the odds and conquer the heavy crush of bad memories, memories of a time when the ocean had almost beaten *her.*

Since the *ama* generally tried not to dive for longer than a minute—who needed hypoxia to end a diving career?—Kat paced herself.

Pulse fluttering, heightening her senses to giddiness, she cruised over to a rock where an oyster had been deposited. At about the sixty-second mark, she retrieved two more, then aimed her body toward the surface.

With a slight pop-splash, she broke the waterline, put the oysters into her barrel and took a second to recover while hanging on to the floating basket. Over the emcee's droning speech, her breathing sang like a whistle. To the untrained ear, it was alarming, but her lungs and heart were the better for it.

Next to Kat, Yoko was hanging on to her own barrel and watching her.

As the announcer told the audience about how Kokichi Mikimoto, industry pioneer, had created the type of *ama* uniform they were now garbed in here at Neptune Point, Kat took another dive. Then, after that, two others.

On the last dive, fifteen seconds disappeared in a flow of growing peace and self-esteem. She held her breath, triumphing.

You're beating the water again, she thought as she fetched her oysters. *Every dive makes you stronger.*

Focused on her task, Kat barely felt it when a hand levered down on her head.

In the back of her mind, she knew it was Yoko trying a new, more effective method of jarring Kat out of the way as she grabbed for the oysters that Kat was holding.

Yoko didn't usually make bodily contact.

But…damn—*damn*! There was something about the pressure on her skull, the claustrophobic weight heaving her down.

As faint as the push was, its power roared over Kat like a storm wave, pinning her, mentally freezing her limbs into helpless stumps.

In slow time, she felt the oysters slip from her hand, felt Yoko pushing off her body in a lunge for the booty. As Kat instinctively opened her mouth, a bubble of treasured air escaped upward, lost to the water.

Panic bathed her, a terrible memory wiping over her eyes—the one from years ago, the one she fought with every dive: water, so gorgeous and deadly and blue as it sheened over her like a glass ceiling. Waves, ebbing, flowing, as Kat, who was only nine, lay on the bottom of the ocean, trapped by the undertow.

Debilitating fear. A few moments that seemed like hours.

But the horrific serenity was slashed wide open as the pressure of the tide spat her back out of the water, coughing, gripping for breath. Her dad had rushed to her side, helping her to expel the water from her lungs, carrying her to a threadbare towel where he dried her and whispered an urgent pep talk of recovery.

Now, as she remembered, she could feel the water seeping into her like a transfusion of cold blood. It became a part of her, almost like the sea hadn't forgotten. She'd been stolen from the ocean once, and it was taking her back, wasn't it? Taking her...

No. No it wasn't.

With an explosion of energy, Kat frantically lashed out with her clawed fingers, blindly catching Yoko as she grabbed for the falling oysters.

Kat choked on a gasp of water, then, quickly shutting her mouth, latched on to Yoko's arm. The other diver's eyes widened under her mask, like they always did when she acted surprised that someone was freaking out about something she considered quite minor.

Breath...air...need...air...

Suddenly, the water was a trap, a box. Kat dug

through it, trying to reach the surface, craving the open sky wavering beyond the flowing barrier.

Reach...up...air...

She burst upward with a screeching gasp, falling and hunching over her basket, wheezing. As she whipped off her mask, quivers wracked her limbs, and she tasted something sour in the back of her throat.

"—gift shop where you can see the luster and spellbinding splendor of the pearl," said the deliriously perky emcee. "Thank you for the honor of your company."

Applause leaked from an audience who couldn't have seen the details of what had happened beneath the water, even though they could sure as hell see one majorly dazed *ama* now.

Weakly, Kat turned her head toward Yoko, who'd also surfaced, taken off her mask, and a second later, begun to swim madly for the boat.

Like *that* was going to get her away from Kat.

Anger took over, helping Kat to reach the deepest strengths in herself. When she caught up to Yoko, she made damned sure they were sheltered from the audience's view.

Yoko only had time to hold up a palm in mercy. "I didn't mean to—"

Kat surged through the water and clamped her hands against the boat, caging Yoko, her face only an inch away.

"You want to bully me?" Kat clenched her teeth.

The other woman closed her eyes.

"Then expect me to fight back."

* * *

"You don't take any guff, do you?" Duke said. His voice, which, imaginably, once had possessed the strength of a hero in a jungle safari film, was now thready—hardly the bark of a man who'd conquered the world.

It was later that day, and they were sitting in their half wet suits on the beach, their sticks—surfboards—abandoned right now even though the conditions offshore were perfect. The five-foot waves curled into barrels that Kat was yearning to pipe.

Duke's smooth, bald head absorbed the early-September sunset. He'd been waiting for Kat on shore for his twice-a-week "lesson." Even though he wouldn't get around to catching anything today—he never did—Kat knew that Duke enjoyed watching her carve the waves more than anything else. They never talked about the fact that he was too unhealthy to be in the water. It was hard to admit, especially since the sixty-five-year-old's hazel eyes still glittered with desperate vitality, the line of his jaw hinting at the wild adventurer he used to be.

But even shaken by his cancer, Duke still wanted to believe that he could climb mountains, surf and basically accomplish everything he wanted to before he died. And Kat never disagreed with him.

"Screw what happened with Yoko," Kat said. "You're not looking so hot today. Isn't the new medication—?"

"It's working fine, don't worry. Been a harder day than most though." His thin voice was wry, amused.

"And let's not 'screw' what happened with Yoko, Kat. Suddenly your livelihood is in question. Locker-room brawls with coworkers don't go over well with most bosses."

Kat shrugged. "It wasn't a *brawl*, just an energetic talking-to. And, don't worry, I'm only under review with pay for a few weeks. At least I'm not fired like Yoko."

After Kat had offered her coworker a scathing crash course in manners, Yoko had once again emphasized that she hadn't meant to hurt Kat, that she'd only wanted to make everyone see that *she* deserved to be in Kat's lead position. Losing face in Yoko's culture was a huge deal, which made Kat wonder why it didn't matter so much to her, too.

Probably because her Japanese mom had died when she was only three. Probably because Kat hadn't been raised to really *have* a culture since all ritual and ethnic identity had been erased when her mother had passed on. Her dad hadn't been much on teaching her about any of that, either.

"I can give you a loan to keep you feeling secure in case you do get fired after this suspension," Duke said, grinning. "Come on, you know I'm good for it."

Temptation chewed at her. But…no. Her pride would eat her alive if she gave in.

"No more offers, okay?" Kat said.

"All right, it's rescinded." Duke sighed and slumped over, arms on knees. "If I didn't have a rule about getting persuasive with women, I'd…"

"Is that what they call it nowadays? 'Getting persua-sive'?"

They relaxed and laughed at her deft switch of topic. During all their beachside conversations, Duke had revealed that he wasn't into dating, not since his wife had passed away years ago. Not since he'd sworn off that notorious party rep: the hard drinking and smoking, the womanizing, the decadence that had earned him the headline nickname of Ride-'em-Hard Playboy.

Actually, he'd told her he'd rather spend his time setting his world to rights instead of setting some poor woman up for heartbreak when his time ran out. Besides, he seemed perfectly happy hanging out with Kat. Somehow, she'd become the symbol of youth for Edward "Duke" Harrington III, a way for him to make up for everything he hadn't made time to do, a reminder of healthy days wasted away. There were times when she also suspected that he felt normal with her, that he could forget all the billions of dollars he had in the bank and all the grief that went with it.

But…a loan from Duke? No way. She didn't like the idea of owing anyone anything. She'd already gotten into enough trouble with credit-card companies but at least they were faceless. It'd be too uncomfortable knowing Duke had something to hold over her, friends or not.

"I'll work the economics out," Kat said, drawing in the sand with a forefinger. "I've been thinking of getting a second job anyway."

"I'm sure I have an opening at one of my companies."

She gave him an exasperated look. "And maybe one day I'll get up enough cojones to take you up on a training offer." Just as soon as she could convince herself that she could succeed in a world like his.

As if.

The mellow growl of waves rolling in and then fizzing to foam paused their conversation.

She was going to get herself on her own feet financially, even if she was just about broke right now. Hell, she'd been the one who'd naively accepted every credit card that'd been sent to her after she'd graduated from high school and gotten her first job at Mickey D's. It'd been free money, right? Uh-huh. Now she had to take responsibility for her own stupidity. Anyway, she was used to being broke, having grown up in one of San Diego's "upper hoods." On the south side of the 8 freeway, she'd learned to live without frills under the care of a father who gambled too much, always leaving them scrambling.

"That chip on your shoulder is showing," Duke said.

And it's probably going to stay right where it is, she thought. It's who I am, even if I try hard not to spit much slang or be that girl from the block.

"That chip gives me character," she said, laughing.

"Yes, it does. You've got spark, Kat." It was a mantra he used whenever she revealed her lack of self-confidence. His pale face was highlighted by the sunset, the waning light showing the lines of exhaustion, the tired fight of someone on his last leg home. "You're the best, whether you know it or not."

She nodded, throat suddenly tight. Figures that one of the only people who never made her feel out of place, one who actually made her think she could be more than she was, would be leaving her so soon after she found him.

A couple of regulars walked by, boards under their arms, wet suits halfway undone to their waists to reveal muscled, tanned chests. One, a brunet with pale eyes and a killer bod, jerked his chin at Kat with masculine nonchalance. Thrown off guard, she glanced at the picture she'd scribbled in the sand.

It didn't resemble anything, the picture. Broken lines and squiggles. Kind of like the state of her life.

Silence roared at her, and she peeked up at Duke, who was staring at her with an unreadable softness in his gaze. He looked away then nodded toward the departing surfer.

"He wanted to say something to you."

"Like what? Let's get married?" Kat was all of a sudden uncomfortable. "Like that's my style."

"It could be if you'd stop hanging around with old men and get out there. Ever since Will…"

"Man, I am *never* telling you about my dating life again." Maybe it'd been the way he'd said it or… Kat wasn't sure. She just knew that the subject was unsettling, especially since he was right.

During the four months since he'd first seen her surfing and wandered right on up out of the clear blue sky and asked her to teach him, she'd made the mistake of telling him about her ex-boyfriend and all her non-romantic romances before. It was one of his "crusades," to learn to ride waves, he'd said, not that he ever felt well enough to actually go out and catch one.

She'd accepted his explanation nevertheless, feeling

a little greedy because he insisted on paying her for the lessons. Intuitively, she knew that denying him this obvious pleasure would take away the pleased gleam in his gaze, and she couldn't do that. Instead, she listened to his exciting stories, marveling at the experiences of his healthier days, like exploring rain forests and living in unindustrialized countries to get "the next big idea" for his Trump-esque empire, which included everything from real estate to redeveloping businesses in corporate makeovers or something like that.

Kat had always wanted to learn more about his successes, and also to take his cue and experience life beyond her own neighborhood. So she'd accepted a lot of his more downscale invitations to tour his companies, to talk with marine biologists at UCSD, to *learn*.

And she was grateful. This kindhearted man had brought new meaning to her life. But she was also aware of her faint fear of disappointing him, of staying in the same rut just because it was easier.

"Even though you're refusing everything," Duke said, bringing her back to the moment, "I've been meaning to talk to you about a different proposition. Something for your education, Kat."

Her education? "What?"

"Sharks. The ocean. Another opportunity for knowledge."

She just stared at the optimistic, crazy sparkle in his watery eyes. His impetuous ideas, his never-ending mental youth, tugged at her. God, how she wanted to

grow up to be like Duke—caring, giving, kept alive by
joy and the refusal to accept defeat.

"I'm chartering a boat out to Isla de Guadalupe, off
the coast of Baja California," he said. "Cage-diving. A
five-day trip. Hell, you're basically on vacation while
Neptune Point reviews what happened with Yoko
anyway, right?"

"Yeah, but—"

Duke's shaky sigh cut her off. Its world-weary tone
spoke volumes. "It'd be a great experience."

Closing her eyes, Kat tried to shut out the thought
of how, these past few months, Duke had eased his way
into the place of a father who'd died unexpectedly
when she was eighteen. She would've given anything
to have had time with him before he was gone, to have
spent every waking second making that dying man
happy.

Not for the first time, Kat wondered why Duke was
being so kind to her. It was something that made her a
little uncomfortable to mull over. They were friends,
right? An older man and a younger woman could
manage that. He'd never made any advances toward her
and, truthfully, she dreaded having to face that kind of
situation. All she knew was that most of Duke's family
had been distant until his recent illness, and she loved
the thought of having a surrogate family like Duke for
herself. Theirs was a symbiotic relationship—good for
them both.

"I'm taking Chris, also," Duke said. "He's on a
shark kick right now."

His grandson and ward. An orphaned thirteen-year-old who looked at Kat like she was the end-all-be-all every time Duke brought him for a surfing lesson. He was one of Kat's worst soft spots besides Duke.

"No fair." Kat took some sand and playfully tossed it at her friend's leg. "You know I can't resist that kid."

"Then pack up. We can get an expert from the Shark Study Institute on board, the finest gourmet food, spectacular staterooms—"

Tempting. *God*, it'd be so tempting if she could just tell herself that he was inviting her as a friend and nothing else. But then she thought of a trip to the middle of the ocean, surrounded by blue. Peace, danger. She thought of how her dad would've loved such an adventure with her, if he'd had the money or time for it.

In her mind's eye, she saw him scooting out the front door, on the way to Viejas Casino. "I can't go to the pool with you today, Kat," he'd say. "See ya later though?"

Then she saw him the way she preferred: guiding her over the surface of the public pool as she floated on her back, the sun splashing over her face. "You're a born water baby, Kat," he'd say. "Like dad, like daughter."

As the memory drifted off she tried to cling to it, but it just disintegrated, like all the possibilities between them.

Duke's voice took the place of her father's. "You want to go. I can tell."

He was right. And since when was she going to let a little thing like discomfort get to her? "I guess I can deal with real life when I get back."

"Good. Good. I like your attitude. But, for now, just have some fun, okay? You deserve it after your day."

Shaking her head, she resigned herself to giving in.

Like it was a hard choice, she thought, going on a cruise to make Duke's day. What a sacrifice.

Little did she know just how much of one it would turn out to be.

Chapter 2

At 8:00 a.m. on the day of the trip, Kat was the first in her party to board the *M. Falcon,* a 112-foot luxury sport-fishing-and-diving vessel complete with eight crew members, docked at Fisherman's Landing.

A deckhand with brown dreadlocks named Larry carried her belongings while Hugh the steward led her to a stateroom decorated in mahogany, teak, brass and tasteful artwork depicting marine sunsets. There was a double lower berth for her to sleep on, her own head and shower, plus a color TV with a DVD player. He told her that they had a library complete with movies and books, too.

Not bad, she thought, unpacking her bag as Larry closed the door. She'd already stored the diving gear

Duke had rented on the upper deck after meeting Shaw, the first officer; Tink, another deckhand; Wayne, the medic; Linda, the chef and Jason, the engineer. She was anxious, feeling like a kid playing hooky from school and wondering, once again, how the *ama* show was going without her.

Instead of pearl-diving these past two weeks, Kat had been amusing herself by going to counseling with Neptune Point's human resources for "confronting" Yoko. But she hardly felt punished. She'd also been spending a lot of time with Duke, polishing up her diving skills on his dime.

Kat plopped to her berth, spreading out her arms as her back hit the mattress. She inhaled the air, the hint of must and polished wood, then tuned in to the creak of the boat as it bobbed. Duke was paying for everything, and as grateful as she was, it got to her. Still, she could tell he was happy.

Again, she tried not to think about why. Duke was a buddy, right?

A swift knock interrupted her thoughts.

"Yeah?"

A muffled voice answered. "It's your captain, here to officially welcome you aboard."

"Oh." Kat zipped upward, scooted toward the edge of her berth, eager to meet the only crew member who hadn't greeted her yet. "Come in."

As the door swung open, she prepared herself for the sight of a sea dog: an aged skipper with a sailor's hat at a jaunty angle and a squint to rival Popeye's.

But what she got instead robbed her of a heartbeat.

A tall, deeply tanned man in his early thirties. Under his white T-shirt and khakis, he had the roped muscles of an athlete. His light-brown hair was cut close, highlighting a green-blue gaze that could cut darkness like sunlight through seawater. With a notable lack of shock at her presence, he grinned at her, but his hand gripped the doorknob, the veins in his arm pulsing to the surface.

For an endless, awful moment, they didn't say anything, too busy staring.

Finally, Kat drew in a breath, exhaled on a surprised, pained laugh. "Will."

"Kat."

A beat passed as they locked eyes again then glanced away. A whole volume of anguish, joy and disappointment was in that one look, and she couldn't handle it—not after she'd spent so much time trying to forget this man. Not after the hurt from everything that had gone wrong between them.

In the presence of Will Ashton, she felt like she was underwater, ultra-alive and afraid, heart crashing against her ribs, skin prickling with awareness and the detection of danger.

Had Duke known Will would be here?

Kat bit the inside of her lip. *Of course* he'd known. Duke was anything but careless or stupid. Unlike her.

One of them had to say something, so she stepped up. "Well. A captain, huh? Wow. From a scrub on that Catalina diving outfit to pure luxury."

Tone down the sarcasm, she thought, standing

because she felt much too inferior looking up so far to this man. She'd spent too much time doing that in the past, and she'd grown out of it by now.

"I've moved up in life," he said, obviously more comfortable than she was with this awkward greeting.

A different grin slanted over his lips now. That damned, I-want-you-now-Kat grin that used to spin her head like a whirlpool.

Just like it did right now.

Kat nodded, trying to calm the bang of blood through her chest. Will, she thought, I wish you weren't here, but it's weirdly nice to see you.

Jerk.

"What've you been up to?" he asked.

She busied herself by tracing a finger over the mini-TV. Stop, she told herself. Just stop it.

She nixed the fidgeting. "Same thing I was doing last year. Work, play, conquering the world. You know. The usual." Eternal pause. "You?"

He spread his hands out to indicate the boat. Kat couldn't help following his every move, remembering how those fingers had stroked her to sleep. How those palms had smoothed over her face when she'd needed it the most.

How those hands couldn't be around to comfort her when they'd gone their separate ways.

She drew to her full, not-so-impressive height, raising her chin so she could give him a look that was half-casual, half-*Can't you see I'm over you?*

"You own this boat or what?" Something sank into her chest, drawing her heart along with it. Nice. The thought of him being a success, of him accomplishing all those ambitions he'd held so dear ate at her.

"No." He shrugged.

With that one word, Kat knew she'd hit a tender button. Even as vindication—the realization that he was almost as restless in life as she was—settled through her, she couldn't help the burning itch that choked her throat. Out of old habit, a silent cry for connection, she reached out to touch his arm, to make him feel better, just because she knew the mediocrity had to be killing him.

But when he looked up, she caught herself, crossing her arms in front of her chest instead. Underneath her Billabong Surf T-shirt and faded jeans shorts, she was wearing a bikini. It made her feel too vulnerable, as if Will could see through all the material, see through *her*.

True to form, he got that familiar cocky gleam in his eyes because he no doubt knew what was going through her mind. He'd always been real good at that.

"But things are happening," he said. "I'm working on owning my own rig."

"At least you've graduated to captain."

"And dive master," he added, his jaw tightening.

It wasn't a quick enough career trajectory for Will, Kat knew. She'd never met a person with more drive and dreams. For a few short months, Kat had ridden his rainbows, too, believing that, someday, a fallen golden boy and a girl who'd been on the free-lunch program in high school could make things work. Sigh, right? But then reality had hit. He'd shown his true colors.

And she remembered every nuance of their breakup down to the last, heart-shattering detail.

She wanted to say something to wound him since she'd been saving up the anguish for so long. Something to reveal that she realized just how much his failure to fulfill his goals hurt. But she couldn't, because she felt the same damned way about herself.

Even after everything, she still needed him, dreamed about him, wanted him to live happy.

"You look good," Will said softly, jerking her attention back to the present.

"And you're still chasing the big pot of gold in the sky." She wished she could stop herself, but pent-up frustration was getting the best of her. "I guess what happened with Captain Macintosh on your last sailing gig hasn't stopped you."

Even at the mention of the dark rumor that had dirtied Will's reputation personally and professionally, he kept his dignity. "I was cleared of suspicion for his death. He was a good guy, but a drunk. I can imagine what happened—him saucing it up and spilling overboard when we'd docked and most of the crew—except me—went into town for some fun. I was under the weather that night, in bed. I never heard the captain go overboard. And when I found his body floating nearby the next morning…"

She knew. And even though there'd been mean whispers from Will's old coworkers about how he could have benefited from the captain's death by taking over the command of the luxury yacht *Sundowner*, she'd never believed any of the accusations. She hadn't wanted to.

Sure, Will had developed a lot of deep resentment because of what life had done to him and his family. Sure he had that temper, but…

"You already explained," she said, "back when…"

Back when she'd made that lone phone call—just one—to see if he'd recovered from the rumors. In pure Will style, he'd assured her that all was kosher— that Captain Macintosh's drowning had been ruled accidental and that he'd moved on by switching rigs. He'd claimed he'd wanted to work out of San Diego again anyway before Kat had said a stiff, I-can't-believe-I-just-talked-to-my-ex-and-I'm-still-in-one-piece goodbye.

Kat shifted her stance. "It looks like you're mingling with your type on a regular basis now, judging from this boat. The beautiful people, right? Have they welcomed you back into the fold, even after all the scandal?"

"I wish."

For a naked moment, his gaze grew a little lost, revealing enough to allow Kat a glimpse inside: the wounded boy whose socially prominent family had fallen from grace because of a father's dalliance with the wife of a colleague. The kid who'd witnessed that same father being taken down by the enemies he'd made, peg by peg, dollar by dollar, until there was nothing left but a strategic, tragic drug overdose. The youngster who'd raised his family, a man of the house before his time. The man who'd put his heart, soul and body into cleansing the good name his father had ruined.

The man who'd disillusioned Kat during one pivotal moment, devastating her.

As if barring Will from reaching her heart again, Kat tightened her arms over her chest.

Mess me over once, shame on you. Mess me over twice...

He must've caught the defensive hint because, suddenly, the cocksure captain was back, leaning against the door, all heartless, predatory grace.

A slash of lamplight made the stubble on his jaw glisten. "So what're you doing with the Harrington party?"

Long story. And it was one she didn't owe him.

"Never mind that," she said, clean out of patience for this unwelcome tension. "Captain, do you have any green tea on board? Hot tea for a cool morning, you know. Good for the soul."

He sent her a glance that told her he knew she was getting some petty revenge, capitalizing on the fact that he was in her service.

"I'll talk to Chef Linda in the galley." He turned to leave then paused, grinning over his shoulder. "Funny," he said.

"What?"

"You on my boat. The world works in mysterious ways."

He was talking as if there was a purpose to her being here, as if they could take up where they'd left off. It riled Kat, heated the blood until it hummed in her veins. Simmered under her skin, awakening her in places best left cold with Will.

She walked to the door, rested her hand on it. "Don't get too excited about the prospects."

He turned, then backtracked a couple of steps, almost like a magnet pulled to her.

A dangerous tingle zipped through her. Dangerous because she didn't want it, had spent a year trying to chase all the Will-tingles away.

Without another word, she closed the door on him, noting his raised eyebrows.

As she rested against the wood, she heard him chuckle, then walk away, leaving her and some awakened yearning for him alone.

Again.

When Duke trudged on board, hand on his abdomen and sweat beaded on his upper lip, Kat was watching her tea grow cold. In a chair on the top deck, she was taking in the morning sun as it nudged through the haze. In the meantime, the crew bustled around, readying for their departure.

"You. We've something to talk about," she said, rising to her feet to relieve him of his small load of gear.

Duke managed a sheepish glance, tugging a baseball cap reading Harrington Enterprises over his eyes with a trembling hand. Not having any of it, Kat eased it off his head so she could really look at him.

"So," he said, calmly retrieving his hat and struggling to readjust it over his brow. "Would this be one of those *talks* like you had with Yoko?"

"It *could* be."

They were both quiet as Larry the crew guy grabbed

Duke's diving gear and headed toward the lockers. Then, with a gently persuasive hold, Kat took hold of Duke's Hawaiian shirt and guided him to a seat.

As seagulls wheeled overhead with their pitched cries of hunger, Kat said, "I met our captain."

"Good." Duke smiled weakly. "I was hoping you would before I got here."

"And…?" Kat braced her hands on her hips, waiting for a response that never came. *"What the hell?"*

Duke paused, eyebrows knitted as if he was trying to recall a thought that had vanished.

For a second, she wondered if his recent progress on the new meds had been erased. If he'd gone back to the confusion, the mood swings, the endless vomiting up dark blood… "Duke?"

He blinked, smiled up at her. "I chartered a trip. And it just so happens that Will Ashton is the skipper."

Thank God he was okay. Now she could let him have it. *"Dammit,* Duke. Do you think I buy that?"

He gestured for her to sit next to him, then laid a gentle hand on her shoulder. The contact had an immediate calming effect. Human valium, that was Duke to her system.

God, if she could only find a man who combined all the nice parts of Duke and Will, she would never complain about the male species again.

But Duke was Duke. A friend. An older friend. Someone who could never strike the sparks in her that Will did.

Kat exhaled. "This is one of your fix-it *crusades,* isn't it, forcing closure between me and Will?"

There was a strained attempt to look innocent on Duke's part.

"Or…please don't tell me you're trying to get us back together or something," Kat said.

Duke stared at the dock.

"Oh, no. No, no, no…"

"Listen for a minute." Sadness etched itself into the lines bracketing Duke's mouth, his eyes. Taking his time, he laid it out for her. "I've heard it all from you, Kat, when you've got enough tequila in you. All the regrets you've had about leaving Will, all the times you've told me how much you miss him. You're not going to be able to move on with any man until things are settled with the ever-present ex."

"If you'd been listening, you'd know I never wanted to go back to him—that he isn't good for me."

Even though Will was innocent, the story of Captain Macintosh darted through her head.

"We'll know that for certain after this trip." Duke shook his head. "The way you left Will… You packed up one night and never went back, never talked it out, aside from that one stilted phone call where nothing was ever really said. That's no way to leave things."

"And I'm fine with how it ended." There was an emptiness around the edges of her heart, a lifeless field that throbbed and ached with every remembrance.

"Are you?" Duke asked. "Are you really fine?"

His reassuring tone of voice persuaded her to meet his eyes. There was a warm, soul-stirring question lingering in the hazel of his irises, a sweet sense of protection from the man who'd once asked her for surfing lessons, the non-threatening mentor who only wanted the best for her.

If you knew you weren't going to be here soon, wouldn't you fix things? his gaze asked. *Use me as an example, and take care of this before you run out of time.*

Once again he was right, and she knew it. Still, she didn't want to do this, didn't want to be around Will, smell his skin when he got too close, remember the feel of his lips on her body.

She wasn't sure she had the courage.

"That's cute, Duke," she said, relieved, drawn to that paternal concern. "Dump me and Will into the middle of the ocean where we can't run from each other."

"Perfect solution."

"Spoken like the ultimate problem solver that you are. You know, there is a definition for people like you."

"Savior?"

"Troublemaker."

He shrugged, grunting with the effort. "Only for the people who matter most to me."

Shaken by his intensity, she frowned. The odd feeling was back—the warning sirens telling her that there was more to Duke than he was letting her see. That maybe he had moments when being friends wasn't enough....

"After that phone call, Will tried to contact you," he said quietly. "I'm sure he wanted a second chance. That's why I'm doing this, Kat, because he tried and you didn't let him in. You deserve the chance to close your file on him. You deserve to move on and know for certain that your doubts about him were warranted." Duke's jaw tensed. "The way he acted when you told him about the baby just…"

Shaking, she held up a hand, cutting him off.

She didn't want to remember that night: The news that she could be having Will's baby. The shock on his face as he realized that he'd permanently connected himself to a woman who would only hold him back from blue-blooded glory, one who would only make him even more self-conscious about his efforts to bring pride back to his family.

The sheer relief on both their parts when her pregnancy turned out to be a false alarm.

Kat closed her eyes, wishing the memory away.

"So you're not going to desert me because of my meddling?" Duke asked.

She opened her eyes again.

"I should, you busybody." But she wouldn't. She wanted to make him happy, make him feel complete and valuable, just as she would for any member of her own family, if given the chance.

Even if it meant avoiding Will for five days.

Hell, she could do it. She had a stateroom, a DVD player, a shark cage to escape to…. She was a big girl who could deal. Duke was more important than Will anyway.

Shooting her friend a smile to tell him she forgave his meddling, they regained their easiness. He was back to being good old Duke and she the girl who learned so much from him.

But the word *baby* still hung between them, invisible and thick.

Leaving the boat, she went to retrieve the rest of Duke's belongings from his waiting Town Car. She then leisurely strolled back to the *M. Falcon*, listening to the clang of sailboat rigs knocking against masts, the slap of water hitting the docks. On deck, she found him rubbing his temples.

Headache city, she thought.

Just as she was about to lead Duke below deck to stow his stuff and get him into bed, they heard an energetic young voice behind them, accompanied by running footsteps.

"Gramps!"

They turned around to find thirteen-year-old Christian Harrington gunning for them up the gangplank at full speed, weighed down by a backpack. His flop of golden hair hid one eye as he waved, then ran into a pole, his pack skewing his balance.

"Oooo," Kat said, wincing.

She jogged over to see that Chris was okay. And...jeez, picking up that backpack, it weighed more than a tub of wet seaweed.

"What's in here?" she asked.

Between excited breaths, he sputtered out, "Shark books. I brought all of mine to show you."

Aw, thought Kat. How sweet.

She ruffled his goofy hair, and his face lit up in a smile. His pale skin was freckled, his lips a vivid shade of Kool-Aid pink, his teeth sheathed in clear braces. He wore the lanky, awkward body of a new teenager stretching to fit growing bones. All these great features and his positive energy hid the fact that Chris had led a real crappy life before Duke took him in. Duke had told her that when Chris was ten his parents were killed in a fire. Ever since, he'd taken care to raise the orphan in security and love, giving him the best in therapy and luxury—including a round-the-clock "butler team."

Kat wasn't sure this was a great thing. All that the attention seemed to produce was a boy who hadn't quite matured out of the age of ten and into what he was now.

She hauled the backpack up to her shoulder. Ooof. "Are all of these hardcover?"

"Most."

The boy shot her his awkward smile before they walked over to Duke. At least, Kat and her enormous backpack were walking over. Chris *zoomed* to his grandpa.

Pepped up, Duke raised his hands to enfold his ward in a hug. "Chris," he said, voice soft.

They embraced as if they hadn't seen each other in months. Kat knew it had only been hours, since Chris had been finishing up a math test with his regular tutor before going on this study-vacation and had just been dropped off.

She lugged the pack to the deck, set it near her feet. "Where's the rest of your stuff?"

"The driver's bringing it." Chris faced her, enthusiasm lighting his eyes. "Kat, did you know that Guadalupe Island hosts one of the most prolific populations of white sharks on the planet?"

His big words always cracked her up. "Brainiac. Thanks for the scoop."

Duke winked at her and lavished such an adoring look on his grandson that her heart clutched.

And that's when she heard the others.

"Lovely San Diego!" called a cultured female voice. Careful footsteps dallied up the gangplank.

As Chris sat next to Duke, Kat's mentor sent her yet another sheepish grin.

The Delacroix tribe. The family who'd been summoned from their out-of-state home because they were the main beneficiaries of Duke's massive wealth.

Eloise, Duke's darker-side-of-her-forties daughter, was the first to step onto the *M. Falcon*. She was as sophisticated as they came, dressed in swanky-svelte sunglasses and a designer sports blouse and slacks with pearls mounded around an aging neck that didn't match the plastic-surgery tightness of her face. A champagne-blond chignon completed her perfect look.

"We're here!" she said, voice bubbly as she lowered her sunglasses to sweep a glance over the deck. Content, she came to watch her father, smiling.

"In all your glory," Duke said, showing grateful cheer at seeing his family. Before Duke's cancer, they hadn't been very close, he'd told Kat. But things were beginning to change now.

Eloise slipped her eyewear back on and waved her baggage-laden manservant on board. When her gaze lit over Kat, Eloise took a step back and said, "Why, hello."

"Hi," Kat said, waving. "I'm Katsu Espinoza."

As Duke formalized the greeting, he bragged about how Kat was "a real mermaid" and hugged his daughter with such excitement that Kat ached. She wished she had her dad here for this, too.

"Paradise," Duke said. "All the people I love, with me on the adventure of a lifetime."

"Sharks," Chris said, giving an excited little hop.

How appropriate, because that's when the rest of the Delacroix brood appeared.

Eloise's husband, Louis.

Duffy.

Alexandra.

And Nestor.

The whole gang was here for one big happy gathering.

Chapter 3

Later that afternoon, the *M. Falcon* cut through the water on its twenty-two-hour trek to Guadalupe Island. The scents of sunscreen and coconut tanning oil mingled with the salty tang of the ocean as Duke's party enjoyed the start of his grand adventure.

One they all knew could very well be his last.

Even as he reclined contentedly on a deck chair, baseball cap and smile in place, Kat could tell that the excitement had sapped the last of his energy.

"Need some water?" she asked.

"Nope, nope. Not right now." He placed a hand over the one she was resting on her own lounge seat.

His enjoyment was obvious. Duke was supremely happy to be around his once-distant family: Eloise, who had already gone below because she'd gotten her five minutes of sun and had to mind her complexion; husband Louis, a thoughtful, gray-haired man dressed like Mr. Howell and enraptured by the passing ocean; Alexandra, the Paris-Hilton-blond daughter who worshipped the sun with her bikini-clad twenty-something body; Duffy and Nestor, the dark-haired sons who drank martinis and talked about stock options while ignoring the fishing poles they'd stuck into holders around the rear of the boat.

And then there was the "other" neighborhood of the deck—the one where Kat felt just right.

From a seat on the opposite side of Kat, a young woman laughed and told Chris a free-spirited joke. Dr. Janelle Hopkins from UCSD. Duke had left the regular tutor behind and hired the African-American shark scientist solely for the trip. She'd arrived just before the *M. Falcon* had departed and, wasting no time, had immediately started tutoring Chris. Kat had been hanging around, too, keenly interested in what the doctor had to say.

And Duke was getting a kick out of watching Kat learn right along with Chris. He'd probably lecture her at dinner about applying for college again.

The older man kept his hand over hers as he leaned back his head and closed his eyes. Kat squeezed his thin, brittle fingers, turning her attention back to Dr. Hopkins and Chris, caught by the pictures they were studying in one of the teen's books. It depicted a monster great white shark—twenty feet in length if it was an inch.

"We might get lucky," the doctor said. "An eighteen-footer was recently spotted near the island. We're going to see elephant and Guadalupe fur seals, California sea lions…"

Chris shifted in his seat. White sunblock chalked his nose and increased his nerd factor. "I can't wait to dive and take pictures of them. Right, Gramps?"

"Ditto," Duke said, even though Kat knew he wouldn't even get near the shark cage.

As if to punctuate that thought, he held his stomach, then slowly rose out of his chair, coming to balance himself on unsteady legs. A gust of wind blew over him, testing his stance with a low, whistling moan. A lone bird screamed and dove toward the water in a suicidal arc.

Kat wrapped her arms over her knees, suddenly cold.

"I'm going below," Duke said, face pale.

She started to get up, too. "I'll come—"

"No. Just need…some rest." Duke walked away, trying to smile at her for reassurance.

Hell, there was no fighting him. He had a pager for Wayne, the medic on crew, and Kat *would* check in on Duke later. Stubborn man.

"Gramps?" Chris asked.

"Just a nap, Chris."

"Then sleep tight," Louis added as the wind tousled his gray hair. Duffy, Nestor and even the near-comatose Alexandra put on cheery grins, too, and bade their grandfather a good nap.

Kat noted that even when Duke left the deck, their smiles stayed intact.

Louis returned to the sea, smiling. Alexandra checked her tan line and turned over to brown her back, smiling. Nestor and Duffy smiled at each other, as if they were the Waltons and this was some kind of "awwww" moment.

Smiles, smiles, smiles. If they were all such a big happy family, why hadn't they visited Duke more often? Funny; and why did they all seem a little...distanced...with each other? Seriously, when they thought no one was looking they deflated a bit, like they were mingling for Duke's sake.

Still, as Janelle Hopkins and Chris started talking again, Kat focused on what Nestor, the younger brother, was saying.

"So, how much Qualcomm stock do you think seven million dollars could buy?"

"Enough to bring you back in the black, you careless moron." Duffy drank from his martini glass, draining the contents and allowing the emptied vessel to dangle from his fingers.

But Kat was still dwelling on Nestor's question. Was he already mentally spending his inheritance from Duke? And was Duffy calling him out for it?

She inspected the older brother. Ruddy cheeks and beefy ex-linebacker physique. Hearty laugh and casual attitude. Cool or not?

And how about Nestor? Did he also deserve more credit than she was giving him?

Willing to give her doubts a rest for just a second, Kat looked at him with neutral eyes. Not bad, if you were into pretty. He was like the most innocent member of every boy band she'd ever made fun of: dimples, shy grin, soulful blue eyes and all.

Okay, maybe it was just the neighborhood girl in her getting all prickly. She had her own prejudices, mainly about richies—besides Duke, anyway. Back in her world, everyone knew that folks with cash got the glory and others never had a prayer. Her outlook colored the Delacroix family, whether Kat wanted it to or not.

Had they come on this trip only to butter Duke up and secure their share of the will?

Hell. This just meant that it was up to her to make sure she defended him against the Delacroixs. She, along with Chris, would give him a sense of family, even if he was surrounded by blood relatives who didn't genuinely live up to their end of the bargain.

Kat must've been staring at Nestor and Duffy because both brothers glanced at her. They even *smiled*.

Kat turned back to Chris and Dr. Hopkins, finding that the woman was out of her seat, up and stretching. Her cocoa-colored legs were long and slender, her breasts pressing against the cotton of her tank top.

Once again, the wind picked up, humming a strange tune in Kat's ears. The sky seemed a little more overcast.

Dr. Hopkins stopped, a slow grin spreading over her face as she glanced over at the boys.

Slyly, Kat peered at them, then back at Dr. Hopkins.

Okay. So the boys had been smiling at the lovely lady behind Kat. Flirts.

When Duffy turned away, pretty-boy Nestor kept throwing charm at the doctor, grinning like a fool.

When Kat snuck a peek back at the doctor, Hopkins laughed, a gleam in her dark eyes.

"Enough of them to go around, huh?" Kat ventured.

Chris wrinkled his nose and looked at his cousins, just like he was Kat's and the doctor's big brother and it was his responsibility to check things out. But, shaking his head, he went back to his book.

That cracked the women up. Kat had no interest in adorable posers or bulky sportsmen, but the laughter bonded her in a small way to Janelle Hopkins, girlfriend to girlfriend.

"So can I get you two anything from the galley?" the doctor finally asked. "It's snack time for me."

Both Kat and Chris said no, and Dr. Hopkins left them with a pert "Okay. Don't do anything I wouldn't do, Kat."

Kat waited until she was gone. "A doctor. She's smart, huh?"

"Yeah." Chris shut the book and laid it on the now-empty chair. "Wouldn't it be awesome to have her job?"

Oh, sure, Kat thought. Like she could ever afford the education. Like she had the brains, anyway.

But before she could answer, Chris was out of his seat, pointing to the rear of the boat. When Kat looked, she saw Nestor's fishing line whizzing to life.

"Hey, they caught something!"

It wasn't a surprise when the excitable teen darted to his cousins, who stared at the bending pole like it was a foreign object suddenly come to life.

When Chris made a grab for it, Nestor interceded.

"Whoa, there, Chris. You don't know what's on the other end." He unhooked the pole from its holder and worked the line, fighting whatever he'd snagged, seeming slightly amused and encouraged by Chris's enthusiasm.

Duffy followed suit, throwing a thick arm around Chris in companionship—a big boy who didn't know his own age, much like Chris himself. An eternal kid.

Yet the teen squirmed away, and Kat paused, taken aback by the vehemence in the boy's reaction.

Right away, Duffy's face reddened, and it didn't take a professor to see that he was hurt by his young cousin's rebuff. But the embarrassment took the form of playful revenge when Duffy picked up the boy, wrapping a beefy arm around Chris's middle. "So, you like the fishies, Chrissy?"

Father Louis looked away from the sea. "Don't, Duff."

Oblivious to Chris's agitation, Duffy ignored his dad and quickly flipped his cousin upside down, pretending that he was about to hang him over the boat's side.

With a sigh, Louis stood up.

"Put me down!" Chris yelled.

"Hey, Nestor, need more bait?"

Kat zoomed over to them. "Cut it out, you idiot."

Duffy seemed taken aback.

The shock of seeing the banked hurt on his face stole her words away, but as he continued to hold Chris captive, anger kicked in. She'd inherited her temper from her dad and had shown little patience for the calm her mom had tried to teach her when she was young, too young to understand.

"Do it," Kat said, "and I'll shove my fist so far down your throat that I'll tie your guts up for Duke's birthday ribbon."

Nestor turned around to shoot a stunned glance at Kat. His pole zipped into the ocean, fish and all.

In the meantime, Louis walked over, nonchalantly positioning himself behind Duffy.

A flat valley-girl cadence sounded from behind them all. "Don't push Chris's buttons, you ass. If Gramps—"

"Okay, okay, Alex." Immediately, Duffy flipped Chris right side up, steadied him on the deck and made a show of straightening his cousin's hair and shirt. "Gramps's favorite. We need to hail your greatness, Chrissy. The great boss demands it."

Louis's voice interrupted. "*Decency* demands it."

Without warning, he grabbed a handful of Duffy's thick black hair and pulled back his son's head.

No one moved as the whites of Duffy's eyes took over his widened gaze.

"Okay, okay, I got it," he said, voice tight. He reached for his father's wrist just as he was letting go.

With one last warning look, the patriarch mellowed, smiled at the sea, then walked below deck, leaving behind a silenced crowd.

Seizing the chance, Kat rushed to Chris and guided him away from Duffy, taking him into her protective arms. As she did so, a mildly interested Alexandra watched them, blue eyes vacant, mouth pouted like a model in some magazine ad.

Was she that much of a blank? Kat wondered. Or that good at hiding what was going on inside?

Kat brushed away everything but Chris, yet she couldn't ignore one thing—the parting gaze Duffy had given her. It was haunting, filled with mortification and…believe it or not…even a glimmer of regret that his stubborn nature couldn't voice.

Then again, she could be wrong.

"Let's find Dr. Hopkins," Kat said, steering the boy toward the galley.

"All right."

"How can you be so nice, Chris? If I were you, I would've slammed a few kicks in Duffy's grill—and that would've been just the start."

The wind crept through the hall, continuing its uneasy tune from the deck. Wood creaked around them, sounding like something was coming unhinged.

"But I knew he'd stop sooner or later."

She'd seen kids like this. Victims of the playground. Kat, herself, hadn't been one of those for long.

"Gramps told me that Duffy sometimes gets too much testosterone in his system and that Uncle Louis says Duff hasn't gotten all that college football linebacking out of himself yet…if he ever will. He's always going to be a big, dumb dork who doesn't have a clue how to contain himself." Chris smiled, eyes wide. Kat could detect the threat of tears in them. "Besides, everyone gets worried about hurting me, so they always end up walking on eggshells and being super apologetic. You know, because of my parents."

She wasn't sure what to say, whether to ask more

questions or not. Duke had always given her the impression that it was a touchy subject and wasn't to be broached around Chris. One thing she knew for sure was that Duke, himself, didn't like talking about the death of his oldest son and his wife. The first time he'd mentioned it had been the last, and when she'd tried to bring it up again, he'd uncharacteristically shut her down. Understandable, though. There was no pain equal to that of losing a loved one.

The teen sighed, just as though he'd sensed her uneasiness, as though he was all too used to it. "I'm tougher than they think. Sometimes, people call mellow kids like me wimps, but…maybe it just takes more to get me mad."

"Or maybe you're more mature than people give you credit for." Kat patted Chris's back as they walked into a dining area, where Dr. Hopkins was seated, snacking from a plate of assorted cheeses Chef Linda had probably put together.

And even though Kat tried to keep her mind on the conversation as it turned academic again, she couldn't. The temper she'd inherited from her dad—*her* very own legacy—wouldn't allow her to forget Duffy's bullying. Because she knew exactly what being picked on felt like.

An hour later, when Kat went back up to the deck to find Duffy, she discovered that everyone had deserted the area to get ready for dinner. Everyone, that is, except Alexandra. And Will.

He was rubbing suntan oil on Alex's back as she sat

upright, holding her long fall of bleached blond hair in one hand as she tilted her head to the side.

An empty twinge needled through Kat's chest, spiking her loneliness, bursting any hopes she'd entertained about... What? Them getting back together?

Numbness gripped her heart and she told herself to leave, that horny captains could touch anyone's back they wanted to. But her feet wouldn't move. They were rooted to the spot, forcing her to listen to Will's jaunty banter, Alexandra's laughter.

As Kat helplessly watched, she could almost feel the trail of his fingers burning along her own back, massaging away the knots of her own muscles. The whisper of his soft voice almost warmed her ear as they talked about their ambitions, their days.

They'd talk about things like Will, investing his money in get-rich-quick schemes that always burned him. Kat, wondering what it would be like to travel to Mexico City or Japan with him someday. Will, playing nice with the men who'd watched his father's pathetic demise in the hopes that they could help him. Kat, assuring the man she loved that he was a better person than the lot of them.

That they already had everything they needed in each other.

She'd been so wrong. So *young*, even if it was just a year ago. But dammit, he wasn't her boyfriend anymore, so why was she still so territorial, so torn up?

Sucker punched by the sight of his hands on someone else, she forced herself to go.

As Kat headed back to her cabin, passing a couple of random crew members on the way, she boiled with frustration, longing, the unfairness of her lingering need for him.

Will. A high-priced cabana boy. Kat suspected that if he had the opportunity to hook up with someone like Alexandra Delacroix and the millions she was in line to inherit, he'd probably do it in a heartbeat, just to make his family name shine again.

By the time Kat found a nook with its own wet bar, she was ready to tear a hole in the wall. Unfortunately, that's where she found Duffy.

He was nursing another martini, elbows resting on the mahogany of a small table, gaze on a TV that was playing highlights of last year's Superbowl.

Just seeing him brought back her rage at his treatment of Chris. Heightened anger, stoked by Will's actions, prodded her.

She leaned against the door frame, her hand braced on a hip. "Is this where the boys come to man up?"

Straightening in his chair, Duffy had the grace to seem guilty. A flash of pity stole through her at the image of Louis Delacroix bullying his son, but it didn't last long. As if sensing her momentary sympathy, Duffy rolled his eyes, putting her at a mocking distance. A sheen of moisture from the beverage lingered on his bottom lip, still giving him some vulnerability whether she liked it or not.

"Chris didn't get hurt, okay?" he said. "So drop the guardian-angel act."

"Listen." She stood, sauntered into the room. "I don't know if that kind of 'playing' is an everyday thing for you, but it's not going to happen again.

Chris is thirteen and you're...what? Mentally twelve? Except you outweigh him by about one hundred pounds and fifteen physical years. That's not a fair round."

"We were goofing off, not that it's your concern."

Duffy took another sip and his blue eyes bored into her. Not quite drunk yet, she thought. But sober enough to know that he's offending me.

Her adrenaline hummed, warming up for a real show. "I think you've got different sandbox rules than the rest of the world. Regular people don't pick on kids, unless they're trying to make up for certain other...shortcomings."

"Well, you're a ballbuster, aren't you? Why the hell my gramps tolerates you, I'll never know. You can't be *that* good of a lay."

She froze.

With as much control as she could muster, Kat lifted up a finger and held it in front of Duffy's face, leaning over to make her point. Even with his fumes of gin and vermouth hitting her she didn't flinch.

"If I see you messing with Chris again," she said, "I will make good on that promise I made earlier, except we won't be talking about guts being all tied up."

She lowered her gaze to his lap, making sure he caught her meaning, then turned around to walk away. God, she was proud of herself for keeping it cool.

"You won't last long anyway. Ever wonder why you're such good friends with Daddy Warbucks, Orphan Annie?"

Yes. Hell, yes. Sometimes she felt like a charity

case or downright pet to Duke, and that even dolts like Duffy could see it hurt her with shame.

He didn't even wait for her answer. "Gramps is a collector, you know. He's done this a hundred times before, so don't let his heroic stories of redemption fool you. He's still a womanizer—always will be—and you're his final project. Girls like you give him a thrill—to refurbish, just like the old buildings he used to buy and sell."

She was actually standing here listening to this, glued to the spot but wanting to run away. But she needed to hear what she'd always suspected: that Duke had ulterior motives, that she wasn't good enough for him on her own merits. With every syllable, Duffy was nailing her further into the floor, the truth ringing in her ears. When she opened her mouth to stop him, to save herself before she crumbled before him, she found she couldn't talk. Dryness—cotton-like on her tongue—evaporated each word.

"Don't worry," Duffy added, "he'll leave you in good shape. But, for now, keep this in mind: you're the hobby of a bored old man, *Katsu*. So don't think you've got any kind of superiority over me."

By now she was quivering.

Duke, one of the only people around who seemed to respect her, to believe in her… He was just a player.

But Kat couldn't really buy that. It was a lie. A way for Duffy to bring her down. And the only thing Kat could do was start walking again, praying that her jelly legs could make it to her cabin.

But Duffy stopped her by grabbing her T-shirt. "I'm not done yet, señorita."

Bristling, she stopped, but not before he slid his other hand under the curve of her butt.

He laughed. "What's good for the old goose—"

She whipped around and swung her arm, knuckles crunching his cheek. In the same motion, she pushed one of his arms away and sprang backward so quickly that he didn't have time to latch on to her clothing again.

"That was a warning," she choked out.

He was holding a palm against his face where she'd connected, mouth agape and eyes wide. It took about a full minute for him to lower his hand.

"You *bitch*." He was wearing the same expression she'd seen when his father had dressed him down. Destroyed.

But did that give him the right to call her a bitch? Little did he know that in her neighborhood, the term was a compliment. A damned badge.

"Number one," she said, her voice edged with a quake of anger, "you don't touch me. Number two, you don't call me señorita, geisha, American pie or any other condescending nickname your mini-brain can conjure up. But…" She fought to bring a tough smile to her face. "…you *may* call me bitch."

The second he angled forward in his chair, eyes blazing with rage, Kat was ready. Her upbringing had tuned her in to the subtlest jerk of the hand, the hint of an explosion. She'd been jumped too many times by punks at school, faced down by skanks on her own block.

So bring it, Duff.

When he did, she'd already widened her stance, taken her right fist into her left, positioned her elbow in front of her body. After a rapid cock backward, she levered her elbow forward, smashing it into Duffy's temple and sending him crashing onto the table.

Just as she was preparing to follow up with a kick, applause hit the air and she lost focus.

Duffy, who'd sheltered his head with his arms as he sprawled on the table, peeked up. Kat eased away—*never* put your back to an enemy—and looked at their audience.

Four of the crew members she'd met earlier were in the doorway, clapping: Larry with the dreadlocks; Shaw, the short first officer who carried a big knife holstered at his belt; Jason, the bearded engineer; and Tinkerbell, a petite, dark-skinned, Filipino woman who'd dyed her spiky hair red. The woman was shaking and staring a burning hole through Duffy. "There's none of that crap on the *M. Falcon*, asshole." Shaw put his arm around her as angry tears filled her eyes.

Larry stepped inside, taking up Kat's back as Shaw and Jason slipped away. "Do I have to ask if you're okay?"

"It's a nice gesture."

Larry smiled, whispered in her ear. "Beat them all to shreds. That's what I say."

His smile reflected genuine respect, and it made Kat wonder just how long they'd been standing there, silently rooting for the underdog.

And from the livid look on Duffy's face, she knew he was thinking the same thing.

* * *

After a delicious dinner of Maine lobster, Dom Perignon and crème brûlée, everyone more or less retired to their cabins for the night.

Duke, who'd been served a meal tailored to his special diet, had wanted to rest for tomorrow, when they would arrive at the island and begin their cage-diving. Civil to the extreme, everyone else had followed suit, obeying his wishes with sugar-sweet speed.

Truthfully, Kat thought Duffy might be happy about the lack of social time tonight. He'd looked at her only once during the polite dinner, and it hadn't been a nice look, either. His bruised eye had made it more of a glower.

In explanation, he'd told everyone that the martinis had gotten to him so he'd tripped and hit his face on the TV stand. During his recitation of the excuse, Kat could feel his hate.

So what. She'd have to walk around with *ojos* in the back of her head to keep track of Duffy from now on. Big deal. It wouldn't be any different than the harassment she'd had to endure throughout school, and *that* she'd survived once the other kids understood that a shrimp like her could definitely deliver some blows. Once her dad learned about her problems, he taught her another trick or three. He hadn't lived through boot camp for nothin'.

After dinner, Kat settled back in her berth, dressed in an oversize white T-shirt and undies, and opened the shark textbook Dr. Hopkins had loaned her. After a half hour of trying to absorb the scientific terms and dry language, she closed it.

Out of my depth, she thought.

Still, as she shut off the light and listened to her stomach wrap itself around all the foods she'd gorged on tonight, she couldn't help wondering about what else was in that book. What she could learn if she took a chance. But…right. This was coming from a girl who'd blown school, a girl whose grades sucked, a girl who'd showed everyone just how dumb she was. Schoolgirls got taunted, harassed, and Kat hadn't needed the extra grief. Kat hadn't…

Sleep claimed her before she could think it through.

Her dreams were full of sharks and cages and a sea that glowed the color of Will's eyes. Peace, just like under the surface of the ocean.

Fear, too, at what was hidden.

Just as she was giving in to the blue-edged serenity of unconscious thought, her world jerked around her, like water thrashing into itself, flooding her. She sprang up in her bed, frozen, heart thudding through her skin. In the dead quiet of night, she listened for whatever had disturbed her.

A shift in movement? A sound?

Thump, thump. Creaaaak.

Her heart. The boat. But there was something else beneath its rhythms. Something she couldn't really…

Kat flicked on her lamp, eyes stinging from the sudden brightness, eyes squinting and scanning her small cabin for the intrusion. But nothing looked out of place.

Just as she relaxed a little, the boat seemed to flicker, or hiccup or…something weird.

She waited. It didn't happen again.

Spaz, she thought. You're still jacked up from this afternoon with Duffy and what he said about Duke. Just chill, okay?

So she sat in bed with the lights on, waiting to get tired again.

She didn't. And…ugh. Her cabin was shrinking by the second, falling in on her.

Throwing on a pair of shorts, Kat knew sleep would be out of the question now. The best thing to do would be to trip down to the library and grab a movie or get an easy book to lull her back to slumberland.

After grabbing a sample-sized hairspray—just for defensive insurance—she eased open her door, then tiptoed into the hall. Night-lights fizzed along the passageway, dim and eerie. There was a long screech like the boat was yawning and…

…silence.

Keep those eyes in the back of your head open, she thought, glancing toward the library. It wasn't very far, so she started to walk, blood thumping, ears trained for sound.

Screeeee…

Spooked, she looked behind her, seeing nothing, then faced front. The library door was only ten feet farther, just past the dark opening to the stairway…

But she never made it that far.

Chapter 4

A calloused hand pressed over Kat's mouth just as if it was pushing a tight gasp of surprise right back into her.

Without hesitation, she brought up the tiny bottle of hairspray, guessing an aim at her assailant's eyes. Makeshift Mace. The Barbie McGyver solution to an attack.

But a familiar voice stopped her with a whisper.

"Kat! Shhh…."

Heartbeat tearing through her skin, she turned around to find Will, who rested a finger over her lips before she could react.

At the gentle contact, her body betrayed her, melting. The skin of his finger was so warm, so natural against her mouth, burning memories, sensations, right back into her soul. Without meaning to, she relaxed, lips softening against him as repressed hunger expanded through her.

All those nights with Will…his fingers trailing down, over her mouth, exploring the pulse of her neck, the angles of her collarbone…weakening her to the point where she could feel herself melding to his body… A sharp pang of hunger twisted in her chest, stinging like barbs on tentacles, leaving her flailing. Ashamed of the power he still had over her, Kat backed away, leaving Will with his finger in the air.

He tightened his jaw and slowly brought down his hand until it rested in a fist by his side.

"Sorry to scare you," he said quietly. "I was making the rounds to see that everyone is good for the night."

While they stood there, awkward as can be, the floor tilted a bit, lifted by a swell in the ocean's rhythm. Kat searched for her balance by reaching for the wall.

But Will was there to steady her, grabbing her hands. Warm…God, so warm…

She stood up and disengaged, her palms tingling, begging her to touch him again. "Choppy outside?"

There we go. Casual. Well done.

"Yeah, we're heading into some Dramamine weather," he answered softly, minding the guests who were sleeping. "I was just going back up to the bridge to cover it. Nothing to panic about."

"Then I should let you go."

He hesitated. "Right."

As he started to leave, her heart sank. But then he

paused again, turned back around. She sucked in a breath at the intensity of his expression in the dim lighting.

"Kat, I just…" He laughed bitterly, shaking his head and staring at the ground. "I'm going to say it straight out. I've really missed you."

Bam. That was the sound of her heart exploding, muffled by all the layers of anguish she'd piled on it. It throbbed, struggling to regain strength and control. She couldn't allow him to decimate her again.

"Just let it go, Will."

"No, dammit, I won't." By now, his whispers had turned ragged. "Can you do me the favor of explaining why you never gave me another chance?"

It was the moment she'd been waiting for—closure. Even though part of her resisted the death of her dreams, Kat blew out a nervous breath, girding herself, and motioned for him to follow her up the stairs. Fighting another rolling wave that tipped the boat up, then down, she eventually led him to the empty salon, where she set the hairspray bottle on the table and stood behind a chair—a subtle shield.

"Maybe you should get to the bridge," she said.

"Shaw's covering it. He knows I'll be along."

His voice cracked on the last word, which proved the trigger for all the hurt and betrayal she'd been buried under to finally give way.

"You remember how disappointed I was when I told you about our baby…." *Pain. Loss.* "Or what could've been our baby."

Guilt flushed over his face. "I'm sorry for the way I reacted. But I asked you to marry me. Didn't that—"

"No." The answer was harsh, full of grief. "You asked me to marry you because you thought it was the right thing to do, not because you wanted me to be your wife. But that's not why I left…at least, that's not all of it."

While she caught her breath, the boat shifted again, creaking and moaning, a haunted thing echoing the ghost-laced wind. He waited, his hands gripping his own chair as he faced her from across the table. He'd gone pale underneath his tan and that made her feel worse because she couldn't accept his remorse. Not after spending a year talking herself out of loving him.

"What did it for me," she said, voice jagged as she struggled to keep it together, "was that one moment where you found out that it was a false alarm. The day I got my period and found out I wasn't pregnant. I could see the relief on your face. I can still see it every time I think of you. Nothing can ever make up for that."

"We weren't ready for a family."

"No, we weren't, and thank God we didn't have one."

Absently, longingly, she drifted a hand over her belly, then stopped. All she'd ever wanted was Will, from the night they'd met until…well, now. She'd never known anyone like him: a guy whose mind was tinted with the same ocean-blue shade of her own life, a man who wanted to make something of himself come hell or high water…a man who she'd once *thought* had some stalwart integrity because of the way he took care of his family.

"Let's face it," she said, "I don't fit into your upwardly mobile plans. I never will. That one moment made everything obvious."

"Kat," he said gently, "that's not true. You've got the potential to outshine any society woman."

Duke would say the same thing. The realization unsettled her. "*If* I would just change, right? But I can't. I'll never be some diamond come out of the rough. Say it— this scatter-blood smart mouth complicated your big goals."

"Okay, yeah, you complicated a lot of things, but only because you'd never let me forget about your race or your damned *station* in life. That doesn't mean I didn't love you."

The breath left her. It was the last thing she'd wanted him to bring up. And the first thing. The only thing. "I loved you, too, but I can't forget that little peek into how you really felt about us. It made me doubt you every day after that."

"This is all behind us, Kat." He offered a hopeful grin. "Can't I make you trust me again?"

What…did he think it was all that easy? Trust was just the tip of the iceberg. But it was also everything.

A flash of Will putting suntan lotion on Alexandra swept over her, flooding away all hope of *trust* ever happening for her again. There'd always be reminders of his priorities, his all-consuming ambitions.

So afraid of the damage, the inevitability of repeating the past, she drew back into herself. "Why don't you save your sweet nothings for Alexandra Delacroix?"

She regretted the words even as they left her mouth.

Devastation—and realization—washed over him. He'd been caught "networking," making nice with the rich girl.

"Kat." Will shook his head. "I'm the captain. You know it's my job to make my guests feel welcome."

But Kat had seen her ex-boyfriend in action before, kissing up to "connections," trying hard to become someone again. She couldn't stand it, especially since she suspected that the Delacroixs thought the same thing about her, too.

The boat was lifted by another, more aggressive wave. The lights flickered then burned on again.

Without another word, Will sent her an indecipherable look, then left for the bridge, his shoulders stiff with wounded pride. The sight almost knocked Kat to her knees.

Was he upset because she'd misinterpreted what he'd been doing with Alexandra today, or because she called him on it?

She sank into the chair, cursing Duke for reintroducing Will into her life and throwing her emotions around like so much debris, cursing herself for letting Will past the cracks in her heart.

But she didn't have long to recover because, soon, she was joined by the other passengers, one by one. Scared people who had been brought to the salon by the shift in weather, by the need for comfort from the mild storm.

Or from whatever was lying beneath their own skins.

* * *

Eloise Delacroix, dressed in a silk robe, was holding a paper bag over her mouth as the bobbing waves shook the boat. Alexandra was dressed similarly, watching her mother closely while Duffy looked on from the spot where he was standing, back to the corner of the salon, seemingly immune to the roiling ocean. Even Louis looked a little yellow as he attempted to pour himself a glass of sloshing water. Kat and Dr. Janelle Hopkins were silk-less in their wardrobe, slumming in T-shirts and shorts and Dramamine patches.

Nestor and Chris, wearing spiffy robes over their own wake-me-for-champagne-brunch pajamas, were occupied arm wrestling at one of the tables. Nestor's dimples were at full salute as he strained to beat his teen cousin. But Chris was methodically gaining ground and forcing Nestor's arm to give way.

Dr. Hopkins winked at Kat, then said, "Nestor, you can't possibly be this weak."

That's what you get from a boy-band-type guy, Kat thought, noting Nestor's designer-gym-honed physique. Surprisingly, Chris had some real *oomph* to him. He was a deceptively wiry kid with the constitution of a steel clamp. Kat couldn't help getting into the contest; it beat thinking about the waves and the nausea. It also trumped thinking about Will.

"And Rocky faces Apollo Creed in the ring," Kat said, refusing to dwell on her issues. "Can. He. Do. It. Folks?"

"Wait," the doctor said. "Is this *Rocky One* or *Rocky Two?* Because we're talking about different finales here."

Duffy wandered over and took a seat next to Dr. Hopkins. Even though he and his black eye were studiously avoiding Kat, she could tell he wanted to be a part of the group. "Since it looks like Chris is about to make Nestor into a girly-man, I think we need to go with the sequel, where the underdog pulls it out."

Chris slammed Nestor's arm to the table and whooped in glee, raising his arms over his head. "Gotcha!"

Nestor shook out his arm, laughing. "Two out of three?"

Just as Chris was about to accept, Duke came into the room, shrouded in a thick robe, his pallor and slow gait halting all conversation. After an awkward moment, everyone greeted him heartily, save Eloise and her paper bag.

"Ah, parties," Duke said, folding himself into a chair and leaning on the table.

Louis crossed one leg over the other, facing away from his wife as she dry heaved. "It was rather impromptu, Edward. Welcome to Misery Loves Company. Care for a Dramamine?"

"I've had my fill of pills, thank you."

"I pulled a Rocky on Nestor," Chris said, giving Duke a play-by-play of the victory.

"Well done." Duke lit up at his grandson's joy. But as the boat listed to the side again, he closed his eyes.

Worried, Kat watched him, even though she was still smarting from what Duffy had said this afternoon.

Am I a project? she wondered. A refurbished building? A lie. Duffy was lying.

"I remember," Duke said through clenched teeth,

clearly fighting his stomach, "when *Rocky* came out. Most of you are too young to recall it, I'm sure."

"Nineteen seventy-six," Kat said, offering a smile to her mentor after he opened his eyes. Even though she was wounded, she wasn't about to let Duffy's comments sabotage Duke's last voyage. Besides, she'd give him the benefit of the doubt before discussing this with him later when he felt better.

"That's when disco was popular," Chris added.

Duke sat up a little straighter, and Kat realized that engaging him in a conversation he'd love—pop culture trivia—would go a long way toward diverting his attention from his pain. They frequently spent hours chatting about movies, TV, music. They were both media nuts, especially Duke. Of course, he'd once owned a syndicated television outlet.

Another wave moaned under the boat, so Kat rushed to distract Duke. "Best sequel ever, Harrington?"

He didn't even have to think. "*Godfather, Part Two.*"

"Man," she said, "according to *Scream Two*, *G-Two* is part of a trilogy, not an actual sequel. You know that."

Chris had already plopped his butt on the table in his exuberance, clearly wanting to be in the thick of the topic. "Favorite scary movie…?"

"*Bambi,*" Duffy said dryly.

Everyone laughed as Nestor added, "*Friday the Thirteenth.*"

"Sequel number?" Kat asked. "One, two, three…?"

"Part two. Boy, you people are sticklers."

"You got a thing for hockey masks?" Dr. Hopkins

asked. "I like my killers to have the guts to show their faces."

Nestor leaned on his elbows and aimed his body toward the dark-skinned beauty. "Jason Voorhees didn't get the mask until part three. And, aside from the pillowcase he wears, you do see his gorgeous puss at the end of Part Two."

"Well, touché then."

As the rest of them offered more titles, the doctor and Nestor just grinned at each other.

Hold up, Kat thought. More flirting.

And—much to her shock—*everyone* was getting along. Even Louis and Alexandra were listening while Eloise weaned herself away from her thankfully empty paper bag.

Soon, they were all laughing with each other, totally at ease, the touchstone subject of movies providing neutral ground. While they tested each other about Academy Award winners, favorite movie scores and worst actors, no one seemed to notice that the weather had calmed.

Until Will walked into the room.

Kat could feel the change in temperature immediately—lukewarm to burning. But maybe that was just her skin, which had blushed to flame the minute she'd sensed him.

When he leveled a meaningful glance at her, Kat looked away to find Larry flanking their captain. Larry looked as ready to rumble as ever.

"How's tricks, Captain?" Nestor asked.

"We're past the tossing and turning."

"Hey, can the boat run by itself?" Chris asked, ever curious. "Why aren't you driving it?"

Will grinned at him. "One of my guys, Shaw, is monitoring the radar while the *M. Falcon* is on auto-pilot. I just wanted to see how everyone was doing."

Kat noticed that Alexandra was busy devouring Will with her gaze. A junkyard-dog instinct bristled inside Kat, making her want to claim him again, apologize to him, even. With effort, Kat tuned in to the conversation, trying hard to distance herself from jealousy. And…good luck. She'd need it.

"Captain Will?" Chris asked. "Favorite…TV theme!"

Louis piped up. "Trivia, Captain. We've been whiling away the time with a bunch of silly talk."

Wait, Kat thought. Silly talk is awesome. She caught Duke's wan, knowing smile. He was thinking the same exact thing. Trivia had gotten them through the worst moments of the trip so far, so thank heaven for it.

Will leaned back against the wall, his pose thoughtful. "I've never really considered this before."

Bull. She should've called him on his coyness. He loved the theme from *Wild, Wild West*. Just remembering the endearing, dorky dance he'd done when they'd watch repeats sent another bittersweet memory through her.

"I like the *Alias* song," Chris said. "It rocks."

This brought up a renewed burst of answers. *Hawaii Five-O. Cheers. Magnum P.I. Twilight Zone.*

"Ah," Dr. Hopkins said. "The best. *Twilight Zone.*"

"Ooooh." Nestor lifted up a finger. "Name the

episode. The one where they've captured the devil and some dumb backpacker guy gets talked into letting him go, thus unleashing evil upon the earth?"

"'The Howling Man,'" Duke and Kat said at the same time. They pointed at each other. "Jinx!"

It was *on*: a competition between her and Duke. Damn, it felt good to see him perk up a bit.

Louis even joined in. "The one where the woman is in bandages in a clinic. Everyone is making a point of how ugly she is, and when the bandages are taken off—"

"I know this one," Eloise said, fanning herself while Alexandra yawned.

"—we see that she's beautiful and the doctors look like pigs…"

"'Eye of the Beholder'!" Kat got it just a split second before Duke could.

"These are before your time," he added. "How…?"

"Wasted days in front of the TV after school," Kat laughed. "I've seen them a hundred times each."

Will laughed, too, knowing her well enough to appreciate the comment. He'd often teased her about watching too much of the tube, but he'd also known why she was in the habit. When she wasn't with dear old dad, she'd often stayed indoors when she was young, avoiding certain kids who liked to pick on her.

Recovering from the intimate moment, she tried to ignore the flutter in her tummy.

A little less energetic by now, Duke offered a tidbit. "The one where the aliens manipulate a neighborhood into thinking—"

Kat was still distracted, so Duffy beat her to it. "'The Monsters Are Due on Maple Street.'"

Flushed and in the moment, Nestor blurted out another. "The one where the dying old man makes his family wear masks that show their true natures in order to get their inheritance, and at the stroke of midnight, when they take off the masks, their faces reveal what's in their souls…"

The room had come to a terrible standstill.

"'The Masks,'" Duke finally said.

Only the howl of the wind, a cold keening that breathed through Kat's bones, kept her from shouting to break the thickening in the air.

Dr. Hopkins tried to improve the atmosphere. "The one where the tiny man with the glasses—"

Duke interrupted. "Let's cut the bullshit. I'm dying."

It was like he'd gently taken out a sledgehammer and knocked them all in the heads with one swing. Kat's ears rung, her heart beat in her throat.

"Father," a pale Eloise said, gingerly rising to her feet to come over to Duke, "let's not—"

"Eloise," he continued, voice trembling, "why are you and the family finally with me?"

Everyone sat in silence.

"Gramps…" Duffy began.

But Duke stopped him with one lift of a finger. "No excuses. It's too late for that. I'd just like to know—"

He cut himself off with a bout of coughing. Kat poured a glass of water, setting it in front of him.

"Before the diagnosis, there were never any family dinners." Another cough. Duke's face grew uncomfortably red. He took a sip of water and collected himself enough for his skin to turn a hard-boiled pink. "There were never even Christmas cards until you saw the light at the end of the tunnel for me."

"Now, Edward." Louis was on his feet. "Let's talk about this in private."

He motioned toward Will and the crew, who took the hint and started to withdraw from the room. Dr. Hopkins followed. Yet when Louis gestured toward Kat and Chris, he received no such response. Kat wasn't going anywhere. Duke was like family. He was all she had.

"Why not in front of us?" she asked.

Louis raised his chin, but Kat could tell he wasn't brave enough to take her on.

Duke was smiling—and it was no longer the soft, lighthearted grin of the man Kat thought she knew.

"It fascinates me," he said, sighing, "to see how people act when faced with the possibility of great wealth. From an aging businessman who's been waiting out his father-in-law's decomposing body—" he nodded to Louis "—to a daughter who's shown complete apathy until recently—" a salute to Eloise, who held a hand to her chest and looked like she was on the verge of getting sick "—to the grandchildren who've spent a fortune they've never had and need a new one to keep themselves proficient in all types of debauchery."

Nestor shifted in his seat. Alexandra straightened her spine and her eyes got watery. Duffy, however, was heating up by the moment, knuckles going white as he fisted his hands on the table.

"And," Duke added, "let's not forget the upwardly mobile class who might have good reason to give in to the temptation of money."

He slid a glance to Kat, then toward the door where Will had disappeared. Her stomach dropped. This trip hadn't been about allowing her to reconcile her feelings about her ex, after all, had it?

She flinched. Was Duke planning to set up Will by putting him in the middle of money, just to prove that Will would always choose family pride and money over her? Was he giving her just cause to shut the book on her ex?

Or... No way. Duke would *never* think she wanted his cash.

Hell, she wouldn't believe the worst until she saw proof. She wasn't even sure why this had all crossed her mind, but the fact that it had scared her. Duffy's rash comments had apparently eaten away at her faith in her friend, hadn't they?

Kat walked over to Chris. His eyes were wide. Confused? Surprised?

When she took his hand to lead him out of the room, he pulled her back to his chair, indicating he wanted to stay.

Maybe he's more mature than other kids.

Okay. It was time to give him a little credit.

Duke paused to rub his temples. "So, really, I didn't invite you here for adventure as much as honesty."

Louis braced his hands on the table, attempting to seem intimidating. "What are you saying?"

Duke faced him in that gentle yet firm way of his.

"I want to know how much my family actually loves me. I want you to deserve an inheritance."

"We do," Nestor said. "Love you, I mean."

All the Delacroixs nodded, backing Nestor up.

"Good." Duke sighed, smiled. "Then you won't care if I've decided to make a few changes to my will."

"Changes," Louis echoed.

Duffy's voice was tight when he finally spoke. "Like what, *Grandfather?*"

"Ah. Honesty in his tone. I like that." Duke slowly, painfully, got up and made his way over to Kat and Chris, resting his hands on their shoulders. "When I get back to land, I'll be making arrangements to leave ninety-five percent of my holdings to Chris."

Eloise sucked in a loud breath while Chris sat quietly. Stunned?

"And five percent to someone else who has proven that they love me unconditionally."

Don't say it, don't say it, Kat thought, dreading it, craving it all at the same time.

"My good friend, Katsu Espinoza."

And with that, Duke started to shuffle toward the door, amidst the rising protests of his family. Springing out of her chair, Kat went with him, ready to fend off anyone who confronted Duke, ready to talk some sense into him, too. Or maybe she needed some sense talked into her.

Either way, that night changed everything.

Chapter 5

Lesson one: It's dumb to wear flashing objects in the water, Kat thought the next day as she removed her earrings after dressing in her wet suit.

And lesson two, among so many more: Never go into the water without realizing that you are out of your element and in something else's world.

As she stood on the starboard side of the deck next to a similarly suited-up Chris, waiting for the moment they could go back to the boat's stern and climb into the shark-observation cage, she knew that caution was the most important lesson of all.

In fact, she added to herself, like the rules of the sea, you should never venture into life itself without realizing that you're in over your head and you might have to fight your way out.

Last night had only emphasized that.

Oddly, the Delacroixs had kept to themselves after the outburst. Even so, Kat had lingered in Duke's stateroom until dawn, just in case one of his relatives got the itch to harass him.

Clearly, Duke was in no shape for this drama. The inheritance confrontation had wiped him out, and after a bout of vomiting which worried Kat more than anything else, he'd been visited by the medic, then hit his berth, falling into a deep slumber. Kat didn't dare wake him, even though there was so much to straighten out. Instead, she'd spent the night in a chair by Duke's side, jangled by all the emotions mingling and confusing her conscience.

What was five percent of billions of dollars?

Even now, standing here on deck, she told herself not to dwell on it. She didn't want to face that tiny seed of greed taking root, the ecstatic buzz of power and control that money would bring to her life. No more debts. A better place for her and über-roomie Tracy to live.

Respect from everyone who'd ever looked down on her.

Just as she was flying high on this fantasy, she crashed to earth again. The price for this false sense of self-esteem was Duke. His death.

Heaviness settled on her shoulders. She'd give millions just to keep her surf-days friend around.

"Kat?"

It was the first word Chris had said so far this morning. He seemed just as troubled and red-eyed as she was after last night. Had he lost sleep after the confrontation, too?

"You ready to go first?" she asked.

"Sure." He was distracted, moody, showing an uncharacteristic lack of excitement. Even at this young age, Chris was an experienced diver; it was one of his passions, one of the things the lonely teenager was *really* good at.

Kat was still determined to make the most of this amazing experience for him. "Think about it—three whole days out here. We're gonna have some fun."

"Right. Fun." Chris fidgeted with his suit.

Kat glanced back to the stern, where the cage was being checked over. Sunlight chased away any reminder of last night's restless weather, and the ocean itself was calm and ready to embrace them. Near the cage, the Delacroix family was keeping to themselves. Alexandra was reading the latest Harry Potter book while Eloise, swathed in layers of white, stared at the ocean from her lounge chair. Louis, Duffy and Nestor fished quietly.

In the background, Isla de Guadalupe waited, its mammoth, hunched rocks stretching under the specter of a lone gray thunderhead. Kat suppressed a shiver.

It was as if something had shifted between everyone, like plates of the earth had rubbed together and were causing a silent quake. Kat dreaded the damage that would come during the next few days.

She was so intent on considering the possibilities that she barely heard Duke greeting them in a reedy, yet cheerful, voice. When she turned around, she saw him hugging a newly joyful Chris, who was obviously excited that Duke was up and around. Kat blinked, unable to believe what she saw. Duke barely looked fit enough to be out of bed, much less on deck.

And he was dressed to dive.

"Uh…?" She indicated his gear.

"I thought I'd give it a go. What do you say, Chris? You want to let the old man go first?"

There's no way his health would allow him this kind of crap…excuse her, *nonsense*.

"Can I talk to you?" she asked, trying to draw him aside.

"Go ahead." Duke placed a hand on Chris's head. That was body language for: "What I hear, he hears."

Okay, if that's how he wanted it. "Your doctor didn't even approve this trip, did he? I'll bet he doesn't know you're here."

His guilty look told the answer.

"Chris, why don't you wait by the cage?" he said.

The teen raised his eyebrows, cheeks turning pink. "But—"

"Small favor," Duke said. "For me."

Chris shot a miffed glance at Kat. "'Kay." He left, looking curiously over his shoulder at both of them.

Duke sighed, leaning his frail body against the wall. "As great as that kid is, he hates being told he can't do something." For the slightest moment, his eyes went empty.

What was with him this morning? "I think he wants to see that you're okay after last night, you know?"

A smile fought its way onto Duke's mouth, but

something still hung behind. Something like yester-day's mournful wind.

The looming threat of his death iced between them. So did the ugliness of his family life.

"So what's up with you?" she asked.

Duke's expression changed to one of pure inno-cence. "I feel fine today, so I'm going to face off with a shark. It's something I want to do before plunging into the great hereafter."

She ignored the implausible scenario, then took a breath, going for it. "About what you said last night...about Will..."

"Remember what I said about you deserving a chance to close your file on him and move on?"

"So you put him in a position where he'd be tempted by wealth? Did you want me to see what he'd do and finally swear off him when he failed?"

A soft smile. "It'll be interesting to see what happens after he hears about the changes I want to make."

Her five percent. "I need to talk to you about that—"

"Don't refuse the possibility, Kat."

She clamped shut her mouth in shame. She hadn't necessarily wanted to refuse—she'd been aiming for more of an explanation, actually.

Dammit, what was happening to her? Was Duke playing mind games with her, too? After all, he'd said he was only *thinking* about changing his will, right?

"Duke, we need to sit down and hash out a lot of things. Okay?"

He smiled, and Kat sighed, giving in to him. Charmer. Then he nodded at someone behind her.

"Morning," he said, chipper as could be.

Kat turned around to find Alexandra and Eloise staring at Duke in his wet suit.

Eloise spoke. "Chris told us you're diving."

The teen appeared next to Alexandra. "Sorry, Gramps. They don't want you to do it."

Duke chuckled. "It's not like it's going to kill me."

A loud argument followed. It was passionate enough to create a scene, drawing Dr. Hopkins and most of the curious crew. Kat pictured the shark cage all by its lonesome, twiddling its aluminum bars and wondering what the holdup was.

When Will made his way to the front of the crowd, Kat's blood gave an excited, wary leap in her veins.

"I won't be responsible for sending you into that cage, Mr. Harrington," Will said.

"It would be worth your while." Duke made the international sign for cash with his fingers by rubbing them together.

Grunting, Will just shook his head and planted his hands on his hips. Even though he had his eye on the big pie in the sky, he apparently had pride in his reputation, also.

Still, too much of it, Kat thought. Pride was responsible for his quest for redemption. Pride was why they couldn't be together.

By now, Duffy, Nestor and Louis had filtered to the back of the crowd, tellingly silent. Kat wondered if they agreed with Eloise and Alexandra about keeping Duke out of the cage or if they wouldn't mind seeing a speedier demise out of the older man.

"Bottom line," Will said, "is that I'll dismantle that cage before I let you get into it."

With that, he headed toward the bridge.

"You're missing a good opportunity," Duke said.

With surging admiration, Kat watched Will disappear, a warm smile on her face. When Duke caught her eye, she lifted her brows, just like she was saying, "So much for him giving in to money."

But when his visage clouded—frustration at being proved wrong?—she stopped smiling, feeling a little owned.

Manipulated.

It riled her temper, her need to find a way out of the net she'd found herself tangled up in.

Cool yourself, Kat, she thought. Losing it isn't going to help at all.

"Let's just go watch Chris from the flying bridge," Kat said to Duke, offering him a graceful way out.

"Hold it." Nestor cleared his throat, reminding everyone of his presence at the back of the crowd. "I say we postpone the dives for a spell, just until we straighten a few matters up."

But Chris was already on his way toward the cage, pulling Dr. Hopkins along with him. Thank God seeing Duke had brought his verve back.

"Let's go!" the boy yelled.

"Not yet," Louis headed off after them.

Nestor took off, too, unsuccessfully urging Chris to come back.

Arms folded over his chest, Duffy watched the chase, then followed his father. The various gathered crew members traded jaded looks, probably used to the drama of the wealthy, then went back to their jobs.

That left Duke, surrounded by disapproving women.

After a tense hesitation, he nodded, his grin sheepish. "Hell, I tried." Then, growing serious, he turned to Eloise and Alexandra. "Thank you for the concern."

As Kat led him away, she noted Alexandra's pleased expression: The almost-hidden relief of someone who'd positioned her chessboard queen in a very strategic square.

Before they'd momentarily left their posts to witness all the hubbub, Larry the dreadlocked and Tinkerbell had eased the cage into the water. So, it was just a matter of getting Chris into the last of his gear, linking him to the "hooka regs"—long-hosed regulators that were connected to oxygen tanks on deck—and helping him inside. Since everyone had been prepped on safety, everything was a go.

As the cage was lowered a couple of feet below the surface, Kat leaned over the flying bridge's railing with Duke and Dr. Hopkins, who had joined them. The clear water gave them an eagle's-eye view of the ocean and cage; they could see Chris holding an underwater video camera, see the bubbles gushing upward with his breaths, see the chum—fish scraps, oil, guts, blood— spread into the ocean to attract sharks.

When the first creature, then the second, appeared,

Kat grabbed Duke's arm, on edge. All that was protecting Chris from a set of dagger-sharp teeth were the cage's bars and the knife that cage-divers wore strapped to their thighs.

The sharks began to take passes at some tuna bait.

"Would you look at that," Duke said.

Dr. Hopkins laughed. "Every time I see them, I can't help feeling like it's my first time."

A ten-footer glided past Chris and the cage. Previously, the doctor had explained that the sharks were conditioned to accept the tourists, but that didn't guarantee safety—not by a long shot.

You never know what a shark is going to do, she'd told Kat on their first day together. *We'll be in their territory, their world, and they own it.*

Never forget that.

"It's always good to give them some healthy respect," Dr. Hopkins added, "but as I've told you before, even though sharks have been around for thirty million years—and they haven't changed much in that time, either—we still don't know a whole lot about them. They still pull the unexpected. For instance, we can be outside of the cage in the water, and never be attacked."

Kat's stomach flipped. "Seriously?"

"Seriously. In fact, shark attacks in the United States are less frequent than homicides or auto deaths. You'd never know it by the kind of attention the media gives them though, would you?"

Duke straightened up, creaking with the effort. "Judging by the news, the sea is full of jaws."

Without much energy, he squeezed Kat's arm as he left the flying bridge, saying something about a nap, while the women chattered and watched Chris. From all the doctor's information these past couple of days, Kat felt confident about her own dive. She wasn't as afraid of these predators half as much as she'd been back in San Diego, where surfing myths about man-eating sharks ruled the day.

By this time, the ten-footer had started to "test" the cage bars, as Dr. Hopkins explained. Its teeth had been scraping the aluminum with every pass and, now, it had graduated to biting the cage.

"When this happens to you," she said, "just remember that it's trying to determine what the cage *is.*"

"Or if it would make good grub." Kat wondered if Chris had peed in his suit yet. But she had to hand it to him; he looked real collected down there all by himself.

Seconds later, one shark had left, but the ten-footer was still hanging out, going back to eat more chum.

When it finished, it tested the rope that connected the cage to the boat—the lifeline. Kat gasped.

"Is that okay?"

"It'll realize the rope tastes awful."

But then it happened.

The ten-footer gave a powerful yank on the lifeline.

"Tell me *that's* okay, Doctor."

Dr. Hopkins backed away from the railing, gazing at the water. She started to walk toward the stairs with Kat.

Tinkerbell started yelling at Larry.

The shark wrenched on the rope again.

Chris's cage began to float…underneath the boat. A trail of bubbles spurted out of the top. His breathing had gone erratic.

Kat took off down the stairs, Dr. Hopkins on her tail.

Grasping for breath, she came to stand by Larry. He'd retrieved another lifeline and was ready to throw it toward the cage for Chris to grab.

"Is that going to work?" Kat asked.

A jagged voice cut the air. "What's happening?"

Will. Calm, in control, green-blue eyes blazing.

"Old Ten Speed got a hold of the lifeline," Larry said, gesturing toward the shark, who'd deserted the rope and resubmerged. A faint thud from the bottom of the boat spoke for the peril of Chris in his cage.

Will leaned over the vessel's side. "Did he tear it? How—?"

Kat joined him, heart thudding until it beat in her ears. "What can we do?"

He leaned over further, inspecting the rope. The length was taut, moaning with tension.

"Shit," Will said, a hint of fear in his tone.

Kat saw the problem. The strands were splitting and every push of the current weakened them as the rope was stretched.

Will looked ready to kill. "I inspected everything *myself* before we started. That rope should withstand more than a test bite."

She knew the cage couldn't be hauled in the old-fashioned way. "Can't we all grab the rope below where it's damaged and bring it in?"

Even as she said it, she knew it was an idiotic question. There wasn't enough length between the cage and the yielding strands for them to get leverage.

Will pushed away from the boat's edge. "Larry, get your lifeline in the water."

"And what happens if Chris can't grab it?" she asked.

She didn't really expect an answer, especially since Will was already holding the rope below the frayed strands, his arms in the water, muscles straining as he battled to keep the cage from floating to the bottom of the ocean.

"Are you loco?" she yelled, her pent-up emotion for him coming out as anger.

"I think Ten Speed is gone!" a voice said from the flying bridge. It was Shaw, on watch. "I don't get any readings on the equipment!"

And then the crap really hit the fan.

At first, Kat only heard the bubbles. But then she saw it.

Chris's regulator mouthpiece, still hooked to the hose. It was dancing in the water like an agitated snake.

Which meant Chris wasn't getting any air.

She didn't stop to think. Pulling the diving hood over her head, Kat dashed over to her fins and mask, boarded the swim step at the back of the boat, spat in her mask, rinsed it then jammed that and her fins on. She heard someone yelling at her, but she was already treading in the warm water before the words made any sense.

"Kat, we're not positive that shark is gone for good!"

It'd been Will's voice, serrated with frantic concern.

But she'd think about Will…and everything else…later.

All that mattered now was Chris.

This is just another day at the pearl show, that's all, she thought to herself, sucking air into her lungs and bobbing up in order to dive under. If she needed more, she could go to Chris's abandoned regulator, but there was no time now.

Slipping under the waterline, she was enveloped and felt welcomed, as usual. Steeped in the blue of a beautifully forbidden place.

A place that could be hiding death.

Balancing between her normal fear and exhilaration, she swam under the boat, the echo of her heartbeat filling the universe. The fear kept her from looking behind her. She was afraid of what she might find.

Instead, she immediately locked on to the cage. Chris was holding his breath, pushing at the top of the structure in order to get out.

Was it stuck?

When he saw her, a bubble of surprised gratitude escaped him, and she signaled for him to calm down. Then, working smoothly, telling herself that undoing a cage was no trickier than collecting an oyster, she pulled at the top hatch, which really was jammed.

Adrenaline spiking her to action, Kat braced her feet against the boat, pushing the cage away from it. Bubbles of air flew out of her mouth, every one a countdown to possible failure.

She was getting dizzy, but it didn't matter. All she knew was that the hatch was opening and Chris was squirming out, that she had to get him back to the boat before…

Chris's eyes widened behind his mask, and Kat didn't look.

Couldn't look.

Her chest drew into itself, her pulse beating through her suit.

Up…boat…get Chris out of here…

Dr. Hopkins's lectures slashed through her mind: *It's their territory, so it's better to leave them to it than challenge them for it.*

Remember, you can meet a shark without being attacked, but don't count on it.

Never make sudden moves; they'll think you're wounded prey.

Carry something to tap that shark on the snout if it gets feisty with you.

Kat's chest was aching, the lack of air tearing her lungs apart. But they were so close to the surface. She could even see arms reaching toward them, warped by the wavering water above.

Three feet… Two… O…

She pushed Chris upward with all her might, expelling almost all of her oxygen. He flew away from her, carried off by the crew.

What happened next took place in the bang of a heartbeat. In what seemed like a soundless experimental movie, she could see Tinkerbell with her dark skin and red hair, her mouth opened in what looked like a frenzied yell. Will was on the other side of her, reaching for Kat, reaching…

Something bumped against her leg.

Kat couldn't stop herself. She looked.

God help me, help me...

As the shark circled to her right, Kat tried not to thrash around, to play the victim...the meal.

But its back was arched, its pectoral fins lowered.

A pose of agitation.

She hadn't brought anything like a shark billyclub, something to pop it with and let it know she wasn't a snack. All she had were her fists, a knife...

...and a second chance.

As the creature opened its mouth, rows of spired teeth gleamed.

Just...

Kat's body tensed.

Do...

She readied herself.

It...

With the last of her energy and breath, she grasped through the water and sprang toward the outstretched hands awaiting her.

Will was the first to grab her, flinging her out of the water with a sucking splash and pinning her to the deck.

"Here it—" began Shaw from the flying bridge.

But he didn't finish.

"...goes!" Tinkerbell completed the sentence for Shaw. "Look at that! Ten Speed isn't interested anymore, the fickle freak."

Heaving breath into her lungs, Kat succumbed to the sky whirling above her, closing her eyes and hugging her knees to her chest as Will rolled away from on top of her. Bright lights flashed over her eyelids, freezing her brain, burning her chest. The strange whistling technique she used during her pearl dives provided rhythm, solace. The shallow breaths protected her heart and lungs.

"You're damned lucky," Will ground out.

Even though he was mightily ticked off, Kat knew he was relieved. She could hear it in the way he breathed, feel it the way he stayed next to her, touching her back. Joy welled—joy at being alive, joy at touching him again.

"As soon as we get you checked out," he added under his breath, "we've got to deal with some nasty stuff."

Panting, Kat managed to ask, "What do you...?" She couldn't continue.

"I think the cage's lifeline might've been *cut*."

Chapter 6

They were all seated around the dining table, most of the crew standing against the walls. Kat and Chris were wrapped in a blanket, his head resting on her shoulder. He hadn't left her for a minute, even while Wayne the medic efficiently looked her over and pronounced her "fit as a fiddle" in his countrified drawl.

Although Kat was wracked by shivers more mental than physical, she didn't pay much attention to that. Chris seemed in much worse shape. His body was drawn raggedly tight like a quivering string on a bow that was ready to break. Instead of talking, the poor kid stared, mouth taut, his victim's gaze a thousand miles away.

The boy refused to go near anyone except her and

Duke. And when Kat had tried to find out the reason, he'd only shaken his head, never answering.

Something was going on, and Kat was on the outside. But she wasn't the only one who was suspicious, especially after she'd told Will about everything that'd happened last night.

"We're going home," he announced now, as he stood at the head of the table. "I'm getting this boat back to U.S. territory as soon as possible."

Louis gestured toward the shredded lifeline that was lying on the wood. "I don't feel safe out here, either."

The edges of the room puckered with the tensing bodies of the crew members. Larry elbowed Tinkerbell, as if saying, "I told you we'd get the brunt of this."

Duke, from his spot next to Will, managed to pick up the rope and inspect the end of it with quivering hands. A tiny, clean cut led to an explosion of frayed, reddened fibers.

"Mr. Delacroix," Will said, jaw tight as he leaned over the table toward Louis, "I'm sure I don't have to say it again, but I will. I inspected the rig, just as I always do, before it went in the water. The cage was left alone for only minutes as Larry and Tink went to see what was going down when Duke came out in his wet suit. There was no way they could predict that someone would start slicing the rope…and rub chum on it."

Kat carefully looked at each face in the salon. No one reacted out-of-line. There were just your basic raised eyebrows and opened mouths at this last bit of news. No indication of guilt from anyone.

So who'd done it?

A terrible thought rose from her worst fears: was Will grasping at straws to save his reputation? Was he trying to avert guilt and keep the job that provided so many connections for him to "get back into the game"? Was he blaming someone else for his failure to keep his guests safe?

Come on, she chided herself. Don't be ridiculous.

"Chum?" Duffy asked, the skin around his wounded eye a palette of angry colors. "Maybe the rope dragged through the blood and guts out in that water."

"You're right," Will said, standing back up, shrugging. "It could've happened. Then again, maybe someone wanted to increase the odds that a shark would taste-test the rope, insuring that the strands would be torn the rest of the way when the shark yanked at it. That tiny cut wasn't enough to do all the damage itself. But...I know. That's a lot of what-ifs. That's also a lot of desperation, and who in this room could possibly feel that way—especially after what happened last night?" Will leveled a glare at the Delacroix family. "Who thought Duke was getting into that cage and could've set him up to die before he could change his will?"

His accusation was out in the open, wobbling like a compass needle that was searching out a culprit.

Louis gave Will a measuring glance. "Do you *hear* yourself, Captain?"

Maybe it was because of the stress. Maybe it was...something else. Whatever caused it, Will lost his temper and grabbed Louis by the starched collar, heaving him off the chair and up to his reddening face.

"Do you remember what happened?" he asked. "Let me remind you. Kat had to dive for Chris while a shark was still lolling around. Something or someone—accident or not—made that cut in the rope, *sir.*"

Louis frantically grasped at Will's hands to free himself, his face still slack with surprise. Will shook the man once, making his point before he thrust the patriarch into his chair. Then, with a plastic smile, he backed off.

"Sorry," Will said through his teeth. "I'm sure you're just as upset."

Pride, Kat thought, pulse racing, heart breaking under the small cracks of her doubts about the man she'd loved. *Temper.*

Alexandra, of all people, coolly interrupted. "We're all grateful for what Katsu did to save Chris."

Kat blinked, taken aback. While the rest of the family seized Alexandra's cue and thanked Kat, Chris's body tensed even more.

But then Kat noticed Duffy glowering at her, his black eye glowing in a slant of wan light, and she came back to earth. *Yeah,* he seemed to be saying, *you're a big hero, Kat.*

Louis kept quiet, his eyes on Will and no one else as the captain spoke to Duke.

"We'll talk about refunds later, Mr. Harrington, but I'd like to get this boat turned around."

"There's no chance of staying?" Duke asked.

He sounded so sad, as if, in spite of what had happened with the cage, he still held out hope his family would come around.

Didn't he realize that he could've been a possible victim today? The saboteur could've made that cut after they found out Duke was planning to dive.

Or maybe Chris, the beneficiary of ninety-five percent of Duke's holdings, really *had* been the target....

Kat slid her arm around his shoulders, only to feel the slight tremors holding his body together.

And maybe Chris damned well knew that already.

Will was shaking his head in response to Duke's question. He lingered next to Louis, a silent intimidator.

"We can't risk that there's someone on this boat with such total disregard for human life. Pretending that nothing happened and continuing this *idyllic* trip isn't even an option."

Nestor raised his hand to speak, probably afraid of Will now. "Who's to say that this person won't try something on the way back?"

"That's a problem I've been mulling over." Will eased the rope away from Duke and inspected the damage, driving home the need for caution. "There's an airstrip on Guadalupe Island. It's a Mexican wildlife preserve, so we could arrange transportation that way."

"No," Eloise said. "I can see us all taking separate planes back home and never speaking again. Father?"

A feeble Duke was slumped in his chair, looking like he'd lost his final battle already. Kat could understand—all his plans to see if his family really loved him had failed.

"Yes, Elle?" he asked. There was still a heartbreaking nimbus surrounding his words.

"Maybe—" his social-matron daughter smiled tearfully "—we could sort everything out on the long trip back. Nobody in the Delacroix family would leave this room until we've resolved every issue. We would never do anything to hurt you or Chris. You need to believe us."

Even though Eloise's plan would keep all the likely suspects in the same place and out of trouble, Kat thought it was a real weird way to deal with an attempted murder.

"Mom—" Duffy began.

Eloise choked him off with a glare so forceful that her son actually flinched. The room froze with the heat of it.

"Your grandfather needs us," she ground out.

Quietly, Will motioned his crew and everyone who wasn't a Delacroix to exit the salon. On the way out, though, he stopped to whisper something to Shaw, the first officer, who gave a gruff nod and stayed in the room.

A watchdog, Kat thought. She'd be watching, too, unless this was all just an exercise in paranoia. Was it?

As she rose from her chair, Chris did, too.

"You need to stay here," she said.

"Kat—" He was scared to death.

"Hey, Chris?" It was Duke, holding open his arms, welcoming his cowed grandson.

Reluctantly, Chris went to him, sat next to his grandfather and avoided looking at the Delacroixs.

When Duke sent Kat a beseeching glance, also, she shook her head, continuing out of the salon. In the dark part of her mind, she saw money falling from the gray sky, just out of her reach, resting on the waves of an ocean that would carry it away forever.

But that was okay, she told herself as she left. She didn't need wealth.

She risked one last peek at Duke to reassure him. He seemed so much smaller and more fragile now than the larger-than-life man of story. But at least Chris was nestled, like a support beam, in the crook of Duke's arm.

They'd be fine without her.

Still, as she headed away from Will, who'd gone to the bridge, she couldn't help guessing what was being said in the salon. Were the Delacroixs going to offer the ultimate snow job to Duke? How far would they go to secure their inheritance and convince him that they loved him?

Hell, all Kat knew was that there was a good chance that someone had gone too far this morning.

But...God. The enormity of what had happened *finally* hit her—a giant fist mashing into her stomach and leaving her breathless.

Chris in the cage. The shark.

How could anyone do it? Was there actually someone on this boat who hated Duke or Chris so much that they would arrange a terrible death for them?

Was it one of the Delacroixs with their appetite for money? Duffy, Nestor and Louis had been late in joining the crowd this morning. They would've had time to mess with the cage after hearing about Duke's planned dive.

Or was it someone who wasn't so obvious?

Unbidden, the memories came back: Will flirting with Alexandra. Will losing his temper with Louis.

Then, just as if Kat was looking at an extension of that memory underwater, where her view was bent and surreal, she saw how it could've played out:

Will, whispering with Alexandra...making a tiny cut to the rope and slathering it with chum...assuring Larry and Tinkerbell that the equipment was secure...confronting Duke about going in the water just to throw off suspicion, then...

Alexandra's chess-queen expression.

In her rampant imagination, Kat saw the future, where Alexandra cried at Duke's funeral, then wrote a check to Will for his troubles. A big check. A check that would guarantee a fresh start for Will and his family. Maybe she had even promised to introduce him into her social circles...

"Penny for your thoughts."

It was Dr. Janelle Hopkins, lounging on a chair, one ankle resting on the opposite knee as she lay beneath a sky that was growing darker by the moment, riddled with heavy clouds. They'd already turned around, headed back to San Diego, and water chopped against the boat as if trying to grab on to them but losing hold.

Kat tried to play it off as if her thoughts weren't even worth a penny. But, truthfully, her doubts about Will had throttled her to the core. Especially since she realized that it was her doubt doing all the mental dirty work. Doubt raised by their breakup and the question of how well she'd really known Will after all.

She sat in a chair next to the doctor, and the other

woman gestured toward the main cabin. Hugh, the steward, was loitering outside, as if watching them.

"Did you notice," Hopkins said, "that the captain left Shaw in the room? He's the security guard, I imagine."

"Making sure no one cuts another family member's throat. Yeah, I noticed. And I see we've got our own cop. But I have to admit—it's not a bad idea to have someone keeping an eye on everyone. It's that or the plane, and I know Duke will argue against that until he gets his way."

"True enough, Don't you think that family's a little slippery, even someone as harmless as Nestor?"

Why did the doc think the culprit might be a Delacroix?

Kat scanned the doctor's open body language, remembering all the signs of attraction between Janelle and Nestor.

"Why have you been...well, getting to know him?" Kat asked.

Janelle laughed a little, more the naughty flirt Kat had hung out with yesterday. "You mean in the Biblical sense?"

Ah-ha.

Now, Janelle's laugh was amused. "You saw it coming a mile away, Kat. I *know* you did. And, in my opinion, it's a hell of a lot more comforting to talk about this than..."

No need to say it. Kat nodded in understanding.

"Anyway," Janelle said, "it was just a 'thang.' He was wrung-out after the blowup last night, I was around, and we got to drinking, then..." She made an "oops" gesture. "You know."

"Yeah," Kat said, having very little one-night-stand experience to draw upon on, herself. Her post-Will love life found her preferring surfing to dating. Lots less trouble.

"What can I say?" Absently, Janelle rubbed a finger over her dusky complexion. "He's charming, fun and so very temporary. And he was willing to slum a little."

"Slumming? With you?"

"Kat."

Janelle didn't have to explain. She wasn't in Nestor's social set. It was a story Kat knew well. But the doctor didn't seem to take as much offense as Kat always had.

The doctor leaned forward, lowering her voice. "You take the opportunities where they come, right?"

"Sure."

As Janelle leaned back and closed her eyes, she started giving Kat more details.

But she wasn't listening. Rather, Kat was thinking about the events in the salon. Wondering when she'd hear about the outcome of the big talk.

As it would turn out, the nightmare started before that could actually happen.

Thankfully the Delacroixs stayed in the salon for hours, taking dinner there, talking into the night. Once, when Kat passed the door to see if they were almost done, she heard laughter, and even though she was happy for Duke to know they were making headway, she was also unable to stop errant thoughts about more dollar bills falling just out of her grasp.

She hated herself for that. Ultimately, she tried to sleep in her cabin, rocked by waves that seemed to be increasing in power and anger. Waves that churned inside her.

For what seemed like hours, she lay without closing her eyes. But then…then everything fell apart with the sudden smash of a head-on road accident.

Something crashed against the boat, a watery anvil jarring her out of the berth and to the floor.

The room seemed to tilt on its side, wind wailing, the boat *yawww*ing like the doors of all the dark abandoned houses neighborhood children were too afraid to visit.

Kat sprang to her feet, aiming herself toward the wall where an orange life jacket swung back and forth.

Storm, she thought. Much worse than last night…

The boat violently pitched upward, then hammered down, practically taking the floor out from beneath her bare feet. Pulse sputtering, she managed to slip into her shorts and light tennis shoes and secure her life jacket over her body. Chest tight with anxiety, she found herself weaving to the door.

The hallway seemed to be swaying on the same rollers as her cabin. The lights bursting on and off were like some demented Morse code pattern. Another door flew open, and Dr. Hopkins, life jacket in hand, tumbled into the hall.

Maybe I did fall asleep and I'm dreaming, Kat thought.

Then—even later, Kat wasn't sure what happened next. She could only recall a monstrous keening sound, a thousand women crying at the top of their lungs.

Smash, slash, boom—

Hit head-on by a stone wall…toppling, heeling over before Kat had a chance to suck in a breath.

That's when her sight broke apart, splatters of wood spearing away from themselves, an explosion that erased the boat from the face of the ocean.

Kat smacked into the dark water below it, salty liquid shoved into her mouth. It felt like an invisible hand pinning her under, drowning her, just like *that* day, at the beach, pinning her to the sand, helpless.

Her brain couldn't register the sensations quickly enough—gulping, choking on brine, arms flailing, head dunking under again and again until…

Her hand hit something on the surface, and she clawed to grab on to it. She pulled it to her, levering herself upward, breaking the surface of the water.

Sinking over the piece of wood, she sputtered and coughed, the wind and waves still attacking her.

The life she'd felt sliding away rushed back. Her vision scrambled and chilled her blood until life thrashed in her veins, pumping her with the will to survive.

Got to get out of here. Got to…

She got her bearings as best as she could in the dark. Lightning flashed, revealing pieces of the boat washing around her like shrapnel. Rocks stood against the crashing waves. A mass of dark ridges loomed nearby.

Was that…?

A sheet of water slammed against her, coupled with lightning and thunder. Rain? Spray? She gulped against it, a splinter of hope stabbing her belly.

Was that land?

She embraced the optimism. She was going to beat this storm, dammit. The water wouldn't get her. It would *never* beat her down.

Another silent blade of lightning revealed, amidst the debris near her, a blond head bobbing below the water, a hand reaching out for help.

Without hesitation, she kicked toward it, using the wood to keep herself afloat. The waves fought her, but she was helped by an unexpected ally—the moon. As if choosing sides, it ripped a shroud of clinging clouds from its face, shining faint light on the ocean.

As Kat struggled onward, Eloise screamed to the surface, arms jerking as she tried to find purchase on whatever would prove solid. Using all her strength, Kat yanked the older woman up and onto her plank. Groaning with the effort, she pushed Eloise until she lay gasping, her fingers taloned as she scratched at the wood.

Wildly, Kat scanned the rolling waves for others. At first, all she saw was floating furniture, abandoned life jackets, a book winging face down.

Chris. Where the hell was he? And Will…?

Her gaze fixed onto a colorful piece of wood about fifty feet away and…oh, no, no, no. The plank bore a shirt. One of Duke's tiki shirts.

Kat turned to Eloise and yelled, "Kick toward land!" Her voice was hoarse, but she thought that the other woman heard.

She didn't have time to make sure. Dammit, how could she swim to Duke?

There was only one way she could think of that

would be faster than fighting the waves. Let the water help you, she thought. Trust it.

She shucked off her life jacket. Without a moment's regret, she heaved in a deep breath. Submerging, she gave herself to the ocean she knew—the one that made her feel akin to it. The one less affected by what was going on above the surface.

She kicked through the restless darkness, swimming around falling debris. When she reached the spot where Duke was floating, she burst out of the water, fetched a bobbing white seat cushion, shoved and held it under his body.

"Duke!" she screamed, trying to turn him over.

She could've sworn she saw his chest rise. Maybe he hadn't been facedown for long.

Please, God, please let him be breathing!

She heard the commotion before she saw it coming—a growing roar.

Taking a huge breath, Kat braced herself for the wave. Her surfer's sense made navigating waves a natural instinct. Luckily, she was at the point where it lifted her, carried her, then deposited her behind its roll, but it had separated her from Duke....

With a smashing rush it pounded over him.

"No!"

In the distance, the white cushion wavered in the foam. Alone.

Before she could scream, another wave swept her up and pushed her toward shore. Sand scraped her knees as she crawled to her feet. Legs rubbery, she could barely stand as rain fell around her. Through its opaque rush, she thought she saw Eloise sprawled on the beach. Someone else was a little farther down, with…was that Alexandra?

Frantically, while the rain slashed at her skin and blurred her sight, she scanned the angry ocean. The wreckage.

She couldn't see if there were any more people out there, she couldn't…

She crumbled to the sand, consumed by utter cold and disbelief.

But she would've saved that sense of horror if she'd only known what the next few days would bring.

Chapter 7

By dawn, survivors had gathered from different parts of the beach, the wind and rain chopping around them.

Kat. Louis. Eloise. Dr. Hopkins. Alexandra. All that was left of the crew: Larry and Tinkerbell.

And…thank God. Chris.

As the bedraggled party huddled against each other under a rock overhang that overlooked the beach, shielding them from the elements and affording them enough light to live by, Kat hugged Chris to her, trying to keep him—*them*—warm. The storm batted against pine and cypress trees, all the survivors shivering from the cold in tattered clothing still wet and clammy. Bruises colored Kat's aching flesh. Scrapes marked her skin like gnawing burns—living tattoos earned from the sand and rocks.

She could faintly see the shoreline of their unknown island from where they sat. Past the curtain of rain the wreckage could barely be seen washing up. Now that the sky was a temperamental gray, giving her the weak illumination to reveal what they were up against, Kat's mind started to shed its veil of numbness and go to work.

"The other survivors won't be able to find us up here," she said, throat stripped raw.

None of them responded at first. Was it because they had no ideas or because they thought the others weren't alive and were too overcome to speak?

Kat wouldn't accept that last part. No way. Duke was out there somewhere, and so was...

Tears prickled her eyes, infusing her with regret. Will wasn't dead. He was too smart, too vital. If anyone was stronger than the sea, it was him.

Duke, Nestor, Duffy, the rest of the crew...she was more doubtful about their chances than Will's.

Louis, holding Eloise to his chest as she squeezed her eyes shut, finally stirred. The husband and wife were mourning the absence of their sons and...possibly...Duke. A shell-shocked Chris had already told Kat that things hadn't changed with the Delacroixs, even after their family meeting on the boat. They had all remained weird around one another.

Louis's coarsened voice hinted at the depths of his sadness. "We have nothing to guide any survivors, Katsu. The weather won't allow us to build a signal fire. It's too wet."

"Too fierce," Larry added. He and Tinkerbell had

crowded against each other for heat. "This weather is a demon. It'll keep Search and Rescue away, even if they received the captain's distress signal and know our location. Just look at that tumbling water. There won't be planes or ships out this way until all of this settles."

"Lovely," said a female voice to the right of Kat.

A nasty cut decorated Alexandra's cheek. Probably in an effort to deny the loss of her brothers…and grand-father?…she'd avoided crying and had wholeheartedly thrown herself into the duty of playing nursemaid to Dr. Hopkins, using a life jacket to prop the woman's head up. The scientist seemed to be in worse shape than any of them, her face tight with anguish as she cowered from the cold. She was in the fetal position, hunching over her hands, which had been smashed by falling debris during the wreck.

"I'm just being realistic," Larry said. Moisture beaded on his dreadlocks. "I've never experienced anything like this. It happened so fast…"

Tinkerbell sniffed. Her dark face looked scoured. "And the storm isn't stopping."

"First, there were whitecaps," Larry continued. "From out of nowhere. Then—kaboom. Everything went to hell." He hugged Tink to him. "Captain did his damnedest to get us out of it, steered us toward this chain of isolated islands—God even knows which one we're on—and shouted his Mayday before the commu-nications equipment went out."

"While that's all very interesting," Alexandra said, "it doesn't help us right now."

As Larry shot the rich girl a dirty look, the wheels

turned even harder in Kat's brain. Kat knew that she, herself, was the last person she wanted to depend on, but it sounded like they needed to help themselves for the time being.

"I'll be going down to the beach," she said, "whether the storm clears or not."

"Don't." Chris clung to her waist.

Alexandra stood, glaring at the beach. "We don't even know what's out there. You wouldn't be safe."

"So what do you want to do then?" Kat gestured behind them, to a dark entrance that she thought might lead to better shelter. A deeper cave than the open-sided shelter they were in now. "Waiting out this storm means we might be here a while. We'll need warmth and light for nighttime, which is going to be here before we know it. We'll need food. Water. We'll need a signal that leads the others to us and attracts Search and Rescue."

"How can we do that without fire?" Louis asked, just as though Kat knew all the answers.

His apparent confidence took her aback. She was no survival expert, but her dad had learned a thing or two in the military. Kat had been his "little tomboy," loving to hear all his stories of wilderness training and exotic assignments because it'd meant quality time together.

But, God help her, it was hard to remember the details of what he'd told her so long ago.

Kat pointed toward the beach. "There're things washing up. Who knows what we can salvage? And I'm wondering…" Okay, would her idea sound stupid?

"What?" Larry asked.

His interest propped up Kat's self-esteem. Suddenly, she realized that she—bullied Katsu—had somehow taken the lead here, that the others were watching her. Depending on her.

"What if we tried to make some kind of sign on the beach for the rescue plane that'll come after the storm?" she asked. "An SOS made out of wood pieces? Larry said this island is just one in a chain. S&R might not know which one we're on, so we'll have to help them out."

"That can be done later," Louis added.

"Are you taking charge?" Tink fired at the Delacroix patriarch as she got to her knees, bunching her fists.

Louis moved away from Eloise, his face going red. "Watch your mouth, you little—"

Larry sprang over to Louis, his hand reaching for the patriarch's throat.

"Stop it!" Kat yelled, darting toward Larry and hauling him back by the arm. She took him by the shoulders. "Calm down. We're depending on you." She glanced at everyone. "All of you. The last thing we need is more injuries. Can't you guys just think with me instead of going crazy?"

Clearly ashamed, Larry backed off as Tink sat him down. He gave Kat an apologetic glance.

The tussle with Duffy, she thought. *That's* the day she'd won Larry's respect.

When she looked at Louis, he seemed stunned. They'd all have to remember to cut the Delacroixs some slack, even though they were all hurting in their own ways.

Duke. Will…

She chased away the renewed devastation in the pit of her belly. "Maybe we can make…I don't know…arrows or something on the ground for the others to find us. Arrows pointing to this cave."

Tink stood. "Perfect."

"We need weapons." Larry shook his head. "As the rich girl said, we don't know what's out there."

Alexandra flashed an irritated glance at the crew member. She was hiding her sorrow well…if she was feeling any, that is.

"But we know what we have up here," Kat said. "And that's nothing. Zip. If the weather doesn't calm down soon, we'll be dehydrated and starving."

When she got to her feet, Chris followed her.

"No," she said. "You're staying."

"I want to go," Chris whispered. His hangdog look told Kat just how much he needed her.

Understanding his reluctance to be with the family he clearly still didn't trust, Kat wasn't sure what to do. All she was sure of was that Duke's disappearance was, in a cynical way, very fortunate for the Delacroixs.

When it came right down to it, she didn't trust them alone with the possible ninety-five-percent heir, either. Not after a possible attempt had already been made on his life.

Dr. Hopkins weakly spoke up. "Come here, Chris. You can keep me company, all right?"

"Yeah." Kat patted the teen's back, then leaned down to whisper into his ear. "I won't be gone long enough for anyone to mess with you."

"You think you'll find…" His words choked to a stop.

But he didn't have to finish.

"I'm sure your gramps is out there," Kat said, voice thick. "Don't worry."

And Will was out there, too. Somewhere. God, please, *somewhere.* In the face of near death, it was clear. Life was giving her a second chance, and she couldn't blow it if he was still alive. Her beating the storm had swept away the doubts for now, made her see what she needed to do.

But she knew she might be riding a stream of misguided hope, even as she cautiously led Larry, Tink and Alexandra down the slope toward the beach. A fevered, wet breeze throttled the harboring trees, the bushes, making every step a terrifying leap into the unknown.

What was hiding behind each piece of foliage? How long would it be before they found out?

Feral aminals, a killer… Immediately, Kat suggested that the group pick up sticks to arm themselves, the pointier the better.

At the shore the wind was so strong that it threatened to gust them to the ground, so they hurried their pace gathering useful wreckage scraps, running from the relative safety of the trees to the beach, then back again. Little by little, they retrieved light boxes, bags, pieces of driftwood that had all been spat out by the churning tide.

When they dug into their trove, they found gems: a box of bagged potato chips from the galley, plastic cups, individual cans of soda, a bag of health and beauty aids, some loose diving gear—including a mask tangled with a holstered knife—plus a screwdriver and a bigger sheathed knife with a wicked blade wrapped in the ties of a seat cushion. Shaw's knife.

They were optimistic for the first time in hours, ooohing at every present. Kat clipped the sheath of Shaw's eight-and-a-half-inch knife to a belt loop, hoping she'd never need it for wildlife protection, but thinking it was good insurance anyway.

Soon, she led one more trip to the open beach with Tinkerbell while the others worked on that SOS sign and those arrows for the other possible survivors. And that's when she came upon the best treasure of all washed to shore.

A battered body dressed in a ragged tiki shirt and khaki pants. He was scratching at the rocks…

"Duke!" she yelled, pulling Tink with her so they could both drag him back to the trees.

Kat laid the bloodied man on the ground. Heart joyful, she tested his pulse, put her ear next to his mouth, hoping to hear healthy exhalation.

Faint, on both counts. God, was he in shock? Kat was no medical expert so she went with her gut instinct—checking his airway.

"Warmth," she said, voice shaking. "I think we need to warm him up, too."

As if lured by Kat's voice, Duke shuddered and coughed up seawater in a violent burble.

Spent and laughing in relief, she sank over him, shot through with so much happiness that she could barely move.

Duke's eyes cracked open. His breath was thick with wheezing. But he'd beaten the ocean, too, Kat thought, and she laughed a little wildly because her body didn't know what else to do.

A few hours later, they were all back at the shelter. Duke, warmed by Chris's body heat as his grandson embraced him, was just waking up from a nap on his own life jacket bed. He'd taken a cuffing from some rocks and his face and body were cut and scraped. He didn't remember anything, he said, just the boat smashing, then him waking up, safe in Kat's arms.

Her heart sparked, but a part of her was still steeped in darkness. Was Will out there somewhere, too? And did he need her help just as badly?

She yearned to brave the storm again in order to find him, but Duke was holding her hand, watching her with such gratitude and tenderness that she couldn't bear to leave him for fear of bringing about a setback.

Will's young and strong, she reminded herself. Duke isn't. And Duke is the one who's alive, the one who needs me right now.

Please be alive, Will. Stay alive so I can tell you how much I still need you....

As she nursed the old man and the Delacroixs made a fuss over his return, Tinkerbell and Larry had risked a second trip to the beach and brought back a few more items, including wood and blankets that were now airing out. Hopefully everyone would be on their way back home before the wood even dried, but it was smart to be prepared anyway.

Best of all, Tink and Larry had found a waterproof bag that held a first-aid kit and a flashlight. Kat had tended to Duke's cuts and Alexandra had seen to Dr. Hopkins's injuries. But now Janelle and Alex were sleeping, leveled by everything they'd been through these past twelve hours. Louis and Eloise had even settled down for their own naps.

Tinkerbell and Larry were using the flashlight, the screwdriver and some heavy pieces of wood—aka clubs—to check out the deeper cave's interior. They would have used the diving knife for defense, too, but in all the hustle and bustle, it'd been lost.

But it's around somewhere, Kat thought, resting her hand on the one knife she'd claimed. When Louis had commented on her find earlier, she'd told him that she intended to protect them *all* from wild animals. She hadn't dared mention anything about people. Louis and the others had let it go, which surprised Kat. It was almost like she'd earned the knife and the trust that went with carrying it.

In spite of their bounty, the party was still missing a few essentials: a radio, more food and Duke's medications. Kat wasn't sure how long he'd last without them.

She helped him to sip from a plastic cup that had been collecting rainwater outside. Chris sat down with them, helping Duke drink, too. The older man couldn't take much though. He crumbled into himself, holding his stomach, retching with dry heaves.

As Chris steadied his grandfather, Kat watched them. There was a bond there—a steel cable that wrapped around the two of them, cocooning Chris and Duke from the rest of the world. Their affection isolated her even as it made her happy to know that Duke had someone so constant.

She only wished she had that, also.

Grief ripped through her again. She'd blown her chance with Will. And now it was too late.

He's dead, along with Duffy and Nestor and the rest of the crew. Stop torturing yourself by believing he's going to come back to you.

The worst part? There wasn't a damned thing she could do to make up for it.

A sob thrust its way out of her chest, and she held it back, covering her face. Exhaustion mingled with her loss, and she fell helpless under the power of them both.

"Kat?"

She felt Chris's hand on her arm.

Angrily, she brushed away her tears. "I'm okay."

"No, you're not," said Duke in a frail voice. "None of us are."

"But I *am*," she said, hating that she was sniffling. Pissed, she willed the sadness to stop. All she had to do was pretend she was underwater, filtering out the fear.

"I can take care of myself." She inhaled, then blew out a cleansing breath. There. Better.

Duke's laugh was weak, yet genuine. "You've got spark, Kat. You're the best…"

She helped him finish the feel-good mantra. "…whether I know it or not."

They both laughed. Better now. Much better.

"Gramps always tells me what gumption you've got." Chris obviously felt special about being Duke's confidant. "He always says how cool you are, and that you never take garbage from anyone."

Except herself, she thought.

"She learned to overcome the odds from her dad," Duke said, closing his eyes to rest.

Kat stroked Duke's damp forehead, comforting him. "And my mom."

She hadn't realized she'd said it until the words echoed in the aftermath.

"I thought she died before you were really old enough to know her," Duke whispered.

"I was three."

Fleetingly, images came to Kat: tatami mats covering the floor, a beautifully arranged dinner on the table, the graceful curve of her mom's arm as she held Kat to her shoulder, the lilt of her soft voice as Mariko sang her daughter to sleep amidst the scent of her flowered perfume.

Now Kat was calmed, as if she was floating in the quiet of water. No fear. No sadness. Just peace, an affinity with everything around her. Her mom would've reacted this gracefully to problems. Dad had always told her so.

"I wish," Kat said, "I'd known her. I wonder how different my life would be. Would I have been less of a tomboy?"

Would she have developed such an attitude about the world?

"You got that from your dad," Duke said, referring to the tomboy part.

"How did they meet?" Chris asked. "Your mom and dad?"

Kat knew what they were doing. Avoidance. They didn't want to see her cry—God, she didn't want that, either—so they were doing their best to distract her. She adored them for it.

"My dad was a lieutenant in the army at Camp Zama. My mom was—" An outcast. *Eta.* "—eager to escape. She loved everything western, Dad told me. And when they saw each other at a market in Sagami-hara, it was love at first sight. She wanted to see the States, so when he was discharged, he took her." Kat's chest warmed. "Whenever he'd talk about her, he'd get this silly grin, then become so sad. He loved my mom so much and, after she was in that car accident, he never recovered."

"Have you ever been to Japan?" Chris asked.

"I could never afford it. And, really, I have to say I wasn't too interested." Not until now, when the idea suddenly seemed so important. So impossible. "My grandparents were shamed by my mom's behavior, marrying a *gaijin*—a foreigner. And to make matters worse, he was like a lower level *gaijin*, with dark hair and eyes. A mixed-blood granddaughter isn't exactly some-thing to brag about. Even though they wrote the occa-sional letter to me, I didn't feel a lot of love or tolerance."

Ironic, Kat thought sadly, because as *burakumin*—social outcasts themselves—her grandparents should've known better.

"Mixed blood," Chris said. "You make it sound bad."

"The Japanese word is *konketsujin*. And, if you'd had to grow up with all the idiotic comments I had to hear from the kids at school, you'd think it was bad, too."

"Bullies."

"Yeah, bullies."

They smiled at each other, the goofy rich kid and the bristly misfit at a complete understanding.

"So," he said, "who taught you how to surf?"

"My dad." Kat's smile grew softer. "Those were the best times we had together, me and him. Not many girls from my area hung at the beach, but it was the best way for me to avoid…well, let's just say 'after-school activities.'"

In the water, none of their taunts could touch her. It had just been her and her dad, floating, her depending on him until, one day, she'd had the power to swim by herself, away from him. Never really to return.

Kat sighed. "He died long ago."

Chris just nodded, and they lapsed into silence, leaving Kat to mull over her regrets. Why had she and her father drifted apart anyway? Did it happen when he'd started seeing another woman seriously—the first real girlfriend he'd had since Mariko's death?

Was it because Kat saw that woman as just another girl who embraced the 'hood philosophy, complete with bad attitude and justifications for not succeeding in life? For not giving her all in school, for not having higher expectations of herself?

Kat noticed that Duke had zoned off to sleep again.

She tucked the life jackets over him, hoping they would keep him warm. Chris, too, was getting heavy-lidded, but he was clearly fighting it, intent on watching over Duke.

He'll keep his granddad safe, Kat thought. He'll keep better watch over him than I did with my own dad.

As long-overdue sleep took her, too, she was faintly aware of footsteps. Tink and Larry, back from the cave?

She'd hear all about their findings later, after...

A blank darkness washed over her, blissful rest which blocked out all her pain, all thoughts of Will who, even now, might be out there, calling her name.

She heard it so clearly.

Kat. Kat!

K...

Aaaaaaaahhhhhh!

She flew upward, clutching at her chest, confused, rocked by a heartbeat that thundered through her.

Tinkerbell was standing at the entrance to the shelter, eyes bugged out as she yelled.

"Help! Damn, Kat, help us!"

Scrambling to her feet, Kat was the first one up, already unsheathing her knife. The rest of them—Louis, Eloise, Alexandra, Chris, Dr. Hopkins and Duke—bolted awake, too.

"What's wrong?" Kat darted over to Tinkerbell.

"Body," the crew member said, voice cracking like a jag of lightning. "We found a body on the way to the beach."

Chapter 8

Duffy was dead.

From all appearances, he'd been tossed around the ocean and rocks. Even underneath the mud slathered on his body, Kat could see that his face was severely cut, folds of skin peeling away from what was once an ex-football-star buff. His body bore the telltale signs of his painful struggle to get to land.

But, she thought, gathering her courage and bending down so she could get a better look, all this mud told her that he'd probably crawled *onto* land. From there, he could've followed the arrows to the cave until he couldn't move another inch. There was even wet dirt caked under his fingernails.

"We were just on our way to the beach to do more

scrounging since the rain had let up," Larry said as he kept a wary eye on the understandably upset Tink.

Kat had told the Delacroixs that she would come here and make a positive ID for them, even though it was a silly promise. All the lost passengers and crew were built differently, so it wouldn't have been hard to tell them apart, to accept Tink's word for Duffy's death.

As Kat stood back up, her legs shook, threatening to take her down. But she wasn't just upset about the effect Duffy's death would have on Duke. And her stomach wasn't turning just because she felt sorry for Duffy.

It's because this isn't Will, she thought, a little ashamed of her relieved elation.

Tink was running a hand through her rain-spiked red hair. She'd had this same look on her face after Duffy had tangled with Kat on the boat: angry, accusatory. Why?

"So what should we do?" the crew woman asked.

"Bury him," Larry said. "The last thing we need is some animal smelling carrion."

He didn't seem real mournful about Duffy, either. Kat recalled what he'd said back on the boat.

Beat them all to shreds. That's what I say.

As Kat glanced at Duffy again, she surprised herself. She wasn't seeing a total villain so much as a lost little boy in a big man's body, a jerk who hadn't known how to interact with everyone else.

"I think," Kat whispered, "we should ask the Delacroix family what they want. Maybe they'll want a last look for some closure."

She thought of how Louis and Eloise had broken down at Tinkerbell's news, thought of how Alexandra had sunk to the floor, steely-eyed, while holding back her grief, thought of Chris and how he'd started shaking and clinging to Duke, who was himself sobbing heavily.

Larry shrugged. "Okay. I guess he's far enough from our camp to keep the hungry creepy-crawlies away."

Tink started back toward the shelter. Larry hung behind with Kat.

"Neither one of you is sorry to see Duffy go," Kat said. "I wasn't his number-one fan, but still—"

"Better him than us." They began walking. "Imagine having him on this island. How long would it have taken for him to pull out that Richie Rich entitlement crap and attack you or even Tink?"

Kat couldn't disagree. But when she didn't answer, Larry added, "Tink wasn't comfortable around him, you know. I'm happy about seeing him gone just for her sake alone."

"Why?"

"Let's just say Tink don't take kindly to seeing *any* woman assaulted."

With a look that hinted at much more, Larry took off at a jog, catching up to his friend. He settled a protective arm around her shoulders, big-brother like.

As Kat followed the united crew members, she couldn't help another twinge of isolation. She wished she had someone to fully connect with, too.

But Will was gone, and there was no longer a chance to work everything out, for her to have that someone.

When they returned, the trio was greeted tentatively by the group; there was a glimmer of expectation, as if Kat might tell them that the body wasn't Duffy's or Nestor's after all.

It killed her not to have better news.

Afterward, while wailing at Duffy's death, Eloise crawled over to her father, who took her in his arms and soothed her. Louis turned to Duke, also. Alexandra remained on the outside of their circle, hugging herself and grinding her teeth. Chris balled his body into a fetal shell, burying his face against his knees and rocking back and forth protectively.

Dr. Hopkins was the only one cognizant enough to ask for details. After Kat finished whispering them to her, the wounded woman asked, "You think anyone is still alive?"

Was she asking about Nestor?

"Yeah," Kat answered, again slightly stunned because it sounded as if the doctor was looking to her for answers…like everyone else. "I know they're out there. But…" When she realized her hands were fisted, she relaxed them. "I feel so powerless."

The doctor held up her own palms. "This is the definition of powerless, honey."

Alexandra had bandaged them with a salvaged rain-washed blouse.

Soon, the Delacroixs had run out of tears and there was nothing left to do but wait. Rain dripped from the shelter's overhang like back-up notes in the bigger song of the storm. The precipitation had eased off a little, but the ocean was still churning, the sky spotted with black and gray clouds that spat occasional lightning.

"Kat, we need fire," Larry grumbled. "We could go inside those deeper caves for better shelter if we had light."

Earlier, Tinkerbell had revealed that she and Larry had found a network of caves that branched off from this shelter. They'd also discovered armfuls of wood—small, dry pieces that had probably been blown inside by the wind before the storm had come. It looked like enough to keep a fire going for a decent time.

But how would they even get one started?

Kat's mind whirled with ideas from her dad's military stories. Maybe if they could fashion some kind of bow and a stick for friction, or find decent, dry rocks?

She stood abruptly. Man, she couldn't just sit here. There were a million things to do. First she wanted to know what should happen with Duffy's body, but she was hesitant to ask the Delacroixs on the tail end of their shock. She was also itching to get back out to the beach and see what else had washed up.

To see if any other bodies were waiting for them.

The sound of plastic rattling came from behind her. She turned around to find Larry gripping an empty potato chip bag. There was a pile of them in the corner that she hadn't noticed before.

"What the hell is this?" he asked.

Louis's voice was flat when he answered. "It was food. We ate some."

Kat took a few steps closer, prepared to stop another fight.

"Some?" Larry kicked at the empty bags. "That was the only food we've found. And you know what? I've been working all day while you people have sat on your asses. I'm *goddamn hungry!*"

Eyes on Larry, Duke slowly shifted backward. Eloise held still in his arms and Louis flanked his other side. His movement unleashed a muffled crinkle of plastic. The sound reverberated through the shelter.

Larry darted over, bending past Eloise and Duke. "Are you hiding something? What've you got?"

"Larry!" Kat bounded over, then pulled him back. Anger was burning beneath her own skin, but it wasn't because Larry was getting aggressive.

Those potato chips *had* been their only food. Had the Delacroixs eaten all of it while everyone had napped earlier? What had happened while she'd been asleep? Larry held up a full bag for Kat to see, dangling it in front of her face, then showing it to the crowd.

"Trying to hold out on the peons, huh?"

Alexandra finally said something. "We were rationing."

Rationing? A flare of distrust and rage urged Kat to let go of Larry. She faced Alexandra. "Who the hell are you to ration? And just how much were you going to get compared to the rest of us?"

The rich girl lifted her chin, cold as a slick of ice over the ground, making each of Kat's steps a dangerous one.

Duke interrupted. "Kat, please don't jump to—"

"What?" She was on fire. "Who do you think you are? Is there some kind of social order here?"

Duke flinched, his eyes hazy from pain and her words. Had she gone too far?

Immediately, the fighter in her answered. *Yeah, Kat, have you overstepped your place? How dare you speak up for yourself to these golden people? How dare you demand the same privileges?*

Duke and his family must've seen murder in her eyes.

"I was making sure Chris would get his fill," he said softly. "That's all."

Chris hadn't moved. It was like he'd escaped into his own place, balled up with his face hidden. Dammit, he shouldn't have to deal with confrontations like this on top of every other horror.

But what was Duke saying? Was he just assuming that everyone was going to step aside for Chris, the new heir to the fortune?

Kat tilted her head as another thought weighed her down. "Do you actually think it's okay to cheat the people who've been working to help everyone survive?"

Duke's skin colored, and Kat almost choked on the bitter realization that he *did* think that way.

"Give us our share," Larry said. "*Now*."

In response Duke looked to Kat, maybe thinking that she'd speak up for him as usual. But for the first time she couldn't see how protecting him was the right thing to do. All of them needed sustenance and, sure, if it came right down to it, she'd give Chris some of hers, just because she could deal without a few extra chips. But to be *expected* to do it…

She held out her hands, asking for the hidden cache.

While Tink, Larry and Kat ate their first meal of the day, her mentor couldn't have looked more betrayed. Hell, was he really so miffed about what his family had done?

Afterward, Kat gathered the rest of the food in the center of the room, grabbed the screwdriver and gave it to Tinkerbell.

"Watch the eats, okay?"

Then Kat started to walk out of the shelter.

"Where're you going?"

It was Dr. Hopkins. Next to her, Chris peeked out of his self-imposed exile, his face pleading for her to stay. They both looked stricken by her leaving.

But she couldn't hang around for moral support. "I'm going to bring back more food. Larry, come on."

"But…" The dreadlocked guy pointed to the chips.

"Oh, those *will* be here when we get back." Kat looked each person in the eye. The Delacroixs and Duke glanced at the ground, giving way to Kat's demand. "And we'll have more food, too."

She hoped. Good Lord, she hoped.

With that, they ducked into the plodding rain.

By the time the weather began fully crashing down again, Kat and Larry had found one measly netted bag of apples, a ruined packet of rice and a small suitcase that contained but a few of Dr. Hopkins's possessions. Hoping to find more, they climbed over a group of rocks to get to the adjacent beach. There, nothing but driftwood littered the sand. They would come back for that later.

"There's nothing here," Larry said, yelling over the wind, which in the past few minutes had picked up to a whistling roar.

Pointing in their shelter's direction, Kat nodded. But just as they moved toward the rocks again, she saw it.

A man in torn clothing, stumbling toward them, yelling.

Adrenaline kicked Kat into a run. Larry followed. *Tall. Built like him. Was it…?*

The man fell to his knees, laughing, panting, reaching for her.

"Will?" she yelled. "Will?"

Her brain felt numb, blindsided.

Will. Here. Alive!

Both she and Larry skidded to a stop, burying their knees in the sand as they wrapped their arms around him, bowling him over. Electrified with happiness, Kat laughed until she was weak. Will yowled, probably in pain, so they backed off. They were acting like fools in the eye of a hurricane, but why not?

He was alive. She knew it. Dammit, she knew it! Well, she'd *hoped*, somewhere beneath all that pessimism.

As they got over the shock, a forceful wave pounded the shore ten feet from them.

"Let's get back!" Kat tried to help Will…yes, Will!…to his feet. She was near to bursting, giddy as a young girl who'd seen a dream come to life.

He shook his head as she told him about their camp and pulled him in that direction. Gesturing to higher

ground where there was an overhang like the one her
group had found, he said, "Kat, help me get my stuff
from up there first." He signaled for Larry to take the
apples and suitcase. "We'll see you back at your place."

With a wink and a hearty pat on the shoulder that
made Will heave in a slight breath, Larry bounded back
toward the original shelter. Good thing, Kat thought,
because Tink was probably having a fun time guarding
those chips.

Will's limp was pronounced as he took her to his
dank and dreary shelter. He'd settled under a rocky
ledge, which provided overhead coverage while bushes
lined the sides. A life jacket, a power flashlight, a coil
of rope, three kitchen steak knives and a duffel bag with
clothing strewn over the ground were all his supplies.

Kat couldn't contain herself. Throwing away every
pretense, she embraced him again.

"I was hoping…" she began.

"Me, too."

They held each other until she gave him an extra-
strength hug that made him suck in a breath.

She backed away, heart twisting. "You're hurt!" But
then, hungrily, she touched his face, running her fingers
over his skin, giddy just to know that he was in one piece.

Will…right here…

"I don't hurt that much." He put a hand to his ribs.
"Maybe here. Bruised. But it's nothing. I was keeping
watch for anything helpful from the wreckage when
you two popped up out of the clear blue. I—" He
stopped, voice strangled. "God, Kat. I can't believe it."

Neither of them said anything for a minute. Instead,

they just stared at each other. She couldn't believe this, either. Will. Alive, alive, alive.

"Wow," was all she could say.

"Exactly. I thought maybe I'd see other survivors after a rescue, but…"

The rain thrashed against the bushes, sending a stream of cold air past them. His green-blue eyes were exhausted, but glowing. She took that as a good sign. A sign that he would be just as excited about taking advantage of second chances as she was.

Will…right in front of her for the taking…

Almost losing him had torn her apart. It made all the doubts that had broken their relationship in the first place seem so petty, just like rocks that couldn't stop the mad flow of a stream.

He cleared his throat. Was she watching him too intensely? Did he have any idea of how badly she'd been rattled by this storm, of how much it had changed her outlook about him?

"Now, where's your camp?" he asked.

Right. He probably thought she still didn't want anything to do with him.

She stepped closer. "We're just over that rock ridge out there." She told him about how the weather had washed away most of their SOS sign, so she and Larry had been forced to correct that and the arrows leading to the cave.

"Only a hundred feet more and you would've found us."

"I only stumbled over this place this morning." His eyes went dark. "It seems like days ago, doesn't it?"

All those months of being with him had given her
a type of Will sonar. She could plumb the depths of his
sorrow in those troubled eyes. She'd been so much a
part of him that she knew just what he needed.

"Don't feel guilty," she said. "You didn't get us into
this situation."

"Then who did?"

"Stop it, Will."

"I…" He swallowed, gesturing at the knife on her
belt. "That's Shaw's custom-made Bowie. I found him
washed ashore and had to bury him. Are any of my
other crew…?"

"Larry and Tink are the only ones who made it.
God, I'm sorry. I'm *so* sorry, but it's not your fault. Stop
thinking that way."

He looked crestfallen at the loss of his comrades, so
she ventured even nearer to him, needing so much to
make him feel better. He smelled of seawater and sharp
musk. Vitality. The tang of his skin triggered something
primal in the core of her—a sublime cry that cele-
brated being alive in the throes of death.

Dammit, she needed proof of their still being really
alive. Needed to feel again, to remind herself of what
it was like to wallow in utter ecstasy instead of sadness.

She knew her eyes were telling him everything
because he couldn't glance away. And even though
he'd been abused by the water, his mouth swollen with
cuts, his skin sliced and chafed, his bones bruised, Kat
knew none of it mattered.

Unable to stop herself, she tilted her face upward,
standing on her toes. She pressed her mouth against his,

softly at first, testing. It was almost like she wanted to reassure herself that he was really here.

His lips were wet, salty. The taste of his blood from the cuts on his mouth washed through her, warming her, rushing around her own veins. A shiver wracked her body.

She hated that he was hurt.

"When I thought you were dead," she whispered over his lips, "nothing could make the pain go away."

He breathed against her, almost like he also couldn't believe she was with him, that she was inviting him. With effort, he raised his hands, took her own sensitive face in his palms and rubbed his thumbs over her cheekbones.

She knew it was agonizing for him—his ribs sore, his skin tender—but she didn't stop him. Couldn't.

"I'm not about to leave you for anything, Kat," he said, voice low and tortured. "Not when we could finally get what we deserve out of life."

She was beyond wondering exactly what he meant by that, if he was talking about the five percent of Duke's fortune she could be inheriting or if he was genuinely wishing they could be together again. But who cared right now? *Why* care?

Beyond control, she kissed him again. Her head spun with the power of their reunion, with the burgeoning affection she was opening herself to again.

But what if this emotion had only been brought on by all the terror, all the uncertainty, all the...

He kissed her back, ending her doubts, burying his hands in her hair and opening his mouth to suck on her lips in erotic rhythm. Nipping, nibbling, his tongue easing past her lips and tangling with hers until she felt her chest nearly collapse from want of breath.

As they slid to the sand, a thrust of hunger pounded Kat. It'd been so long since she'd *felt*, since she'd sighed under Will's muscles against her own skin, their bodies slick with friction and sweat.

Blood pooled and heated in her belly, between her legs, making her swollen and stiff, in need of a touch, a hard caress. Ignoring her own bruises, she took his hand, guided it down there, breaking their kiss only to moan at the contact. While he stroked his thumb across the denim of her shorts, she bit his neck lightly, craving more.

Her hands traveled up his arms, into his hair, restlessly exploring, encouraging.

"I want you to come inside me. Now."

I want you to keep me feeling alive.

"Kat…"

"Do it, Will. Come on."

He didn't hesitate. Pressure built deep within her, packed by all the fantasies she'd let expand.

Had he suffered through the same yearnings this past year? Had he dreamt of her, too, driving himself to distraction as he counted the minutes of an alarm clock in the dark?

As he worked off her shorts and the knife, her sex pulsed second by second, long and maddening beats of time, just like that clock. Her body was counting down to an explosion, a final betrayal of all the mental battles she'd fought against Will. Looming above her, he eased off his wet top, groaning because of his ribs. But he didn't seem to care. Next came his ragged pants, and then he slid the life jacket under her head.

His body… She'd forgotten how it made her skin hum with electric currents. Wide shoulders, strong arms, a lean and tanned work of nature, like the beautiful cut of a wave. His right-hand ribs were a dark ménage of bruises. Sparse hair sanded down his chest. His flat belly led to…

When she saw how ready he was for her, she felt herself go wet, slippery with heat.

Alive. Next to me. Skin on skin.

She moved to take off her T-shirt, but he stopped her. "Let me…"

He exhaled, his gaze filled with a longing so profound that it swept her under, pinning her until she was almost clutching for breath.

His eyes…a mirror of her own desperation for him.

Reverently, he traced the outline of her small breasts against the dark T-shirt. She hadn't been wearing a bra when the boat wrecked, and with the play of his fingers, her nipples hardened, strained against the cotton.

He circled them with his thumbs, bent down and took one into his mouth. Sucking, he slipped his hands to the small of her back, urging her hips upward against his belly but away from his bruised ribs. She rubbed up next to him, demanding more.

"Wait," he whispered, pushing her shirt up so his lips could find bare skin.

He coasted his mouth down, up, tonguing, teasing, latching on to her other nipple.

Kat winced, digging her heels into the sand. Her

body was thudding toward a big bang. Pounding. Pumping.

Enough. She wiggled, seeking to position him between her legs, dragging over his erection. Her undies were the only barrier between them, his stiffness prodding her, making her crazy.

With a harsh laugh, he stripped off that barrier, wasting no time in coaxing his fingers between her bare, drenched folds. There, he caressed her, expertly nudged her until she was ready to scream.

This was really happening, she thought. Together. We're together.

Alive.

As he entered her, moaning with pain and pleasure, filling every last empty space she'd guarded against him, Kat locked her legs around him, rocking in cadence to a faint alarm signal that was growing louder, louder...

Danger. Danger. Danger...

Like starving creatures, they consumed each other. He drove into her, and she moved with every hammering thrust.

Hungry. So hungry.

Danger...danger...

The alarm was getting faster, blinding her, searing her head until she became dizzy.

When she reached the breaking point, her sight went red, warning lights flashing through her bloodstream like embers flying from a burst of fire.

Danger, danger...

He climaxed first, breath leaving him, body tensing then shuddering to closure.

But Kat was still going, fed by pure euphoria. Will helped her along with his mouth, his expertise, his knowledge of what would make her implode.

Out of time, her body pulled itself apart, blasting into a shower of flame. Sparks dug into her skin, hot, cold, spiking her. Hurting her in such a good way.

Then, while the dying sparks echoed the sound of falling rain, Kat opened her eyes.

Cleansed, she thought, catching her breath, holding Will against her as their heartbeats slowed. A second chance with the man she'd never stopped wanting.

Chapter 9

Epiphany or not, it'd ended up being a little awkward—and wonderful—after the sex. Not having any with your ex-boyfriend for a year did that to a girl. So did wondering if skipping the pill—which she'd been taking only to regulate her erratic periods—for a day would matter in the scheme of things. Still, it was beautiful, lying against him, not having to say a word, yet.

After reclining next to each other in the sand, stroking and caressing, Will whispered to her that, if they didn't get back to camp soon, their privacy would end anyway: someone would probably come looking for them.

She knew he was right. It wasn't like this island was some Club Med where they had all the time in the world to mend themselves together again. There was food to be gotten, people to be taken care of. Responsibilities.

Still, while they got dressed and traded shy smiles that promised more to come, Kat couldn't help floating on air. There was an animating glow lifting her up from the inside out.

They carried Will's belongings and held hands while dodging the raindrops melting from the trees. Thunder rumbled the sky, sounding like a contented animal to Kat.

An animal just blinking its eyes awake.

Will was limping, but he was too proud to ask her to slow down. Embarrassed by her flighty loss of common sense, Kat eased up, slipping his arm over her shoulders so he could lean on her without making an issue of it. Still, she loved carrying his weight, feeling him sink against her.

"This should be real fun," he said, "seeing the old crowd again. Is Louis still as feisty as ever?"

Kat paused. "No, Will, Duffy died."

Will seemed to lose his balance, stopping for a moment, stiffening. But then he began walking again, unreadable.

His reaction… Kat tightened her grip on Will, silent, unwilling to give credit to a growing suspicion that maybe he'd overreacted for her benefit. Ridiculous, right?

Instead, she prattled on about everything that had happened in his absence.

"You know Harrington's going to be worried about you being gone so long," Will said, voice tight. "Your man will be upset—"

Kat ground to a halt. "My man?"

Slowly, Will dropped his arm from around her shoulders.

"What do you mean, 'my man?'" The way he'd said it held all sorts of derogatory meanings for a woman who took such honor in caring for herself.

Will paused, ran a hand through his sandy hair. "I... Okay, dammit, I have to ask before we get back because it's been gnawing at me. What is Duke Harrington to you?"

Excellent question.

"I don't sleep with him, if that's what you mean, like he's my sugar daddy or something. Is *that* it?"

"I don't know, Kat. The way he looks at you..."

She didn't want to hear this. "You don't think a man and a woman can be friends, Will? Is that so hard to imagine?"

A knowing grin covered his mouth, as steamy as the kisses they'd just shared. The Will Ashton charm. Kat almost wilted.

"There isn't a guy on earth," he said, "who'd pass up a chance to be with you."

Heat bolted into her, and her face flushed under its sheen of rain. He'd always known just what to say.

"Duke's not that way," she said, putting his arm over her shoulders again and resuming the walk.

Will's only answer was a strained laugh.

"What?"

"He's got you snowed, Kat, if you can't see what's really going on."

Jealous?

It was the official end of the afterglow. Slowly, as they continued to make their way to the shelter, reality crept back into Kat's pores, taking her over bit by bit.

"We're just friends," she said. "And that's it."

Will's silence ate at her.

"Don't you believe me?"

He waited a beat too long to answer, making whatever he said next irrelevant. It'd been the same kind of heart-crushing hesitation that had marked her with doubts about Will in the first place, the harsh pause of a man who, deep inside, really hadn't wanted a family with her. A man who would lie to her.

No amount of explanation or apology could erase such a revelationary reaction.

It also couldn't blot out all the doubts she'd had about him on the boat, after Alexandra, the shark cage, the accusations about Captain Macintosh.

We could finally get what we deserve out of life.

Idiot, she thought. You fell right into Will's trap again, didn't you? How stupid were you to think that sex could chase away all the problems you two had?

But…dammit, what about everything she'd told herself when she'd thought he was dead? Where had all her I'd-never-let-him-go-again spunk disappeared to?

Soul-sick, Kat ducked out from under Will's arm as they came upon a bevy of colorful shirts amongst the foliage. Their party. Holding makeshift umbrellas of bags and life jackets over their bowed heads to ward off the rain, as they stood over Duffy's body.

As she and Will approached, she heard Alexandra

speaking kind words about her brother in a eulogy. Louis and Eloise were propped against each other, weeping. Off to the side, Larry stood back but neither Dr. Hopkins nor Tink were around. Duke was on his knees, wiping dark red moisture from his mouth as Chris hovered over him. It looked like Duke had been vomiting into the bushes.

Blood, Kat thought, dreading the return of his symptoms, knowing there wasn't a thing she could do to stop this.

Louis saw Kat first, his eyes going wide and hopeful. "Nestor?"

But as soon as he said it, he clamped his mouth shut. Eloise started crying even harder when she realized that her son really wasn't with them.

When Duke focused on Kat, she couldn't help thinking that he'd aged ten years in the last few hours. He tried to smile through his anguish, and she remembered what Will had said about the way Duke looked at her.

Gaze soft, yearning, as if he'd do anything for her.

Kat glanced away, wishing everything was simpler.

When Duke turned his attention to Will, the change in the air couldn't have been more obvious.

Shock, hurt, puzzlement.

It didn't take a genius to see that Duke suspected what had gone down between her and her ex-boyfriend.

The older man squeezed his eyes shut, pressed his palms to his temples. Immediately, Alexandra ended her praise of Duffy and bent down to her grandfather.

"My pills," he said.

No one had an answer for that. There were no pills.

There wouldn't be any until the party was rescued. And, unless the weather let up, that wouldn't be happening soon.

The sky flashed lightning at them, kind of like a punk giving them all the middle finger.

Duke groaned. "That damned smell is still here."

"What smell?" Kat asked, coming to kneel next to Duke, too.

Alexandra patted her grandfather's arm, her eyes red. She held her shoulders just as if the weight of the world was pushing down on them. Much to Kat's surprise, she felt sorry for her. Kat knew what it was like to be a protector, too.

Another taut rumble shook the sky.

Alexandra heaved a shaky breath, rising. Then she gave her parents an odd, accusatory look and walked away. Weeping, Louis and Eloise followed at a distance, stumbling as they held each other. Will and Larry stood still, obviously not knowing what to do with themselves. Trembling, Chris plopped down in the mud, facing a tree, his dark shirt clinging to his body, his back turned to Duffy's waiting corpse.

I'll be here for you, Chris, Kat thought, her own hackles rising for him.

She glanced at the body, shivering. "Let's bury him."

Will and Larry nodded and picked up big, flat sticks, trying to conquer the mud. It didn't go over too well, especially with Will's injuries, but they continued to do their damndest.

Duke slowly rose to his feet, and Kat rushed over to help him.

"A word?" His voice was hoarse, his body slouched and quivering.

She walked him to a spot nearby, where there'd be enough distance for privacy. The rain splattered over the life jacket he was trying valiantly to hold over their heads, but she took over the job for him, unable to endure the noble, failing gesture.

When he began to pant, she stopped their progress, waiting for him to recover.

"So you found him alive," Duke finally said.

Even now, as Kat fended off all the old doubts about Will, happiness rushed back. She'd never forget how it'd felt to see him running down the beach toward her.

"By some miracle," she said, voice quivering from an excess of emotion, "he's back."

Smiling sadly, Duke seemed to note her change in attitude, her obvious affection. "You still want him."

Kat searched for a response. What she felt for Will couldn't be described with a yes or no answer. She wanted to love him so badly, but her street sense told her to back off, to shield herself.

"When I arranged this trip," Duke said, "I was hoping you'd find an answer one way or another. But… Hell, who knows if I'll get a chance to say this to you again."

He leaned against the bole of a pine tree. Water slithered down the bark of it, splashing over his bald head and his withered, slumped body, but Duke didn't seem to care.

"The last thing you probably want to hear," he said, "is sentimentality. But balancing on a line between life and death makes everything else seem a little…"

"Unimportant," she finished for him. Who knew better than her? Her pulse was pattering, dreading what he wanted to tell her. "You need rest and—"

"I've loved you since the moment I saw you, Kat," he said gently.

Oh, God.

She closed her eyes against the sudden, naked admission.

Was this part of his "refurbishment" ritual with every female "project"? But he sounded very sincere. Or was he just so overcome by the past day's trials that he was getting dramatic, romanticizing his fondness for her?

Just like she might've done with Will....

When she opened her eyes, she caught the hopefulness, then the gradual devastation on his face.

"Duke..." She didn't know what to say next.

"Don't answer. I surprised you, I know. And I had to say it before I die, just like I had to go on this one last ill-advised fandango with my family. I only wanted to leave this place knowing everything is set to rights. That's all."

But why had he told her this now, after she and Will had finally taken a step forward? She chided herself for the cynicism. If Duffy hadn't ruined her with his "project" comments, those kinds of thoughts would've never entered her mind.

"I mean it, Kat," he said. "Just having you near me does a world of good." He managed to stand again. "Not that I can compete with the dashing Captain Ashton. But I only hoped that we..."

Flushing, he staggered away, stranding her in mortified silence.

And aching in regret for not being able to love him in return.

Needing some alone time, she waited for Duke to go back to Chris, then wandered over to where Duffy's body was laid out. When she got there, Larry was on another one of his rich-people rants, which, Kat thought thankfully, let her concentrate on something other than Duke's confession.

"Captain, I'll take orders from you," the crew member was saying as rain dampened his face, "but not from them."

He pointed to Chris, who glanced at Kat, confused. Still huddled into himself, he was coping with tragedy in the only way he probably knew—by fleeing from it, planting himself on the outside, where, like Kat, he was the most comfortable.

"All I did," the teen said, "was tell him to hurry."

She could see that Duffy's grave was a slosh of mud, courtesy of the rain.

Will tugged on Larry's shirt, defusing the situation only a little. "We're going to have to bury Duffy in a drier place. The shelter I found this morning could work. Or those caves in the back of your shelter that Kat told me about."

Chris's eyes filled with tears. "Gramps…?"

Kat responded right away, scooping the terrified boy into her arms and bringing him to Duke. The older man led Chris away. In their wake, a blast of wind wailed through the trees, shaking branches. Thunder grumbled like some muttered curse as Duke cast one more heartsick glance back, then disappeared.

Larry threw down his stick. "So I'm that boy's slave to order around? I hate to point out the news flash, but I'm not exactly serving drinks on the boat anymore."

"Larry, that family's hurting." Will glanced at Duffy, like he was figuring out how to move the body. "They're acting out."

"That excuse is getting real old," Larry said.

Distracted, Kat kept silent, going over to Duffy.

"He looks so undignified. No one should go out like this. Not even Duffy."

Not even the guy who might've messed with the cage...?

She dismissed that line of thought, not wanting to return to all the suspicions she'd also had about Will.

Telling herself that this was the right thing to do, Kat took a large leaf that had gathered water, then poured the moisture on Duffy's face. She cleaned him. Hell, she would've done the same for anyone— her dad, her mom...Duke.

Will and Larry respectfully waited, turning their backs as she wiped away the mud, the blood. Soon, she was down to his ripped skin and...

She gagged.

Was everything getting to her or were these cuts a little too...

Precise?

She cleaned some more. Was she wrong about this? No...precise. That was a good description.

Duffy had been mutilated, and it wasn't in a random slammed-against-the-rocks way. His lips had been cut to make his mouth hang down, and his eyes had rings around them. Someone had taken their time carving him up.

Feverishly, she pushed aside his ripped clothing, wiping away dirt and blood there, too.

Stab marks in his chest?

"Guys," she said, "I think I've found something—"

And before she could regret sharing her findings with two men she didn't entirely trust, they were at her side, witnesses to Duffy's freakishly odd wounds.

Even though Kat and Will had wanted to keep mum about the upsetting information until they could figure out how to handle this, Larry spilled the news the minute they got back. He "didn't want no one murdering him, too," so he thought honesty might flush out a guilty face from the crowd right away. There was no stopping him.

"Are you saying my son was murdered?" Eloise asked. She now officially resembled a ghost, her blond hair disheveled, her white clothes tattered and torn.

Suddenly Louis rushed Larry, pushing the crew member. But when Larry held his ground, Kat thought she detected a perverse pleasure in him.

"You, with your mean streak," the Delacroix patriarch said. "Is this because of the chips? Are you bent on getting some warped revenge for your lot in life by lying to us?"

In the real world, it would've sounded ridiculous. But this wasn't real. It was a nightmare.

"Dammit, do I have to stop another fight!" Kat went to the center of the shelter to stand between the men. "Maybe we're wrong about Duffy's wounds, but they're sure as hell out of the ordinary."

Eloise's hand flew to her neck as she sank to her knees. "Do you think there are…*natives*…on this island?"

Natives. Primitives. Anyone with darker skin color, right? Kat tried not to take offense at the very offensive question. Eloise wasn't in her right mind.

None of them were anymore.

"Maybe it was a wild animal," Alexandra said. Her calm voice would've been the perfect example of rationality—if her brother hadn't just been cut up.

"There could be a thousand explanations," Kat said. "But one thing's for sure—we've all got to be on guard."

"That's right." Louis leveled a glare on Larry. "Stick together. Shouldn't we do that? Safety in numbers? Well, let me inform you that I don't plan on turning my back on half of you in here, lest I get stabbed."

Panic was not on the agenda. "Okay, we—"

But he was already across the shelter, grabbing his life jacket, a bag of chips, a plastic cup and an apple.

Duke watched him. "Where are you going?" he rasped.

Louis gestured for Eloise and Alexandra to gather up their belongings, too. "Anywhere. Didn't Tinkerbell say that there's another overhang to the right of our shelter?"

"Yeah," the crew woman said. She was sitting out of the way with a silent Dr. Hopkins. "Back about fifty yards. It connects to the caves, too."

"You're separating yourselves?" Kat said, floored. "That's more than dangerous. It's...well, *stupid*."

Unless there really *was* a killer among them and the killer wasn't a Delacroix.

Kat glanced at Larry, an obvious suspect. Then, unable to stop herself, her eyes focused on Will. It occurred to her that he hadn't shown up until late morning, and that would've given him the chance to...

No, she told herself. What are you thinking? That's Will, the man you made love with a couple of hours ago.

The man she couldn't stop doubting.

Louis was already at the shelter's edge, ready to leave. "Chris? Grandfather? Are you coming?"

Kat's nerves screeched. Even with everything that had gone on these past few days, she wanted them here; they'd be mincemeat with the Delacroixs one way or another.

"No, Duke," Kat said. "Stay with me."

She couldn't have chosen better words. He lit up like fireworks and broke Kat's heart all in the same second.

"I prefer to stay with Kat," Duke said.

His son-in-law bristled. Determined, he darted over to Chris, who was curled up and facing the wall.

"Let's go. Now."

The boy shook his head.

"No arguments, Chris." Louis put his hand on his nephew's shoulder to turn him around.

Startled, the teen whipped Louis's hand away, eyes wide and full of terror.

"I won't go with you!"

Kat stepped back, struck by the level of fear. And why not? Chris had already been a near-victim, too, and who better to suspect than the people who'd benefit the most from his death?

Breathing hard, Chris resumed his cowering position.

As the other man slunk out of the shelter, Eloise followed him into the rain, but Alexandra loitered on her way past Will.

Softly, Kat heard her say, "Want to come?"

A million heartbeats kicked at Kat's ribs.

Will shook his head, watching the ground as Alexandra shrugged and went on her way. Slowly, he raised his gaze to meet Kat's, forehead furrowed.

Was he thinking of the day she'd accused him of cozying up to the rich girl? What had Alexandra's invitation been about anyway? Jealousy rocked through her.

As everyone else began chattering about the latest turn of events, Kat saw Duke in the corner, comforting Chris and glancing at her with sympathy, reminding her that she really didn't know everything about Will. Reminding her of Duke's love confession, too.

As if reading her discomfort, Will drew Kat into the opening of the back cave with a gentle hand on her arm. The contact tingled with a buzz that robbed her of all sense. Semidarkness filtered over them, and a cool wind, like the breath of something hidden, fluttered the drying blankets and clothing, chilling her.

"It wasn't what it looked like," he said, referring to Alexandra.

Was it ever? "Okay."

"No, Kat, don't say 'okay.' We've got a lot to talk about, and Alexandra is just one of those things. Here, ask me anything you want and I'll answer it. I've got nothing to hide."

A torrent of questions assaulted her. Where should she start? With Alexandra? The shark cage? His whereabouts when Duffy had been killed?

His comment about "getting what they deserved"?

"What, Kat? What're you thinking?"

She sighed. "I don't know what to make of anything anymore."

"What are you saying?" In the dim light, realization transformed him. "Don't tell me—"

"Will." She held on to him. "Someone might've killed Duffy."

"Right…and you think that someone might've been me?"

"I didn't say that."

Will shrugged away from her hand. "You don't have to. Kat, I don't know what's gotten into you or how you came to think the worst of me."

Alexandra. Captain Macintosh. The temper he'd shown on the boat with Louis. Ambition. And worst of all, the pregnancy scare. Weren't those enough?

His shoulders lifted. Pride had taken him over now. "You think I'm capable of cutting into a face like someone did with Duffy. You think I could leave a kid stranded in a shark cage."

"I don't *want* to think it."

"But you do, goddammit."

Limping, he stormed back into the shelter. She was on his tail.

Paranoia. It'd gotten to her. But it had always kept her safe on the mean streets after school, the act of always looking over her shoulder and trusting no one. "Will…"

"I'm going to ask Larry to help me bury Duffy somewhere dry," Will said over her. "And then I'm going back to my shelter. Alone."

And before she could convince him to stay, he'd collected most of the items he'd brought with him, recruited Larry and was gone. Just like that.

Hit hard by her confusion, she couldn't do anything but watch the rain for a while. Larry came back, unusually quiet after he explained that they'd found another cave near the beach to bury Duffy. The weather grew angrier as the sky grew darker, and she wondered how Will was doing on his own.

What if an animal attacked him? What if he got killed by the person who'd gotten to Duffy?

She calmed herself down. Maybe there wasn't a murderer on the loose. Maybe they were all overreacting, edgy from exhaustion.

As she went to the middle of the shelter, standing between Duke and Chris and the "other" group—the blue collars—she didn't know where to go. Where she belonged.

But then Chris looked up with those saucer eyes. Duke held his head and hunched over like his stomach hurt.

She knew where she was needed.

They settled down to sleep, wracked by cold, the air blackening around them.

Chapter 10

Kat hadn't slept well.

She'd been on alert for trouble, her mind snapping with scenarios about Duffy's death and suspects who would want to see him gone. And she'd been hoping Will would come back, too.

But, at the first crack of light, gray from storm, someone had indeed returned—Alexandra.

"I feel safer here," she said quietly to Kat. Then, finding a spot nearby, she sank to the ground to sleep.

Soon, Louis and Eloise returned, huddling next to each other without another word. Their eyes held a sadness so deep that Kat couldn't even begin to grasp. Not only had they lost one son, the other was still missing, maybe even dead.

In memory of the baby she'd almost had herself, Kat's hand rested on her own belly, then fell away.

"Kat," Louis said softly as Eloise closed her eyes, her mouth twisting as she cried, "we've been talking. We're all going to work harder with you to find Nestor and to get us home."

Awakened, Alexandra watched them, her eyes narrow.

"We don't want to be alone anymore," Eloise whispered. "We want to find our other boy."

Kat suspected that the Delacroixs' lack of light had also played a big part in their return. Without flashlights, every little sound would be magnified: every clap of thunder, every slap of rain, every cry of the wind.

But she never did answer them, because they all fell back asleep, exhausted before Kat could think of the right words. The family must've been scared out of their noggins to slink back to the group like this. But how long would their willing attitudes last?

Minutes later, Chris and Duke were awake and aware of the Delacroixs.

"They just came back to get your help?" Duke asked sadly.

The family hadn't said that they had come back to be with Duke, Kat thought. They weren't here for him.

"Can't we just go to the other shelter?" Chris whispered, staring at the Delacroixs. "The one the captain went to?"

The edges of Duke's mouth turned down. Kat wondered if he was reacting to the mention of Will.

Or did he want to stay and make amends with the family? Maybe *Kat's* anxiety about making amends with Will showed. Or maybe they could tell that she didn't necessarily believe that things were a hundred percent safer with him.

Anyway, she hesitated, weighing their options, since she didn't trust the Delacroixs anymore than Chris did.

"We've got to get away from them," the boy said. "Please, Kat?"

Duke closed his eyes. A tear slipped down his weathered face. "Chris is right. Now that we have the option of another decent shelter, we should go there...separate ourselves."

But before she could acknowledge that might not be a bad idea if it made them feel safer—after all, she'd be there to watch over them—Duke was talking again.

"How can I convince you, Kat? How much would it take? When we get home, I can see to it that you get that five percent. You'll have everything you ever wanted."

She tilted her head, absorbing his meaning. "Are you bribing me to guard you or something?"

Duke didn't say anything.

"You don't think I would've helped you anyway? Duke, even if I'd consider the extra incentive—which I won't—you can't just go around buying people."

He gave her a look that clearly said, *But I've made a living at it.*

All of Kat's fears resurfaced. Was she just one of his investments after all?

In the wake of his love confession, her relationship

with him had stretched at the seams. Now, a thread of her fondness for him popped and broke, weakening memories of the man she'd known back home.

Or was she overreacting? Was she making a tsunami out of a swell?

"I'll take you," she said, "because I care for you two. I want you to be safe."

"Thank you, Kat!" Chris hugged her. From the force of his embrace, Kat realized how relatively drained she was. A lack of food and sleep was squeezing her dry.

But there was no time for excuses. They had to get fire. More food. She could do that at Will's shelter, if she needed to.

"Let's go," she said, avoiding Duke's bleary, searching gaze. She couldn't meet it—not after he'd thrown her such a curveball.

They gathered those possessions they considered theirs, taking care not to disturb the others while she awakened Tinkerbell, who was sacked out next to Larry's empty spot. He'd probably gone to the bathroom or something. Wanting to avoid a confrontation with the Delacroixs, even though it would come at some point, they left the shelter and covered themselves from the rain. Kat looked back only once. Alexandra was watching them go, her eyes blinking against the gray light.

Mud sucked at their feet and strange cries from the greenery paced them. Duke could barely move, so Kat made like a human crutch again and helped him walk while holding a club in her other hand.

Maybe it was her imagination, but she thought she heard something behind them. A rustle of foliage? Footsteps? Or maybe it was just the rain.

When they got to Will's shelter, he wasn't there. Neither was the flashlight. The rest of his stuff was bundled in a corner, covering the hilt of a steak knife. For all she knew, more blades could've been under the small stash, but Kat guessed that Will had probably taken at least one for protection.

Kat eased Duke to the ground for some sleep while Chris set their belongings close by and busied himself with unpacking, soon relocating across the shelter. Fanged butterflies abraded the lining of Kat's stomach as they waited for Will's return. Had she done permanent damage to their relationship? How could she justify her lack of trust?

To distract herself, she started to undo a strand from the rope lying on the floor. With this, an anchor stone and one of those slim pieces of wood from the cave, maybe she could get a fire going, bow-and-stick style. She stuffed the strand in her shorts pocket.

Out of the gray, a crash of lightning and thunder screeched, and, in the distance, something crashed. A tree?

She barely heard what happened next: A nearby cry of horrendous pain.

Whipping around, she found Duke, mouth contorted, eyes bugged out. He was holding his thigh.

Where a knife was sticking out.

"Duke!"

Both Kat and Chris rocketed over to him. It felt like

she couldn't get there quick enough, her feet moving in slow motion while her vision scrambled in fast forward.

Who…what…?

Blood fizzing, she wildly glanced around, seeing only the surrounding foliage moving restlessly. Mockingly.

Instantly, her attention was back on Duke, to where Chris was shielding him with his own body.

God, how would she be able to get this blade out of him without causing more pain?

Before she came up with an answer, something even more obvious hit her.

The weapon.

It was one of Will's steak knives.

One of the possessions he'd taken with him when he'd left last night.

They were all back in the original shelter, minus Will, who was still missing. After Kat had carefully removed the knife from Duke—finding the blade had wrought minimal damage, thank God—she'd done her best to staunch the flow of blood and wrap the wound with some wet clothing she'd found. At that point, she'd thought it vital that everyone group together for safety instead of scattering.

More importantly, though, she wanted to ask some questions.

"Did anyone besides Larry leave the shelter and come back?" Kat had her hands on her hips, pissed as hell. Tink had vouched for Larry's return soon after Kat had left with Chris and Duke, so they were square on that point—even if Larry's whereabouts still niggled at her. "And don't bullshit me, now. One of you had to have seen something."

"I went back to sleep," Alexandra said, glancing around warily.

Was she lying to cover herself? If she wasn't, then no one would've been awake to witness the attacker sneaking out to follow Kat, Chris and Duke, since Tink and Larry had supposedly fallen right back asleep, too.

But how would that person have gotten Will's knife?

She was trying to not think about that, and they all seemed to know it.

"Not to point out the obvious," Dr. Hopkins said from her isolated corner, "but the rest of us were here, and it was the captain's weapon. And no one has seen him for hours."

"Anyone could've gotten ahold of Will's knife," Kat said.

Tinkerbell, who'd torn off part of Duke's pants and was tending to him with what was left of the first aid kit, stuffed a bloodied piece of gauze into an empty chip bag in disgust, rolling it closed. "The captain wouldn't throw knives at people from the bushes anyway. Lay off him."

"Well, someone did it." Louis's eyes went glossy with sorrow. "And I know a lot of you might believe that my family is responsible for making an attempt on Duke's or Chris's life, but what about Duffy? You could not possibly believe we would hurt *him*. We are not the culprits, here."

The whisking sound of blade over wood cut through the silence. Kat turned to find Larry fashioning a pointed stick with the knife that had been lodged in Duke.

Kat's suspicions boiled again.

"What're you saying, Mr. Delacroix?" Larry shot a contained glare at Louis.

The man's face went red. "I am saying that there is a person here who needs to be brought to justice. The same person who sabotaged the shark cage, the one who threw a knife at my father-in-law." A sob escaped him, though he battled to hold it back. "The animal who killed Duffy and maybe even Nestor, too."

It was as if a dam had broken inside Alexandra. Without warning, she sputtered into tears, covering her face and bowing her head, her body convulsing.

Out of pure instinct, Kat went to her. The other woman didn't draw away as she might have done back on the boat—back in that other world. Instead, Alexandra looked up at Kat, anguish spearing through her blue irises like white streaks of melting snow.

Kat tried not to dwell on all the theories swirling around her head. Tried not to picture Will and Alexandra conspiring together. Or him making plans to win over Kat, Duke's suggested five-percent heir, with every ounce of charm he had. She tried not to think of him making love to her with an agenda—the possible assurance of a fortune that would set him back up in society. She tried not to imagine him hiding among the foliage and winging that knife at Duke, missing the killing blow and then dodging away, furious at his failure.

Was this forced isolation causing her to go nuts? Was it warping all her judgment?

While Alexandra looked at Kat, her mouth trembled as a smile emerged. A real smile, Kat thought.

Then she dissolved into tears again, the former ice queen crumbling to chipped pieces.

Finally, Kat thought. She's human.

Unless she was just putting on some kind of show.

Repelled by her unchecked skepticism, Kat stayed at the woman's side, proving that she was bigger than fear.

Duke, prone and pale, turned on his side and began to retch into an empty container. Chris scooted over to his grandfather, his hand on the older man's back until Duke stopped.

"There's just one thing I keep asking myself," Dr. Hopkins said, drawing everyone's attention from the scene. "Where *is* the captain?"

And they were off again, speculations, accusations. As Kat's nerves frayed to dust, she listened, weighed the comments while Will stayed ahead in the race for best suspect. The evidence got to the point where even Larry looked a little anxious.

Tinkerbell might've been the last vocal Captain Will Ashton supporter in the room. She cursed at everyone and got to her feet, starting back to her seat next to Dr. Hopkins.

"I swear," the redhead said, "you've been drinking jungle juice if you think the captain has it in him."

As she walked past the opening of the back cave, something caught Kat's attention.

Faint, almost dimmed by the darkness.

Red eyes.

Deliberately, Kat got to her feet, but not before the eyes got closer. A sort of inhuman snort bounced off the rock of their shelter, vibrating over the splatter of rain outside.

"Tink," Kat said, "don't move."

Too late. It crept closer, nearing the cave opening. Kat pointed there, and everyone looked. Slowly, they each tore their gazes away, eyes seeking Kat once again.

Hushed terror strung them all together in motionless agreement. No one flinched. Kat could barely make out a creature with bristly dark fur and a straight tail. Its ears stood alert.

A wild boar?

It wasn't really big—probably a youngster—but that didn't matter. In general, Kat had heard they were perilous and fast. And if this was a baby, Mom might be close by. And she'd be one ticked-off, protective, hefty lady.

Kat scanned the outer shelter, taking stock of the group. They were all weaponless. But three feet away, there was a long screwdriver. It was near Louis, who was directly in the beast's path.

Kat's knife seemed to weigh down her left side.

In spite of the act she'd put on for everyone else, did she actually have the guts to use it?

No chance to think anymore because, before Kat's next strained breath, the boar had bounded into the shelter.

Kat dove for the screwdriver, skidding in the dirt, pushing it at Louis.

"Use it!" she yelled.

He picked it up and scuttled away from the boar.

Almost everyone scrambled, clearing the shelter area, except for the wounded Duke and Chris, in the corner. The young teen brandished a wooden club to keep the boar away from his grandfather. Even Dr. Hopkins and her useless hands had managed to scoot away to the far ledge.

But it was happening too fast. In the confusion, Kat bounded away from the animal while it circled the shelter and locked onto Tinkerbell.

Who still had blood from Duke's wound on her hands.

A flash of lightning escorted Kat to the only place the boar wasn't—the deep, dark cave from which the beast had come. There were other survivors running into the opening, then the network of tunnels spreading out in all directions.

Mindlessly searching for safety, their bodies pressing against Kat's in the yawning blackness, screaming for their lives.

When a frenzied grunt from the boar invaded the tunnel, everyone separated, leaving Kat in darkness, like that of the deepest water. A black place of terrifying isolation.

Where was it? Had it gotten anyone?

Kat unsheathed her knife, sweat making her palms slippery. The heartbeats of a million fears flooded her temples. Dark, so dark.

Someone was crying for help. God, someone…in trouble.

And Kat had a weapon.

Self-preservation sounded so right. It was only reasonable to stay out of the way.

But something her dad the soldier had told her time and again came back to Kat.

Inside every person is a coward, he'd said, smiling at her because he knew that wasn't the kind of girl he wanted to raise. *And it's up to that individual to do what they can with it. Because, in the end, that coward could haunt you...if you don't kill it first.*

A woman screamed, shaking Kat back into the horror of cold tunnel walls, reverberating pleas and utter blindness.

Sucking in a breath to sustain her, Kat flattened one hand on the rock. Then, she took her first step toward the screaming.

Ba-bump, ba-bump. Her pulse flashed through her head.

Another scream. Which way was it coming from? Near the shelter? Or from the depths of the tunnels?

She wanted to yell, just to let the other person know she was coming. But what if she attracted the boar?

Trailing her hand along the wall, Kat continued, her breathing keeping time with a drip, drip from somewhere above.

"Help!"

Closer.

I'm coming, she thought. I'll be there soon.

Ba-bump...

Then, another frantic shout.

From another direction.

"No, no, nooooooo!"

The acoustics were playing mind games. Which way was the victim screaming from? Should Kat go right or left…?

A death keel from the right drew Kat into action. The sounds of snarling and grunting confirmed where she needed to go. Pumping up her pace, she held the knife ready in one hand and trailed the other along the wall for guidance.

Light ahead, around the corner. Or were her eyes playing tricks, too?

Dim, dim, light—

The screams abruptly stopped, but the grunting continued.

Kat turned the corner into a foreign cave, open to the rain.

And stopped when she saw what was in the faint light.

The boar was rooting at Tinkerbell's neck. Kat could see her red head bobbing as she thrashed in a silent scream. The woman was beating its skull with a rock, trying to push the creature off of her. But all she was doing was pushing it toward the ground, the movement of its tusks tearing her into movement too.

Fear and strength crashed together in Kat, a wave flaring against the rocky shore and destroying everything in its path.

Including the everyday coward.

With a yell, Kat flew at the boar, knife poised. Its throat gleamed like a target and, with all the stamina she had—something almost superhuman in this moment of terror—she drove the blade through the creature's trachea.

It spazzed, its squeal hoarse as it bit at her. Kat jerked away from the bloody teeth and yanked the knife out from the tough hide. The blade sucked out of the wound. Spurts of blood hit her like bullets as the animal shook its head.

There was no sound from Tinkerbell now, but Kat barely registered that fact. Instead, she became aware of someone else screaming behind her, running forward and jumping onto the boar's neck.

Louis?

He seemed possessed, using his designer shoe heels to stamp on the animal's face, keeping it from biting Kat.

Instead, it was biting *him*. But Louis kept kicking, his expensive slacks tearing, his cries of pain splitting the air.

Knowing this was her only chance, Kat went at the boar again, mindless with the rabid instinct to survive. She stabbed and stabbed its throat, figuring that the first try had worked so she should go with a proven thing.

The knife sunk into flesh, bloodying her hands.

Leave…us…alone!

Every thrust was an attempt to save herself from what was happening on this island. She wasn't just killing Tinkerbell's predator; she was keeping everyone safe. Kick, stab, Kick… She was so afraid to stop because it might start up again.

Louis had fallen to his knees. He yelled like a warrior, forcing the screwdriver into the boar's eyes.

But the animal wasn't attacking anymore. It wasn't…

Kat stopped, stunned at having so lost control.

Her lungs heaved. She scrambled away from the creature, knife in the air for another strike.

But it didn't move. Tink didn't move.

Kat stopped Louis. "I think it's dead."

She didn't know how long she hesitated, holding his wrist and listening for the boar's breath. It never came. Blood covered her, hot and coppery.

Numb, she checked Tinkerbell's silent pulse. When she yelled into the dark that they were safe, her voice sounded like another woman's, one who lived on a different plane of existence.

It wasn't Katsu Espinoza. She'd never gone this crazy with fear before.

As she and Louis scooped up Tink and carried her back to the shelter—*where should they bury her?*—she asked herself again and again: Who am I?

They blundered through the dark tunnels, Louis wincing with pain and stumbling with his injuries. But somehow they found their way back, even if Louis had to crawl most of the way while Kat dragged Tink.

When she saw their own shelter's natural light, Louis and Kat guided Tinkerbell gently to the ground at the lip of the tunnel's opening. The bottom of Louis's slacks were steeped with blood, maybe his own.

"This would be a good place for her to rest," he said, voice anguished while pushing back Tink's red hair from her forehead, just like a loving father putting a child to bed for the night.

Kat left them both there for now. Somewhere, in the

part of her mind that was still working, she knew it needed to be that way. That Louis was thinking of Duffy and wondering if Nestor was in the same shape, without a family to lay him to sleep. She could deal with first aid for his legs soon enough.

At least, she thought, we got our attacker. At least that boar won't be after us anymore.

But her words slapped against her conscience like a deadened sail.

Really, they *hadn't* gotten their attacker. Not at all. They'd only tried to protect themselves from nature's food chain. The real threat was still out there.

And that became more of a reality than ever when Kat stepped into the shelter.

Because that's where she found the second body.

Chapter 11

All alone except for the body of Alexandra Delacroix, Kat could only stare.

She couldn't even feel the new bruises piling up on the old ones. Blood from the boar was like a heavy anesthetic on her skin, seeping into her.

How could someone do this?

It was like the murderer had been making some kind of statement, a sharp blade robbing Alexandra in death of the beauty she'd owned in life. Her lovely nose had been slit deeply on both sides and pushed up in a mockery of humanity. Her cheeks had been scraped, giving her a pink flush. Her ears had been sharpened to points.

Bile rose in Kat's throat. This wasn't real.

She heard a dragging sound behind her. Louis.

"Stay back!" she said, her voice garbled with protective panic. "Don't come in here."

Driven to action—she couldn't let Alexandra's father see his daughter like this—Kat searched for something, *anything* to cover the dead woman.

A drying suede jacket that had fallen to the ground would work. Kat grabbed it, eased it over Alexandra's face. It covered the blood on her chest, too, but not the stab wounds in her stomach.

When Kat turned around, Louis was kneeling where the cave opening met the shelter. He'd obviously crawled away from Tink. Kat pictured the boar bites on his legs, the shredded muscle and deep punctures.

"Go back in there," Kat said, angry because he'd disobeyed. Angry because she wouldn't be able to stop him from finding out that his daughter was desecrated.

He glanced at the body's legs: the threadbare high-fashion pants Alexandra had slipped over her bathing suit right before the big meeting with Duke. The elegant deck shoes that no doubt cost more than Kat made in a week.

As Louis's mouth opened, a tiny breaking noise was all that came out. He collapsed to the ground, then yelled. The tenor of his pain shattered Kat.

Before she could go to him, she heard someone gasp from behind her.

Dr. Hopkins. The bandages had come off her muddied hands, and she was gripping a club in one of them. Kat focused on the weapon, but the doctor dropped it to the ground and cradled her hands to her chest while pulling in a breath of agony.

Her hands...

The scientist took in Alexandra's body. "Another?"

Kat nodded, too dredged in grief to ask questions about how the doctor had managed to hold a club.

Louis was moving on all fours to Alexandra, sobbing uncontrollably. He'd violently lost two, maybe three, children within days.

A nightmare, Kat thought, wishing she could just stop it. For all of them.

Janelle Hopkins limped over to Louis, kneeling beside him, offering words of comfort. Kat joined them, unsure of how he would react if she moved Alexandra's body right now. But she didn't want to shock Eloise with the sight of it when—or if—she came back.

But soon, the woman did return, tentatively entering the shelter with Larry, who held his knife out cautiously. When Eloise saw her husband mourning by the body, she wilted to the ground.

Maybe she'd already cried all her tears and there hadn't been time for more to be made yet. Maybe she was just too shocked to feel anymore. But Eloise sat, thunderstruck, mouth slack, eyes empty.

Larry lowered his knife, his face cloudy.

Determined to make everything okay, Kat tore up a blouse and made bandages for Louis, who refused her help. She couldn't argue with him, especially after he dragged himself over to his wife, where they huddled grieving together, her tears released by his presence.

Larry moved over to where Dr. Hopkins had joined Kat, who had torn up enough extra material to rebandage the doctor's hands after washing them in the rain. As Kat worked, she inspected those hands. Dr. Hopkins pulled away, obviously sensing Kat's suspicion.

Larry lowered his voice so as not to let the Delacroixs hear him. "Her face…?"

"You don't want to see."

Both Larry and Dr. Hopkins sucked in a sharp breath between their teeth.

"I don't know what to do for them," Kat said, motioning to the bereft parents across the shelter. "I can't imagine what it must feel like."

"You can *feel?*" Larry asked. "During all this?"

Yeah, Kat thought. Besides the obvious, she could also feel the boar's blood thick on her skin. The minor injuries that were just now beginning to redden and swell.

Suddenly self-conscious about the blood, Kat looked down at herself. Red-tinted hands. Splattered clothing.

Both the doctor and Larry had followed Kat's gaze. Now, they were getting a funny look in their eyes, like…

Like she'd done Alexandra in.

Kat rushed to explain about killing the boar. Janelle and Larry just watched her, a hint of…she couldn't pin it down…suspicion? Cautious respect? Raw confusion? What was it?

"I was with Louis the whole time," Kat emphasized, in case they missed it during the first telling.

Larry's expression didn't change. "And Tink? Is she okay after all that?"

Kat hesitated, but it was enough.

Once again, she saw that earth-crumbling hesitation in Will's eyes during a moment that should've been so wonderful.

I think we're having a baby, Will....

Hesitation was always enough.

Too overcome to speak, Kat pointed to the cave opening. Larry sprang to his feet in a panic and ran. His cry of rage and distress poured out of the cave.

In the midst of this, Chris and Duke finally returned.

And they'd brought someone with them.

As a rain-soaked Will entered, a thrill—sexually treacherous, wary—bored through Kat, scraping against all her suspicions about him, just like steel on flint.

Louis and Eloise stiffened, tracking their captain with swollen-eyed glares.

In addition to helping Duke walk—even through his own limp—Will was carrying a duffel bag with his possessions, his face pained because of his own bruises and cuts. On the other side of Duke, Chris toted a few oranges that spilled from his arms. While Kat's ex shot her a measuring glance—he was checking out her blood-stained clothes—Chris and Duke distanced themselves from Will. Even before looking around the room, the teen began explaining why they were with the man who was suspected of attacking Duke.

"Will saw us hiding in the bushes out there," he said as they guided Duke to his life jacket bed.

"I found Chris holding a big stick and ready to whomp anything that came near him and Grandpa," Will added.

He trailed off when he noted their faces. The sound of Larry's strangled, muffled cursing came from the cave.

The body.

"Lord," Duke said, dissolving into tears and shaking his head. "Lord, Alexandra."

As Chris lurched away and turned his back to the room, Louis struggled to his feet but fell to his knees, clearly lacking strength. Kat had forgotten about his leg wounds.

The ruined patriarch pointed a finger at Will. Louis looked like he'd been living on the island for years, gray hair bushed away from his skull, eyes reflecting pure hell.

"Where were you all this time?" he asked.

The question echoed the island paranoia in Kat. Where *had* Will been when Duke was stabbed? Where *had* he been during Duffy's and Alexandra's murders?

Her ex-boyfriend was still staring at the dead woman, face cryptic. Was he baffled? Struck down by tragedy? Wrung out with sadness at the loss of a lover?

"What happened?" Will asked, avoiding Louis's question.

"Alexandra…" Speechless, Kat motioned to her face.

Comprehension dawned on Will.

Louis's voice rose in volume. "Where the hell have you been, Captain Ashton?"

"I…" Will cleared his throat of its scratches. "This morning I was beachcombing, where I found some more stuff." He dropped the duffel bag to the ground, his hand immediately going to his sore ribs with the movement. "I was just coming back here to tell you that there's meat on the menu. I found a big female boar caught under a fallen tree nearby. Lightning. Nature did some hunting for us."

Mama boar, Kat thought in a disconnected haze. Odd that it had maybe been her offspring they'd killed today.

Will straightened his shoulders and met every single penetrating stare, including Kat's. Their eyes locked, questions, sadness, hope, all building toward a personal implosion. He was the first to tear away, his eyes haunted with something Kat would give her soul to identify.

"Don't look at me like that," Will said. "Can everyone else account for every minute of their day? Was someone always with every single one of *you*?"

From her corner, Eloise spoke, grief and spite hardening her tone. "Your knife was in Duke's thigh, Captain Ashton, and not only that, you're the only one of two unaccounted for when he was stabbed, and I know Larry was just with me during…" She quivered, obviously avoiding Alexandra's body. "And where are the other knives you had?"

Will's hand rested near his hip, on a makeshift canvas sheath he'd fashioned for his blade. "There's one more in my bag, too. And…" He glanced at Duke's thigh. "You got stabbed?"

When no one spoke, Dr. Hopkins took up the slack, levelheadedly catching Will up on the attack on Duke, the trouble with the boar, Tink's and Alexandra's deaths.

At the end of it, Will looked like he'd been jumped at midnight by a flock of street punks—beaten and robbed. And pissed as hell.

"What reason would I have?" he asked, turning to Kat for some support. "What motive?"

Five percent of a fortune, she thought automatically. The five percent he might've hinted at just before they'd made love. The millions of dollars he could grab after he charmed his way back into Kat's life.

I don't want to think it, Will, said a soft spot in her soul. *Can't you give us an alibi…something…that would get you off the hook?*

Resting his hands on his hips, Will shook his head. "I don't believe this. I guess I'm the scapegoat, huh? Come late to the party and look what the hell happens."

"It's more than that." Louis was on all fours, hunched over, breathing heavily. Rabidly.

"Goddammit," Will said, "let's start from the beginning. Why would I make an attempt on Chris's life on the boat? And then, why would I kill Duffy?"

Against her will, Kat's mind switched gears, her original Alexandra/Will conspiracies playing in her head.

According to that theory, almost every act of violence would've had its purpose for Will and Alexandra. He'd be getting rid of the obstacles for his could-be lover. But if Will and Alexandra had been in cahoots, getting rid of *her* wouldn't have made sense.

Unless… God. Unless theory number two was the one. Could Will be killing off all the Delacroixs to keep them from laying claim to Kat's possible five percent? From that point, Will could work his wiles on her, talk her into a relationship, then marriage, which would give him the fortune he so desperately needed for his family and his self-esteem.

But…jeez, that still didn't make sense. Why would he have tried to get rid of Duke before he'd redone his will?

Damn, listen to her. Kat pinched herself, a small form of punishment and a wake-up call.

"Wait," she said. "This is a bad time for accusations—"

Eloise interrupted. "Captain Ashton's going to kill again if we don't work this out now."

Kat's stomach clenched. "We need proof before we—"

Before she could finish, Louis darted a hand out to his side, grabbed a huge stick of wood and bounded forward with a banzai yell. With a decisive slam, he nailed Will in the back of the head, falling on top of him and bringing the captain to the ground.

Spurred by shock, Kat flew at them. "Will!"

His eyes had rolled back in his head.

She pushed Louis. "Stay back!"

From his pocket, Louis grabbed the screwdriver he'd extracted from the boar and waved it at Kat. "*I'm* keeping us safe this time."

Psycho. That's what he was. Out of his mind—loco with sorrow.

Before Louis could strike, Kat threw her body over Will's. "No! We don't know he's guilty. You don't want to murder an innocent man, Louis, you don't want to be like the person who's killing your children."

She'd said it on purpose, knowing it would throw him off…or make him crazier. It was a gamble worth taking because she didn't know what else to do.

As everyone else froze, the space hummed with tension while Louis poised the weapon, up…up…. He waited, hand shaking. Kat's pulse beat into Will's skin as she prepared to fight Louis off.

But just as she was about to spring at him, Louis crumbled. Eloise came to him, counselor and conspirator.

There was a vengeful streak running through the older woman, one that left the champagne-blond, happy lady from the boat among the sea's wreckage. "I say we kill Captain Ashton to be sure. Keeping him alive is a risk."

"Kill? We're going to be rescued soon," Kat said desperately. "The authorities can decide what needs to happen. And Will…" She swallowed. "Will couldn't have done what you're accusing him of. Please. Don't do this."

The other woman assessed Kat in a way Alexandra would've. Kat knew where the daughter had gotten that hardened air.

"You haven't wondered about Will?" the older woman asked. "Not even with those rampant Captain Macintosh rumors?"

God forgive her…yes.

"We're overreacting." Kat was quaking in denial

now. "We're letting the island, the craziness, get to us."

A glint of conscience darkened Eloise's eyes. Quieted, she pointed to Kat's sheathed knife. "Would you be able to protect everyone from him if you're wrong?"

Kat's brain scrambled. Think, girl, think.

"For peace of mind, we can restrain him," she said, grasping at straws—anything to keep him alive, so she could find out the truth and maybe even save him from this forming mob. She wouldn't be able to live with herself if Will wasn't cleared. "Will has some rope."

Dr. Hopkins spoke up from the other side of the shelter. "I know some good knots that I picked up during my time at sea."

A volunteer, Kat thought. Did the doctor also think Will was guilty? Or was he just a convenient culprit?

"That's okay—I know my knots. And I'll watch over him," Kat added, her meaning twofold. She'd either be guarding Will from these people or...

...guarding *them* from Will, the possible killer.

Something tender, hopeful in her shook in grief. It *couldn't* be him.

"But first," Kat added, "I want a motive. Why would he be doing this?"

Deep down, she needed to know if she was the only one thinking Will might be playing her.

"Motive?" Eloise asked. "Money's a pretty tidy one." Tears gathered in her eyes again. "We're not all blind, Katsu. When you brought the captain back from his shelter, it was obvious what had gone on between you two. Didn't you ever think he was sucking up to you, his ex-girlfriend—the woman who could be very, very rich once we get back to civilization?"

So Kat wasn't making things up in her mind. Others had noticed.

Eloise watched her. "You'll stab him if there's trouble? I'm not entirely comfortable with the rope idea."

A lump had jammed in Kat's throat, but she talked around it. "I'll take care of him if it turns out I'm wrong."

God, she thought, please help me be right.

Or was she a fool for ignoring her misgivings, especially after having trusted Will and being betrayed before?

Eloise held the weeping Louis, gaze fixed on the unconscious Captain Ashton. "I'm trusting you, Katsu, and only because you were with Louis during Alexandra's last moments. You've got the alibi the captain *doesn't* have."

Before Eloise closed her eyes and rested her forehead against her husband's, something lit through the woman's irises. A fire.

And it shook Kat down to her core.

After Kat bound a disarmed Will's hands and ankles, there was nothing much for her to do except wait for him to wake up. Kat didn't envy the pain he'd be in, based on the cramped position of his body, but it couldn't be helped.

If she hadn't stepped in, Will would be dead. Tying him up had saved him—for the time being.

Surprisingly, the wind and rain had died down and the sun began to peek out from the clouds. It forced everyone to suck it up and work. If they didn't take advantage of this reprieve and put their terror into little inner compartments, they'd never survive long enough to see a rescue. Later those pressures could spring open like jack-in-the-boxes. But first they needed food and fire.

Chris and Eloise, two of the healthiest in the group, had taken Will's knives for protection as they'd stumbled down to the beach, intending to salvage more materials. Kat hoped they would be alert enough to mind any predators, though. On the way out, both of them had moved like zombies, with Chris at a distance from his aunt.

Kat gave Larry, who was still mourning Tink, a flashlight and set him to work using the bow, stick and a rock slab to create fire in a protected area where there was no wind. Small pieces of wood and bark from the cave, as well as light planks found at the beach, would be their dry fuel, she hoped. At first Larry had pitched a fit about Will's incarceration, and Kat had needed to explain why his captain was being tied up, that it was better than a screwdriver to the throat any day, that the Delacroixs were crying for Will's blood and this was the agreement that saved Will's life.

His eventual acceptance of the captivity made her realize how much Larry trusted her. Or was it because he, too, thought his captain was guilty? Was he also wary of all the rumors surrounding Captain Macintosh's death, even though Will had denied them? And had Will's attack on Louis back on the *M. Falcon* shown too much of a violent temper, one that made it easy to believe him capable of anything?

Or maybe having a suspect made them all feel a little safer, like the trouble had been neutralized.

At any rate, as she stood guard over Will, knife at her hip, she tried to stay frosty. Lack of sleep was getting to her, and her throat was stinging. Her chest was tight and her limbs were starting to feel heavy and achy.

The last thing she needed was to get sick, exposed to the elements as they all were. She'd heard the others beginning to cough and sniffle, too.

Louis, who had finally bandaged up his shredded ankles, was sitting and staring blankly at the rain. Dr. Hopkins was tending clumsily to an exhausted Duke, who was still having bouts of nausea. He was soothed enough to fall into a partial sleep. Kat was growing anxious about Louis's boar bites. Would they get infected? And how much blood had Louis lost from his wounds?

An excited voice from the cave made Kat flinch away from her thoughts.

"Fire!" Larry cried. "Fire!"

Kat waited, listening, craving more good news. Even this pitiful amount of it had perked her up.

"Is it still going?" Kat yelled back.

Will stirred. She reluctantly undid the knife sheath.

Louis got to his hands and knees, making his way toward the cave. "I'll help him."

Minutes after he crawled away, Chris and Eloise returned, arms laden with coconuts. As the teen told everyone how the fruit had been knocked to the ground by the winds, he went about getting the meat from them. First, he drained the nut by skewing one of the kitchen knives into the softest "eye" on top, pouring the juice into cups. Then he put the nut in Will's duffel bag and slammed it against the wall to break the shells.

As Kat jerked from the crack of the contact, a victorious whoop and another, more victorious cry of "Fire!" made her start, then smile for the first time in…jeez, had it been hours? Days?

Maybe now they'd be able to bring back that mama boar, have maybe Larry or Louis skin it, then ready it for some roasting over the flames. Stomach growling, Kat wondered if they could even find Will's boar under that tree.

As if hearing his name go through her mind, Will groaned. Kat tensed, her fingers touching the rubber of her knife's grip.

"Uhhh," Will said, shifting. His eyes shot open once he realized he couldn't move. "Kat? What…?"

All activity in the shelter ceased. It was only when Kat didn't answer that everyone got back to work.

"It's the only way I could keep you alive," she said, tentatively smoothing back the hair from his forehead in spite of herself. "Louis, Eloise and maybe a few other people who're playing their cards close to their chests wanted to put you on some kind of wham-bam trial where you'd come out hanging."

He shut his eyes, like he was trying to remember. Clearly, he did—right up to the part where Louis had whomped him.

"Untie me." He started forward, then winced. The cuts on his lips were still mean and red.

"Everyone has a lot of questions about you."

Crack went Chris's coconuts, the sound making Kat ultra-aware that Dr. Hopkins, Eloise and the boy were listening.

Torn between being a guard or a supporter, Kat offered him a cup of rainwater. He refused at first but seemed to reconsider and drank greedily, his eyes half-closed in difficulty. Then he looked disgusted with himself for giving in.

"Don't fight this," she said, "because it'll end up being worse if you do."

He finished, licking a stray drop from his lips. Kat's body fired to flame. Even all tied up he had the power to overcome her better instincts with one innocent, suggestive move.

"Does that mean you're going to kill me?" he asked.

He gave a deliberate look to her knife.

"Listen," she said, feeling Eloise's glare on her back. "Someone's running around carving up faces and stabbing people. Got it?"

"And I'm the killer. Why? Why would I be?"

She steeled herself. "One theory going around is that you're after my five percent, and you're killing off the present heirs to get to it."

"Right. I killed Duffy. And Alexandra."

Kat lowered her voice to a whisper. "Yeah, even your favorite passenger." Bitterness. Envy. Her tone was steeped in both.

Will offered a defensive laugh, lowering his own voice so that Kat had to lean in to hear him. "And now you're buying into it all? For the record, since you seem to need reassurance, I wasn't interested in Alexandra. We had a few conversations, that's it. I was the captain who was making his guests feel at home—"

Without warning, he strained at the rope, catching her off guard. Shooting him a fiercely conflicted glare, she sprang to her feet, levering her shoe against his chest to keep him down and putting her hand on the knife. She wasn't going to look around the shelter to see everyone giving her I-told-you-so glances.

The area was quiet now.

"Kat." Under her control, he was panting, voice soft, so damned persuasive. "How could we go from loving each other to this?"

Her heart flared, then seemed to tear apart, raining cold and dead inside her chest.

But she couldn't give in. Not until she absolutely knew that Will was in the clear. Because of the Delacroixs, it was a matter of life and death, a symptom of the fever attacking them all now.

Through her disturbed fog, Kat became aware of someone entering the shelter from the cave. Larry.

He came to stand before her, giving an apologetic, cautious nod to his captain. Larry looked like a kid who'd come to the zoo just to see the nice tigers he worshipped in the picture books he'd read. And now that he was on the other side of the cage, where the only barrier between him and the threat of a beast was a rope that had been cut in two and secured into knots that might not even hold, he wasn't so sure about this animal he thought he'd known.

Was it as warm and fuzzy as he'd once believed? Or would it attack?

"Larry?" Kat asked.

He roused himself. "Delacroix is feeding the fire with the gathered wood. What can I do now?"

There it was again—the assumption that she was in charge of their survival.

And with the speed of a flash flood, she then realized that she pretty much *had* been ever since they'd wrecked.

God. Katsu the leader. The world had really fallen on its ass, hadn't it?

Still, she couldn't stop a surge of pride from pumping her up. It was pretty nice to be valued.

Katsu. The leader.

But then reality edged its way back again. Darkness, heavy, liquid and all too scary.

"I hate to ask you this," she said, "but I can't leave Will, and no one else…"

Larry's direct gaze didn't waver. "Just ask me."

She inhaled, then exhaled on a trembling breath. "Alexandra and Tink."

He got it. Earlier, Kat and Larry had moved the socialite's body next to Tink's, wondering when they would be able to bury them. It had to be taken care of before nature took its course and made their location a target for predatory animals with good noses…like boars.

Now, the dreadlocked guy—the baddie of the group—pursed his lips. He was fighting back tears, Kat thought.

But he quickly gathered himself, puffing up his chest as his eyes got watery. Hiding his face, he lurched toward the cave opening, holding up a hand to tell Kat that he was all right and she didn't need to pursue him. He would get the job done. Complainer or not, Larry was dependable.

And that left her with Will, who was watching her with narrowed eyes, his last question hanging in the air.

How had they gone from loving each other to this?

As a rumble of thunder shook the sky, Kat unsuccessfully tried to come up with an answer.

Chapter 12

I've got to get out of these putrid clothes, Kat thought later that afternoon.

She couldn't take it anymore. The scent of the boar's blood—though partially blocked by a nose that was getting more plugged by the second—nauseated her. Calling Larry over, she told him to guard Will, knowing she was taking a risk, gambling that Larry was indeed on her side. She knew he was aware of the consequences if he were to betray her by setting Will free.

And when she told Larry that Will wasn't his captain now—that he was a prisoner—the crewman didn't argue with her, so that was hopeful for maintaining order.

She quickly set about scrubbing herself under a

palm whose fronds were splashing water to the earth. Afterward, Kat felt as decent as she could, dressed in a pair of her own surf shorts, a T-shirt and a lightweight jacket they'd found on the beach. In fact, when she got back to the shelter, the others went, bit by bit, to freshen up, too. Chris helped Duke, Eloise helped Louis and Dr. Hopkins managed by herself right before Larry took his own "happy shower," as he called it.

They could afford the luxury, now that they thought they had the killer restrained.

But Kat still wasn't so sure.

Tink kept haunting her. So did Duffy's and Alexandra's altered faces. There was something about Duffy's eyes, mouth... Something about Alexandra's nose, ears...

What was eating at Kat? Why couldn't she put her finger on what was bothering her about the way they had looked?

A near miracle was the only thing that ended up keeping her sane: an hour later, the sun struggled through the clouds and cast a streak of gold over the ocean. Kat was the first to see the spot on the back of the newly lit water. It was a spot so tiny that it looked like a black ant ready to drop off the edge of the world.

She stood near the overhang with its beach view, trying not to forget that Will was still behind her.

"Come here!" she yelled.

Everyone did, lured by Kat's urgency.

She pointed, and Eloise grabbed her arm.

"Is that...?"

Impulsively, she hugged Kat, and they all yipped and danced around as well as they could. Even Louis, who couldn't stand fully, was included soon. He'd crawled over on his hands and knees, caveman-like. He was still wearing patches of the boar's blood on his face, where Eloise obviously hadn't scrubbed hard enough. And even though he sported a new set of clothes, they were too big. Hugh-the-steward's grubs. Earlier, Eloise had begged Louis to let her wash his leg wounds again. And, from the way he was dragging around, Kat suspected it wasn't a bad idea.

Trouble was, they had no more ointments in the first aid kit. How much good would rainwater do Louis?

"A ship, a ship!" Chris sang, dancing around.

Kat ran down a mental checklist. Was their SOS sign intact for a plane to spot? Could they build a signal fire out there? She needed to get out and make sure.

"A ship!" Dr. Hopkins said, knocking hips with Chris. "When it gets close enough, let's light up a few torches and run down to the beach. They'll see that, right?"

"Thank you, God," Will said from his corner.

Louis stopped his celebrating. "I wouldn't get so excited if I were you, Captain. You'll be turned over to *them* next."

"I've nothing to hide."

As everyone else went back to watching the dot on the ocean, Kat's gaze lingered on Will, remorse holding her to him while he stared back, disappointment shading his eyes.

When Duke started to moan in his bed, holding his hands to his head, Kat sighed roughly, the spell broken. Chris hopped over to help his grandfather.

"Rescue!" Louis said. He didn't sound happy so much as starving. "Back home."

"Back to the swimming pool," Eloise said. "Back to massages and martinis with three olives."

Both Louis and Eloise went quiet, no doubt thinking of how tasteless those martinis would seem without their children to enjoy them, too.

From his bed, Duke growled, then roared, sitting up. There was a twist to his gaze that made Kat's breath catch.

"And who'll pay for all of that, you leeches?"

Kat took a step backward.

"Father," Eloise said, voice thick. "How can you ask such a thing? After all we've—"

"Don't 'Father' me when you aren't half the daughter I needed."

It was a strange Duke. A man Kat didn't know—one with a mean, baffling flare in his darkened eyes, one whose temper had mounted his pain and been made bigger, more intense.

The shelter suddenly seemed to have a heartbeat of its own, a pulse that pounded through Kat and shook the air.

Shoulders drooping, the fevered billionaire lost his fire, shaking his head in dissipated anger. "I know everything, Eloise. Remember that."

As Kat stood helpless, Duke suffered all alone, sinking into his bed and pulling a newly dried canvas jacket over himself. Chris retreated and sat nearby, gauging his grandfather, probably afraid to go near him.

The rest of them tried to ban the ugliness from the shelter by turning back to the spot on the ocean and planning how to best attract its attention when it got closer.

But it never got any bigger.

When the sun faded, they all got a little nervous.

The wind picked up and Kat's eyes started to sting with disappointment. Thunder declared itself again; lightning answered.

Suddenly, the ocean looked like a pot of boiling water, agitated and dark. Rain crashed down, erasing the beautiful black spot and the golden waves it moved upon.

Kat never got to talk to Duke because he soon became violently ill, then succumbed to a deep sleep. Best thing, really. He was in a lot of pain. His body needed to shut down and replenish—if it could.

They all ate their boar meat in near silence. It was surprisingly tender and likely delicious, even though Kat couldn't taste much of it. Not many of them could with their worsening colds. But, still, as Kat sniffled and struggled to grasp its flavor, she could feel the protein strengthening her.

Now all she needed was sleep.

And so she cut a deal with Larry: alternating shifts, where they would take turns napping.

The group moved themselves to the cave opening,

near the fire. Luckily, more exploration produced more dried wood, and it was given to the person on watch to feed the flames during the night. They'd also salvaged and dried enough blankets and clothing so that they could bundle under a decent pile of warmth as they went to sleep.

"'Night, Kat," Will said as he huddled near her, still restrained. "Hope your dreams are as sweet as mine."

There was an edge to his tone. Even while hardening herself against it, she felt his anger slash into her. It wouldn't have been so bad if it'd been *just* anger, though. There was also a tinge of regret—a reminder of a fork in the road and the different directions they'd taken. A reminder of how they'd lost each other along the way.

Kat swallowed. "You know this is the last thing I want to be doing—holding you prisoner."

"And being trussed up is *my* last choice." He paused, then raised his voice so everyone could hear. "I may have a temper, but I've never killed anyone—not Duffy, not Alexandra, not Captain Macintosh."

"I wish," she said, "you'd just see that I'm your protector and not your jailor."

No one said anything in the cave. Only the crackling fire and some sounds of the winds provided commentary. Maybe everyone was already asleep.

"Will…?" she whispered, trailing off, not knowing where to start.

His exhausted sigh spoke more than a thousand words ever could. "As I said, sweet dreams, Kat."

Her throat was too choked to pursue it, so she took

her knife in hand and blinked her eyes, forcing them open. But she couldn't help watching Will, piecing together her confusion, her apologies, their past....

A downtown bar on a summer Saturday. A popular Brit-rock band had been slumming it in a small venue. She'd caught Will giving her a grin from across the room and, when she'd gone to get a second beer, he'd told her that she had the most beautiful eyes he'd ever seen. Flustered by the force of her immediate attraction to him, she'd accused him of recycling a bad line that'd probably worked before. They'd listened to the music together, bodies brushing against each other in innocent contact. They'd talked about their favorite bands, their favorite movies, their favorite types of Mexican food. Then, they'd walked to the harbor in the dead of night, watching the sun come up and talking about their favorite breakfasts. And...

Kat's vision went blank.

Blessed emptiness where she couldn't think about everything she'd done wrong. Where she couldn't dwell on every ache in her body that was being magnified by the pounding rain and wind...

She jerked back to consciousness, her heart quivering. The fire had hushed to embers, darkening the area. Dammit! She'd fallen asleep. For how long?

With a frenzied glance, she saw that Will was still there, a peaceful slant to his brow as he slept. Before she could get drawn into how achingly gorgeous he was, injuries or not, she glanced around. Everyone else was tucked in, too, heads and bodies buried under blankets.

Don't you fall asleep again, she commanded herself.

As the rain softened, tapping on the leaves outside, Kat realized she needed to go to the bathroom. They'd all agreed that using the cave was unsanitary and might draw predators, so she had no choice but to wake Larry.

He grumped a little, but Kat made sure he was alert enough to watch over Will and the fire. When she grabbed a flashlight and sneaked out of the cave, Eloise woke up, too.

"I have to go," she whispered, rolling out of her bed. "Buddy system."

Both women used jackets to keep the moisture off them, but it wasn't worth it. As if playing a joke, the rain began to pound down harder as soon as they stepped out of the cave. Still, they managed to follow the markers they'd previously tagged onto the branches and took care of business soon enough.

At least, Kat *thought* both of them were returning. Mrs. Delacroix wasn't with her anymore.

"Eloise?" she called, the sheets of rain absorbing her voice.

Kat backtracked with her flashlight. What if one of those boars had gotten to Eloise? Kat probably wouldn't have heard it in all this racket.

As the rain took a turn for the better, it stopped sounding like Kat's voice was bouncing around the inside of a steel box. She put on her jacket. "Eloise!"

No answer. Just the rain, the low sound of night hiding its creatures.

Pulse picking up nervous speed, Kat walked back toward the john. The other woman wasn't there. "Come on, Eloise! I'm tired."

She spent a few minutes tripping around the area. Dammit, where was she?

You know where, said the scaredy-Kat within.

In the near distance, something barged through the foliage. Kat gasped, whipped out her knife.

Run away. Now.

Fearing for her life, Kat did start running—here, there…she wasn't sure where.

The flashlight's beam bobbed over the trees and bushes, rain like white needles as she stumbled toward the shelter. She could see it looming above the swaying green leaves, but it was so far…

Trapped in a maze, she thought, darting toward safety, confused and frustrated, going around and around to nowhere. Minutes, hours, how long was this taking?

Her breath got wheezy, and she coughed. Her chest squeezed together, cold and phlegmy. Still, Kat forged ahead, blood freezing, the foliage alive around her.

Get back…hurry…

Putting on the power, she tripped over something. Hands outstretched in front of her, she hit the mud with a smack, her palms skidding over an exposed root. Her knife and flashlight spiraled over the undergrowth, the light zigzagging over the trees until it disappeared beneath them.

Jarred, she couldn't move for a second, the oxygen knocked out of her. The tang of copper…blood?…leaked from her lip. It pounded with pain from where she'd bitten it. The heels of her palms were flaring because they'd lost skin when she'd broken her fall.

Get it together, Kat. Right freakin' now.

Forcing herself to crawl for her possessions, she fumbled, spying the light peeping out beneath a bush, her knife nearby, grabbing them just in time to see a thick snake slithering through the foliage only three feet away.

A cry strangled her.

Freaked, Kat shone the light all about, behind her, near her feet, finally catching a sight that made her suck in a horrified breath.

Empty eyes stared back at her.

It was Eloise—blood and water running over and through her sliced face.

Hours seemed to pass as rain cleaned Eloise's features, revealing a fresh, simple, red-etched pattern.

A clown, Kat thought in a shocked haze. *She looks like a sad clown with those slices making her mouth turn down and cuts that look like giant tears.*

Unbidden, Duffy's and Alexandra's faces ripped through Kat's awareness.

Duffy. The cut bags under his eyes. The distended lips. Morbid decorations that made him look like an ape.

Alexandra. The slitted nose that enlarged her folded-back nostrils into a snout. The tweaked ears that made them point at the ends. A pig.

Kat put her head in her hands, her mind scrambled with things she couldn't possibly be seeing. Tremors edged through her belly, traveling upward, outward with white, jittery heat.

With building terror, Kat glanced at Eloise again. *Crash.* Realization blasted through her.

This victim's cuts had been made quickly…just like Kat had rushed the killer by backtracking and finding Eloise so soon.

Her mind spun, covering all angles from day one until now. Every confrontation, every conversation…

Faces. Slices. Patterns.

Duffy the ape, Alexandra the pig, Eloise the clown.

The answer clenched her by the throat, shaking her with its sharp razors, blinding her, robbing her of breath.

"Masks," she whispered, zipping up to a crouch and clenching her knife and flashlight as weapons. "Goddammit, they're *masks*."

And she might still be out here with the thing that had done this.

Rain splattering around her, Kat bolted upward, feet spread apart, knife ready. Scared, so damned scared.

It was her constant companion, fear, that possessed her to do what she did next.

Let the killer know you have your knife out.

"Are you ready for me, you freak?" she screeched. "'Cuz I'm all set for *you*. Get over here and let's end it!"

Her voice carried, giving her a sense that she wasn't so vulnerable after all. After a slow moment, she started moving toward the shelter, constantly looking around her, hoping she didn't see someone hunched in the bushes, waiting.

But sometimes even the worst bullies backed off when you bluffed. So she did it again.

"Hey! You afraid of *my knife?* Because it's calling *your name, asshole.* You know I'm gonna use it, too, *don't you?* You know I'm gonna *get* you *good*."

In the distance, a voice yelled, "Kat?"

Relief pushed her into a stumble towards the sound. "I'm here! Over here!"

"Kaaaaat!" It was more than one person now.

Heart exploding, she ran for all she was worth, arms pumping as she sought the voices calling her name, leaves lashing at her face.

When she got to the cave, everyone but Louis was outside, panting and sopping wet from the rain, panicked.

Who was it? Which one of them had been out there with her?

"Why were you screaming?" Dr. Hopkins asked, coming over to grip Kat's arms.

While Kat wheezed in answer, Larry led her into the cave. Chris followed anxiously as he helped a frazzled Duke along. All of them were touching Kat—on her shoulders, her arms—just like she was a mirage and they were convincing themselves of her solidity.

They guided her to the fire, where the bound Will was sitting ramrod straight, tracking Kat with a concerned gaze. He and Louis were the only ones with dry clothing and hair.

He's innocent, Kat thought, more relief…and guilt…seeping through her. Dammit, she'd been so wrong about him.

Hands bloodied and quaking, Kat immediately began undoing the rope that held him, even though it wasn't easy with her scraped palms.

"Eloise," she choked out.

And that was the extent of it, because Louis gave a wrecked shout that shook the air. Rain running down his face like tears, Duke merely slumped to a corpse pose, moving his head back and forth and staring up at the cave's ceiling, lips slack.

"It's my fault," Larry said, slapping the cave wall. "I fell back asleep when you left, Kat. Dammit!"

Kat wasn't about to get all judgmental on that failure. As far as she was concerned, Larry was a suspect, too.

"Did you notice who was missing before you ran outside?" Kat asked. Ignoring her burning hands, she massaged Will's legs and arms, attempting to say she was sorry in every way she could.

Not surprisingly, he took her hand, removed it from his arm. But then, as if reconsidering, he turned it over, inspecting her injury. He gently turned her face to him, running a thumb over her cut mouth.

"I'm so sorry," she said, throat closing.

"Later." He took over the job of massaging the circulation back into his legs and arms, then stood up and went to a pile of bandages, then outside for a cup that had been collecting water. Even though Kat had taken care to rub his limbs every hour while he was roped up, he still walked stiffly.

As he used the rain to clean her hands and then bandaged them, Kat told the group about what had gone on out there, taking care to watch their faces. Larry was covering his in remorse. Louis was hunched over. Chris had dead-walked over to a still-stunned

Duke. And Dr. Hopkins hugged her wrapped hands to her chest.

Kat glanced down at her own hands, being swaddled in the cloth. *Hands.*

Larry pushed away from the wall. "I've got to get Mrs. Delacroix's body."

"Wait until it's light," Will said. He finished with Kat's bandages, flashing a heart-wrenching glance at her. She could tell he was carrying the scars of her betrayal under his skin, and all she could do right now was vow to heal them and never to lose faith in him again.

As Larry ignored Will's advice and went outside to find Eloise's body with just a flashlight and kitchen knife, the fool, Kat tugged Will out of the cave and into the front shelter, away from everyone.

"You're the only person I can trust right now," she whispered, touching his face with her fingertips, needing to feel him so badly. "It's obvious that you couldn't have killed Eloise—"

She paused, then erupted. One big sob. Delayed reaction.

Will skimmed his fingers over her arm. "We'll get through this."

Kat batted back her emotions. No time for them. No use for them. Still, she couldn't help it. The tears needed to come. It was a physical release her body was relying on.

Steadfast, Will kept stroking her arm, even as she struggled to collect herself. Finally, after what seemed like years, she was able to talk.

"I think I know what's happening with those cuts." She sniffed, shivering and ill from the faces, the blood. It all washed over her, terror screaming through her veins, deafening her own thudding heartbeat.

"What is it, Kat?"

Blades…slashes…blood…

"Remember that night on the boat?" Her voice had risen, rushed and desperate. "The seasick night when we were playing trivia in the salon? You're gonna think I've lost it, but…" Kat swallowed, closing her eyes against the ghosts and the fear that was rushing around her. "Those cuts on the faces remind me way too much of *The Twilight Zone*. That one episode Nestor talked about. 'The Masks.' The one where—"

Will's eyes went wide, and he paled. "The old dying man makes his heirs wear masks that transform their faces into their true natures. I know. I was there."

"Why would somebody do that?"

He shook his head, mouth drawing into a frown. "Because they had the time and the psychosis."

"They had the time," she repeated.

Slash…blood…death…

She armored herself against the terror. "Duffy wasn't found for a while. And I heard Alexandra screaming before I found Tink and the boar. That gave the murderer a lot of opportunity to cut, even though they were taking a big chance on getting caught."

"They probably thought the boar would keep everyone away for a while. Maybe they could hear you fighting from the echoes in the tunnels."

When Will took Kat's hands in his, she melted,

holding his hands up to her cheeks, laying herself to rest against him. They were back to their old selves, connected, the people who'd talked until dawn on the first night they'd met. The couple who had possessed such great potential.

But then it came: a sting of memory she couldn't ignore. Kat's possible five-percent inheritance...Will making love to her in his shelter...

Was that why he was being so forgiving? Because he still thought he had a chance for millions, especially with the Delacroixs all but gone?

You're wrong, she thought. So, so wrong even to think it.

Refocusing, she grasped his hands and held on to her own sanity at the same time. "It makes weird sense. The faces reflect what's really inside, you know? Duffy was an overgrown bully, an ape who couldn't control himself. Alexandra could've been interpreted as vain, greedy..."

"She was a lawyer. You know, people usually think of them as swine." Will looked away, focusing on running his thumbs over the back of Kat's bandaged hands. "That's what she said on the boat, anyway."

The comment had all the force of a slap. She wanted to ask what exactly he and Alexandra had talked about. If it had gone further. If he'd—

No. Will was one of the good guys. She had proof now.

Kat continued, her heart still a little bruised. "And Eloise, a clown?"

"A sad one, you said. I don't know...maybe because she kept whining in that ridiculous way on the boat...?"

They were reaching, but who could really explain?

Just the killer, Kat thought. Just the person who might have more plans for more faces.

"I don't know," Kat said, shaking her head in frustration. "Why would anyone want to do this, anyway? Why would they get Duffy, Alexandra and Eloise and make an attempt or two on Duke's life?"

For a lightning-blast moment, Kat thought she saw an answer in Will's eyes, but when she looked again, she told herself she was wrong.

"Who knows," Will said. "Maybe they've somehow connected themselves to a possible heir and are thinking they can somehow get hold of Duke's money after he and his family die…?"

She hadn't wanted to hear him say that, not what her heart hoped he was too good to even consider.

Kat fixed her gaze over his shoulder to avoid his eyes, unwilling to find her worst nightmares there. But in that pause, something else saturated her thoughts, making her skin feel as if it were being peeled back.

"We're forgetting something," she whispered.

She dragged her gaze back to Will, finding his expression inscrutable. It didn't give her any comfort.

"In that *Twilight Zone* episode," she continued, "there were four heirs."

She made a low noise of pain as his hands tightened around hers, then let up when he realized what he'd done. Neither of them had to say it out loud.

That meant one more victim to go.

If the killer was keeping count according to the episode.

"But will they stop there?" he asked.

"I don't… The killer's just been inspired by 'The Masks,' they're not following the script. There could be just three victims, or maybe five, or…"

Her blood iced.

Or maybe everyone on this island would end up butchered.

She didn't have time to voice her fears. A screech filled the cave next door. Both she and Will flinched as the undecipherable yips and words mingled with each other in complicated knots.

Kat bolted over to the entrance only to be stopped in her tracks.

Because Dr. Hopkins was hugging one of the missing.

Chapter 13

As Larry told it, after having buried Eloise and braving the rain to secure more coconuts, he'd found Nestor ducking into some bushes nearby, "hiding from predators." The island had been rough on him as well. His clothes were falling apart, his pretty-boy skin bruised and scarred.

Now, they all sat around the fire, Nestor resting next to Duke, Dr. Hopkins and Louis. He was giving them his story, and it sounded a little like theirs, detailed with debris on the beach, constant rainwater and terrifying nights. The only difference was that Nestor had washed up on the other side of the island, which he confirmed was rather small, before making his way to them.

"When I first swam ashore, I saw a couple of bodies," a withdrawn Nestor said. "Crew members."

Nobody but Kat seemed to notice Will's subtle reaction: a self-hating tightening of the mouth. They'd been his to watch over, Kat thought, and he'd failed them.

She wiped at her runny nose as she sent a soft, encouraging smile to Will.

"Then," Nestor continued, "I happened upon those arrows and followed them here. And when I heard this guy—" he pointed to Larry "—I took cover, just in case it was something bigger than the stick I was carrying."

Dr. Hopkins, delirious to see her one-night stand, hugged Nestor and attended to his every need. He'd been crushed by the news of all the deaths and the additional attempt on Duke's life, and she was trying to make him feel better.

Funny, Kat thought. The doc's hands seemed good to go with Nestor around—they were functional when needed. Obviously Kat would have to comment on this at the next possible opening, after Nestor filled them in. She wished she'd had the chance to confide in Will, but there'd been too much to talk about as it was.

Meanwhile, Kat continued observing Dr. Hopkins. Was the woman feeling the same way Kat had when Will was missing? Was she over-romanticizing even a slim connection with Nestor so it would convince her that she was still vital, that she could survive anything, too?

As Kat mulled it all over, she focused on Louis, who was lingering near his newly "found" son, reaching out to touch his hair every few minutes, a grin on his face.

But, in spite of Nestor's fan club, Kat obviously wasn't the lone doubter of their group. While everyone else was engrossed in the survivor's story, Will had stood and gathered up the rope that had held *him* captive, and he was staring holes into Nestor.

She knew what he had in mind and couldn't agree more. Tie the fool up, she thought. He's a definite candidate with perfect opportunities for murder. And no matter how "out there" this happy reunion made it seem, Nestor even had a motive: clearing away most of his competitors, family or not, to be the sole heir to Duke's fortunes.

And *that* possibility meant Kat had to watch her back more than ever.

As Kat readied herself to help Will, Chris snuggled next to her, maybe sensing what was about to go down.

"Kat," he whispered.

Even though her hands were raw, Kat held Chris tightly. She couldn't let him out of her sight because, like her, Chris could be the next to find his face cut up. And so could Duke, who was resting again after a brain-crunching headache.

"I'll take care of you guys," Kat said in the boy's ear.

"Gramps needs you the most," Chris said. "I'm so afraid he's going to die."

Me too, Kat thought.

Neither of them said anything about the fact that, murderer or no, Duke was on the road to dying anyway, thanks to his lack of meds. Or that even if they should miraculously be rescued in an hour, he would soon die back home.

As the old man struggled for breath and comfort on his makeshift bed, she could only imagine his pain. No pills. His family destroyed.

She just wished she could do more. And, really, she could, right?

You know he wants to hear that you love him, she told herself. So why can't *you* say it? Why can't you tell a little white lie to give him even an hour of hope?

Embattled, she pushed back the pain, looking to Will. Even with a limp, he was sauntering toward Nestor with the rope in hand.

"Bad news, Nestor," he said.

Kat patted Chris's hand and got up.

Nestor was watching the rope. Dr. Hopkins wagged her bandaged finger at Will.

"We don't know if he's—"

"Guilty?" Will asked. "That didn't keep me from wearing hemp bracelets."

"You're entertaining the notion that I killed my siblings and my mother?" Nestor looked astounded, eyes red and swollen. "What kind of monster do you think I am?"

Kat came to stand next to Will. "We all need to start talking, Nestor. *Pronto*. And we're going to hear from you first. Then I'd like to hear from Dr. Hopkins."

"Why?" the woman asked.

One gesture to her hands was enough to make the doctor's face flush. "They're healing, bit by bit. I've been helping around here though, so don't you say that I've been lazy."

"Your lack of hard labor isn't what I'm talking

about, Janelle." Kat took her knife in hand, then gripped it. "If you can hold a club or squeeze my arms in welcome, you can do *this*, too."

Kat's meaning permeated the cave's atmosphere just as effectively as the cold of the rain had. She sheathed her knife.

"I'm not the one," Dr. Hopkins said.

Will held up his hands, the rope dangling from them. "Then who is? Nestor?"

"No! All I did was…"

"What?" Kat asked, taking a step toward him.

Nearby, Larry leaned his arms on his knees, sniffling and giving in to a cough. It jarred Kat to a cough, too. Then it became a chain reaction, encouraging a round of coughs to spark around the room.

They were all wearing down.

"Go ahead," Kat said. Her own coughs had brought a headache, a piercing throb throughout her own body. Great.

Nestor was watching Duke, regret etched into the lines bracketing his eyes. Lines that hadn't been there a few days ago.

"Gramps," he said, "after you threatened to disinherit us, we were angry, of course. You know that."

Duke stayed silent, staring at the ceiling, bled of color and listless.

Trying again, Nestor spread his arms out in a plea for understanding. "After you brought up the new will we were out of our minds. Then when you went to bed, and to let off some steam afterward, Duffy made some kind of crack about maybe securing our inheritances by getting rid of you before you could change things. Really, Duffy wasn't serious, and everyone laughed because it was so ridiculous. As we calmed down, we started to make our own jokes about ways to kill a billionaire. It was harmless, you know? Harmless." Nestor sighed and lowered his hands. "But my anger didn't go away. I was controlled by my emotions even after you threatened to disinherit us, and…"

"And what?" Kat prodded.

Nestor closed his eyes. "I did something I regret."

Harmless? Kat thought. Bull. "Harmless" jokes could be so funny and cutting exactly *because* they had a sharp grain of truth to them. She imagined that the Delacroixs *had* probably been half-serious about planning ways to get to Duke. They'd felt betrayed and angry enough to take satisfaction out of an imaginary demise for the old man.

She also imagined that the jokes might've been a way of testing each other out to see if anyone would be open to killing the man who could ruin their lives.

Money had the power to drive people to murder, Kat thought. Money…and love.

"The shark cage?" Kat asked through clenched teeth. "Was that one of the crazy ways you guys came up with to secure your fortune, either by offing Chris *or* Duke?"

Nestor hung his head. "When Chris came out to tell us that Gramps was going diving instead of him, I stayed behind for a second when everyone left to talk Gramps out of it."

Oh, no. He wasn't going to say…

"I wasn't thinking straight," Nestor said, shame-faced, opening his eyes. "I've got a lot of debts to pay off and I was desperate. I wasn't thinking."

"What did you do?" Kat asked, dreading the answer.

"It was just *one* moment, a second of warped logic. I used a diving knife to start cutting the rope, thinking Gramps would have a little scare if the cage started acting up." He drew in a rough breath before continuing. "I wanted to be the one to point out the cut, to win Gramps's respect back once he was saved. Dumb, I know. And I realized that. I changed my mind and stopped slicing right away. That's why the cut was so tiny. But what happened after that—the rope dragging through the chum, the shark biting the rope…I didn't mean any of it."

Duke moaned, facing away from Nestor, who reached out to him, then pulled back. Chris's body balled up, once again, trembling as he put his head down.

Will heaved the rope at Nestor. The jerk dodged out of the way.

"Why the hell didn't you tell us before Chris went in the cage?" Will said.

"I started to, but then I figured I hadn't cut the rope enough for it to matter! I mean, good God, what were the chances of it happening like that?"

It wasn't a good enough excuse. Kat stalked over to the rope, intending to use it.

"Wait, wait," Nestor said desperately, "I told you the truth. Why would I admit it unless I was innocent of all these killings, right? The cage had nothing to do with what's happening on this island. If I was going around murdering people, I'd have kept my mouth shut about the cage, too. You've got to believe me. I'm telling the truth."

His story made sense in a dopey way, but Kat was beyond trusting him. Besides, a smart killer would lie to them in order to gain their faith, just like Nestor had done.

Beyond forgiveness, she darted forward and pinned Nestor down with a knee, making him wince. When Nestor started to resist, Will and Larry came to Kat's aid, Kat doing the honors of tying the suspect up while Larry restrained Louis.

Duke, in the meantime, went back to staring at the ceiling with glazed eyes in the aftermath of Nestor's confession. A final knife in the heart. The ultimate betrayal of his family.

Chris was crying, shaking his head like he was denying everything that had happened.

"Who else knew about the shark cage, Nestor?" Kat asked, tying off the knots. "Your family?"

"No." He struggled one last time, coming out the loser again. "It was just me."

Kat pushed off from him. "You're disgusting. Every single one of you, dead or alive. All of you treat Duke like crap. And Nestor didn't even try to stop Chris from getting into that cage."

"It was a small cut," Nestor maintained.

Dr. Hopkins wobbled to a stand. "Kat, maybe he's telling—"

"Oh, *hell*, no. Are you going to take his side?"

Slowly, the doctor shook her head, dark eyes melting. "Right." She gave up and went to the fire, flexing her hands as if to exercise them.

"I guess we're back to guard shifts," Will said.

His gaze snagged Larry's and the two traded an odd look. Was it because, this time, they were guarding the right suspect, or because Will wasn't the one tied up?

With Will's announcement, a sense of gray calm fell over the group. They isolated themselves in corners, cowering from the killer in their midst.

Will came over to Kat, stroking her hair back from her forehead. "I can watch him while you finally get some sleep."

Sleep. It sounded so nice. But…

She coughed again. "I'll manage?" she offered weakly, to try and be strong.

"Listen to you. Get some rest." He motioned to where Chris huddled into himself. "Besides, someone needs you over there. Maybe you can…?"

"Absolutely. Will?"

He crossed his arms in front of his chest, suddenly kind of shy and unassuming. "What?"

Unsure of what she wanted to say, Kat just smiled, affection radiating outward. "Thank you."

For not hating her?

Hesitantly, he swept his knuckles over her cheek, then backed away, taking a seat next to Nestor, where a staring contest began between captive and captor.

It looked like everyone else in the cave was claiming the sleep they hadn't gotten last night. Kat craved it so badly that she started to shake.

She grabbed her blankets and sat next to Chris, spreading her material out and laying him down, too. He wouldn't let her hold him, but that was okay. All she needed to do was let him know that she was here.

As the storm wind whipped through the trees, Kat finally went to sleep.

But, when she was awakened later, it wasn't because of a noise.

It was because there was too much silence.

Except for a body across the cave, the place was empty.

Blinking awake, Kat averted her gaze and automatically reached for Chris. Gone. Just like everyone else. Except for...

Please, God, no more victims, she thought, afraid to look closer, to see who it was this time.

But she couldn't stop. Slowly, her sight combed the cave, making its way to the flat, still body.

Blankets, nice and neat, undisturbed. Fire flickering over the walls, snapping over the sound of raindrops. A man dressed in a T-shirt, sandy hair...

Will.

With a tight gasp, she tripped her way to where Nestor should've been sitting. Their suspect was gone, along with his ropes, the doctor, Chris, Duke, Larry and Louis.

All gone.

"Don't you be *dead*," she said. "Don't you dare."

When she saw his chest lift slightly, Kat laughed in joy. *Alive.*

"Will? Wake up. Will!"

She stroked his forehead, trying to soothe him awake.

He groaned. Oh, thank God. She was never so happy to hear a groan of…was it pain?

As she kept persuading him to come to, she darted a gaze around the cave, on watch for anyone else. What had happened? Where was everybody?

She searched for the knife at her side, seeking its cold comfort.

But it was gone. Nothing useful for defense was around.

As she searched for it, Will stirred, then moaned even louder, holding the back of his skull.

"Bang," he slurred out.

Kat just stared at him. "Will, talk sense to me. Are you okay?"

"I'm breathing, if that's what you mean." He closed his eyes and ruefully shook his head. "That bitch."

"What?"

"Dr. Hopkins. She was getting up for a drink, she said. But next thing I knew—bang! I was on the ground seeing stars. And now?" He pointed to Nestor's empty space. "They're not here."

A club to the head, she thought. For some reason, Dr. Hopkins had only meant to stun.

"And everyone else?" she asked.

Will finally seemed to realize that they were alone. The pupils of his eyes enlarged, then adjusted. Kat reached out a hand to steady him as he wavered.

"They were all here," he said.

Kat tried not to lose the last of her sanity. With all

the calm she could muster, she glanced around the cave again. There, in the corner. Louis's screwdriver.

The only weapon she could see.

She went over to grab it, to cling to it like the most morbid of security blankets. In the same move she got rid of the bandages on her hands. They would only get in the way when she needed to use the screwdriver, and she could deal with scraped palms and the pain if it meant living.

"My knife is gone," she told him. "I had it when I went to sleep."

A flash of lightning left half his face in shadow.

Thunder answered, shaking the ground.

"I don't like this, Will," she added.

The first scream cut the air.

Faint, distant.

"Shit," Kat whispered.

The first thing she thought of was Dr. Hopkins and how she'd "saved" Nestor by freeing him and taking off with him.

Will tried to struggle to his feet, then crashed back to the ground, cursing and holding his head.

"Stay here," Kat said, breath choppy. "You might have a concussion. You're not in any shape to go anywhere."

"This is our chance to stop all this, Kat. We can't sit here listening to someone die."

"I know." She'd never be able to live with herself. And now that she thought more about it, Chris or Duke could be the one screaming.

She *had* to go.

A crack of thunder seemed to rattle the earth itself, but Kat took strength from it, knowing that the weather didn't scare her as much as whatever else was out there.

She took a step toward the storm, but the touch of Will's hand on her belly jarred her to a stop. He spread his palm over her, tilting up a face full of desperate yearning. In his eyes, she could see the past, the future, the chance for forgiveness. Affection awakening once again, she slowly pressed her hand over his, guessing what he was thinking. When they'd made love, there hadn't been any protection. There'd been no time, no need, no access.

Had their impulsive affection given them another chance for a child? Was he indicating that he would take the news differently this time?

"Be careful," he said, resting his forehead against her hip, hiding his eyes before she could look deeper, before she could fully read what was beyond the blue-green surface.

Kat's heart folded into itself, but another agony-wracked scream yanked it back into a flat, pulsing plane where all her worst fears were gathering.

"Back soon," she said, voice shaking.

Her promise seemed so out of place amidst the screams and chaos. So empty and full at the same time.

She only had time to touch Will's head before breaking away, bursting into the rain and running toward danger.

"I'll come when I can," he yelled. But already, he seemed so far away.

The screams, thunder, lightning all drowned him out.

In spite of the tenderness of her palms, of her confused emotions, she raised the screwdriver and headed toward the mangled voices. She hurtled into the unknown, past looming trees, sharp branches, clawing leaves, into a lightning-lit clearing where she found two bodies sprawled in the undergrowth.

Where she also found the victim tied to a tree.

Louis Delacroix opened his mouth in a soundless screech.

The next few minutes were spliced together like a movie—zigs and flashes, scrambled and much too fast for eyes to make sense of:

Walking toward Louis…

Two bodies she couldn't identify on her right side, but now behind her as she came near the gaping victim….

Is Louis dangerous? Is he trying to trap me?

Who did this to you, Louis?

I can still save him.

Then…

Louis's eyes, getting bigger as they fixed on something behind Kat. Louis, face half-designed by bloody cuts, starting to scream again.

Mud scooped in hand, screwdriver raised, Kat turned around to fend off whatever was closing in.

Something had risen from the foliage in the lightning.

One of the two bodies that she'd thought was dead.

As Kat froze, the shadowed form flew at her, one arm raised and holding a club, a predator who had successfully lured its prey with bait.

Louis. Did it use Louis to get me here?

Before she could even scream, it smashed the base of her skull.

Stunned, Kat was driven to the ground, mud slapping against her face. A flash of pain shattered her sight, scrambling it.

It'd happened so quickly, she hadn't even processed the killer's face…just the eyes…

Those blazing, determined eyes.

As dizziness breathed through her, she groaned, beaten by anguish, physical and mental. This wasn't how a girl from her neighborhood was supposed to go down, she thought, almost humorously. This was too crazy to be real, it didn't make sense, it couldn't be happening.

But it was, dammit. And she had to stop it before—

Gathering the last of her strength, she let loose with a moan of rage, rolled to her back, raised the screwdriver.

The face of the killer hovered over her. A blur. A…

Just before the killer hit her with the large branch again, she sucked in a horrified breath of recognition.

The world started going black, the swollen ink of an octopus filling her watery vision, tightening pain around her head.

Never turn your back on the enemy, she thought as darkness crept over her. You know better than that, Kat. Never…

Rain splashed on her face, lulling her. She tried and tried and finally turned her head toward Louis as his screams grew louder.

And then stopped.

Through the consuming black haze, she could only watch as the killer raised his knife to cut further into the face of his uncle, a sob tearing out of his chest as he grated out frantic, unintelligible words.

It can't be. Not him. Not...

Pure shock blanked her, took her under.

Mercifully sparing her the sight of Chris's blood-soaked rage.

Chapter 14

The cry of a bird woke Kat up.

At first, she thought she was home in bed, hearing that annoying robin that twittered outside her window every morning. But then she shifted and mud slurped at her body. As she coughed, her head felt like it was caught in a vise. Her skin felt raw and exposed, strung together only by cuts and bruises.

Island. She was on the island. God...no...

Still on the island.

A ragged dread prickled over her, chills raising the hairs on her arms. She turned her head to the side, and there she saw him. Louis...or what used to be Louis.

Under a patch of sunlight that had taken over the storm, his shirt was drenched with water and blood. His mouth was cut to resemble jagged teeth, like a shark's. Withered little flaps of skin dripping blood.

Kat moaned and held back a heave of nausea. Chris. She'd seen him killing Louis. Where was he now...?

In answer, she heard someone breathing—crying—on the other side of her.

Slowly, she turned her head, wincing, sight half-shrouded by pain and fear.

When she saw him, shock, white and burning, lit through her head, her body. Her throat closed with grieving denial.

He was watching Kat, eyes like two reddened wounds, torn and swollen. His back was to Louis, just like with Duffy and Alexandra, when their bodies had been discovered.

A child in so many ways, his hands were wrapped around his knees as he rocked back and forth, the vulnerable innocent Kat had protected all this time.

Then her eyes lingered on his hands, watered-down blood staining the skin and the darker tips of his fingernails. They held the diving knife.

Not a child. A killer. A sick murderer.

She opened her mouth to...scream?...but all that came out was a twisted groan of incomprehension.

"Kat?" he asked, voice wobbly, unsteady as the graph of an earthquake. There were crimson splatters on his face and neck, his dark shirt hiding God knows how many other badges of murder. "I really didn't mean to hurt you."

It took a few seconds for her to get it together, to

understand what he meant. But even after some deep, sustaining breaths, she sounded broken.

"Then why did you lure me here, Chris?" she was finally able to say, but not in anything more than a tremored whisper.

He tilted his head and a tear squiggled down his cheek. He looked somehow betrayed. "Lured? I *had* to tie him up. I wanted Uncle Louis to be quiet, but he kept screaming." Chris forcefully gestured at Louis with the knife. "He wasn't hearing me out, so…"

A quick, upset slicing motion illustrated the gruesome point.

Her veins turned to rubber. Questions were pushing at her head, straining against her skull. Would she have the chance to ask them? Or was she next?

Dammit, she had to get ahold of herself before he flew into another fit. She had to think rationally even while her head was fuzzy. *Calm down.* Most important, she had to admit that this was real, that the bloody diving knife that had gone missing the first day was actually in Chris's fist, taunting her with its horrible reality.

She had to be ready for him to strike out at any second, even if he'd said he didn't mean to hurt her.

Because he already had.

And what would set Chris off again? The wrong words? The lack of words?

In her disjointed mind she saw the sweet guy she'd known. The trivia-loving Chris. The Chris who'd withstood Duffy's abuse. The Chris who was strong enough to beat Nestor in arm wrestling and break coconuts against the wall.

Kat decided to go with what was working. He seemed to be sympathetic toward her, so she'd play into that while her head cleared.

Then...what? What the hell could she do?

"Why?" she tried to ask gently, like a friend.

As he abruptly stood, he pointed the blade in the direction of the shelter, glaring at her like the answer should be obvious. "You think it was for the *money* or something?"

"No." She rushed to answer, seeing how much the mere thought was disturbing him. "I know you'd never do this for an inheritance."

He nodded, clearly relieved she understood him. His words were hurried, hateful. "Right, Kat. I had to do *something,* because they wanted to kill Gramps. I heard them planning just like Nestor said they did, and they meant every word of it, too. I was right outside the door that night, and I knew I had to help Gramps. You understand that I had to protect him, I know you do. You've been keeping him safe, too."

Rattled by his interpretation, Kat shrank back. Her protection hadn't been anywhere near the same as Chris's.

Still, his answer seemed so rational, as though he knew he was right and no one could tell him he was wrong. But maybe that's how it was in his world.

When he started to tear up again, Kat's heart thudded double-time, expecting him to lose it. Yet all he did was fidget with his weapon, screw his face up in agony and glance toward the trees and the caves. The pause seemed to soothe him, somehow, like he was thinking of Duke.

It hit her that maybe the only thing that had been gluing Chris together *was* Duke—being around him. But what would happen when Duke died of cancer? How would Chris react then?

A dry sob thrust its way out of Kat's chest as she struggled to get up. When she realized she was too dizzy to manage it, she rested, saved her strength.

Calm, she thought. Do *not* show your frustration or fear.

"I need to get back to Gramps, Kat, but I wanted to see that you were okay, too. I didn't want you to be dead…" Chris was shaking his head now, breaking into a strangled wail. But it was softer and more controlled. "They were trying to take advantage of Gramps, and he needed someone on his side. He can't take care of himself, Kat. He needs more help than ever."

"I know."

"No, you *don't!*" Chris bunched his fists and jabbed the air with the knife. "There's a *brain* tumor."

Kat's spinning world stopped.

Brain tumor? Had his cancer spread and Duke not told her? Had his meds been keeping *that* under control, too? She had no medical knowledge at all, but suddenly Duke's island decline took on new meaning: his worsening confusion and moodiness, the strange smells he'd been complaining about, his nauseating headaches.

"The Delacroixs never knew," Chris said, squeezing shut his eyes. "They didn't visit him enough to care." He opened his gaze, irises blazing with rekindled anger.

"But they could see he was getting closer and closer to dying."

Kat pressed her face against the mud, hot tears leaking into it, making her feel heavy—so heavy and unable to cope anymore.

Slash…blood…death…

Her next words were garbled by the mud at her lips. "Their faces, Chris. Just tell me…what did you do to their faces?"

With one last look toward the shelter, Chris hitched in a deep breath. It seemed to steady him. He smiled through his tears as he knelt to a reassuring pose beside her.

"It was justice, you know? Justice that they would be wearing their true selves forever. The only thing is…"

Weakly, she glanced up at him. He was a blurry, warped shape, like an image on the water's surface seen from below.

He swallowed hard and stared at the knife. A ten-year-old in a teen body. "It's impossible to look at them, with their raw faces like that. It's the scariest thing I've ever seen. When their true faces were hiding, you could kind of tell yourself that the masks weren't real. But with the cuts looking like this, you can't ignore them now. You can't lie about what these people are anymore."

"God," she said, a bewildered moan. "God, Chris." She couldn't stand to look at him anymore.

She had to get away from him. Had to get back to the caves before he decided she was a threat…or that Will was a threat…

Groaning, she tried to sit up, but her swirling head rejected her again. She fell back to the mud. Coughing, she wanted to cry and scream and run away.

"I see something in every face," Chris added softly. "Even yours."

Kat stopped moving. Chris drew a circle in the mud with his knife, embellishing it with eyes, a mouth, long hair.

"Your face," he said, "keeps changing to me."

What did he mean? Did he see evil, or…no, it wouldn't have anything to do with how she saw herself, caught between worlds of race, economics…no. This was more primal than that.

Through wide, reddened eyes, Chris was inspecting her, just like he was trying to translate what he was seeing on her features now. Terror? Heartbreak? Disgust?

Using all the strength she had left, Kat forced an understanding smile. Trying to throw him off, it was her "front," as they'd call it back home. A disguise to make the enemy think she was brave and tough, unaffected.

Even if she was broken inside.

"Your face is all blurry to me," he said.

He sniffled and unexpectedly jabbed the knife upright on the opposite side of him with sudden anger.

Kat winced.

"It's like you haven't decided who you are yet," he said. "Weird, huh?"

"Weird," Kat whispered, sucking in a breath.

The word hung in the air as Kat braced herself and

struggled to her elbows. Withstanding the headache and dizziness, she glanced around, her head turned to the second body in the undergrowth.

"I didn't mean to do *that,* either." Chris grunted, getting upset again, shooting her a lowered look like he'd disappointed a favorite teacher who used to think the world of him. "When I got up from my hiding place there, I wasn't meaning to scare you, and I didn't want to hit you, but I thought you might stick that screwdriver into me."

"Who is it?" she asked, referring to the body.

Chris started plucking at his blood-laden shirt again. "Larry."

She clenched into herself, wanting to smash something with her fists, to set the world back to its normal tilt, but she was powerless, beaten down....

But not if she bought more time, she thought. Not if she could use it to recover and take care of business.

Questions. Ask questions and act as nonthreatening as possible. It's the only way you'll regain enough strength.

She looked up at him. "What was Louis doing leaving the cave? He was more paranoid than anyone."

Chris scrubbed at his eyes in growing agitation. "I think he wanted to see where Nestor went. Uncle Louis was so messed up by then that I'll bet he wasn't thinking about anything but his *wonderful* son. He didn't even care that Nestor almost killed me." He narrowed his gaze. "See, I knew I'd have the chance to get him after Dr. Hopkins woke me up when she clobbered Captain Ashton and untied Nestor. I pretended I was still asleep, because when I get Nestor, it'll have to be alone. It's easier that way."

Chris cocked his head, watched her carefully. "You were really cutting some zzzs. I didn't think anything was going to wake *you* up. Larry had gone to the bathroom. Then Nestor and Dr. Hopkins escaped. Then, when I saw Louis crawling out of the cave, I knew it was time. I…"

He stopped and roughly cuffed at his runny nose, seeming to think for a moment.

His pause needled Kat. Something was off. But what?

"Chris?"

He stood up and looked into the bushes, yet Kat didn't sense anyone nearby. Or had Will recovered…

Exhaling, Chris whipped back to Kat. She could tell his anger was riding just below the surface and he struggled to contain it. Would getting him back to Duke help?

"I grabbed the rope Nestor had left," he said, finally abandoning his lookout.

"Why the rope?"

"Because I knew Uncle Louis'd fight. He was like that. He slapped and yelled and pulled hair…"

Chris's face grew red, and her pulse jerked.

Out of pure panic, she blurted, "It's okay. There's no chance of him doing that to you now."

Jaw tight, Chris forced out a nod. "Gramps told me that Uncle Louis only treated Duffy that way because he was disrespectful. So I was prepared to face the same treatment when I gave him trouble, too. My uncle actually took your knife with him, Kat, like that could stop…"

He swiped at his face and a new spate of tears.

"You never woke up," he continued. "I was watching my uncle with my eyes half closed. It looked like he was going to wake you up, but then he didn't. Shaw's knife was the best weapon in the cave, and he wanted it bad. He probably knew you wouldn't give it up, so he was quiet when he took it. But," Chris said, kicking at his own blade, which still stuck out of the mud, "I knocked him out to make things easier, then took Shaw's knife away and threw it into the bushes. He never got to use it on me."

Kat felt more helpless, wishing Chris had forgotten to take her screwdriver away. Still, unwilling to give in, she pushed herself up higher, until she was sitting. She reeled, fought the nausea and the coughs.

Have to get away....

"I dragged him all the way out here," Chris added, crossing his deceptively wiry arms over his chest, emphasizing how scared he was, how alone. "No one would hear us or find us out here until he apologized."

"For plotting against Duke?" she managed to ask.

"Right. He didn't say sorry though. He screamed at me and got obnoxious. I didn't like that, so I tied him up, just like I knew I'd have to." Chris raised a fist, then collected himself, glancing at the shelter again. A sigh weighed him down. "That's when Larry came and tried to stop what I had to do. I could tell he thought he could take me easy."

Larry, Kat thought, chest burning. You big, dumb, brave wannabe hero.

"Don't worry," Chris said, clearly concerned by

Kat's accidental show of sorrow. "I didn't do Larry's face. It was quick for him. Don't be all upset."

"No, no, Chris." She rested a hand on her head. "I'm…God, I'm just not feeling so hot, here. Understand?"

"Yeah. Jeez, Kat, I said I'm sorry for hurting you."

There it was again, the subtle plea for approval. Such a normal kid thing to do…but this wasn't a kid anymore.

Her Chris was gone.

He continued, face darkening with memory. "Duffy was easy. Everyone was sleeping then, too, but I heard something outside. When I looked, Duffy was coming up the slope, slipping and sliding like the gorilla he was."

Kat just tried to keep from imagining the scenario; she couldn't stand to admit that it was possible for Chris to think this way. Had he been projecting his own fears and ugliness onto Duffy's face, warping the other guy's cries for help into accusations that had made Chris angrier with each scream? She didn't dare ask.

Chris pretended he was holding his weapon again, teeth gritted. "I'd taken the diving knife. No one knew. For the animals, you know? To protect me and Gramps. But I used it on Duffy. It was like that jerk was still teasing me and holding me over the side of the boat, even after I stabbed him. Then I remembered the conversation about the masks. It felt good to shut Duffy up and get the last word… But then I had to put mud on him to hide his true face."

After a short burst of nervousness crossed his expression, he shook his fist in a flurry of pantomimed cuts, capped by an angry choke of quivering rage.

Threatened, Kat pushed herself a little higher up, muscles straining as her blood ran fast and cold.

"After that," Chris said, coming to a sudden, sharp stop, his shaking hands useless, "I wanted to leave the shelter so bad. Just looking at that family's faces was scaring me. That's when I asked you to take us to the captain's place."

Duke. This was going to kill him. "That's where you attacked your gramps?" she ground out, overcome with sadness for her sick friend.

At Chris's widened stare, a pressurized pause, Kat prepared to defend herself, to grab the knife that was sticking out of the ground between them if she had to.

"Yeah. That's where I attacked him."

No, Chris. No.

"Why would you want to kill Duke if you were protecting him?"

His face screwed up again, and he glared at the ground. "I just wanted to frame Captain Ashton. Gramps wasn't stabbed anyplace that would kill him, all right? It didn't hurt him so much. He didn't even realize I was the one who threw the knife from across the shelter to make it seem like it came from outside. He was resting with his eyes closed so he never knew any better."

Lay off, her common sense warned. Don't push him.

As if trying to outrun the thought of hurting his grandfather, Chris absently picked at his shirt. His breathing increased in speed.

"And what came next?" she said, needing Chris to talk and give her more time to get to her feet.

He stopped his fidgeting. But that left him confused and not knowing what to do with his hands. "I lucked out with Alexandra. Everyone was running from that boar. Gramps and I found a hiding place outside where we could see the shelter. We stayed there, even after we heard the boar go into the cave tunnels. We wanted to make sure it was gone before we went back into the shelter. Alexandra wandered in first, though, and I gave Gramps the club to defend himself while I checked to see what was happening. He was so out of it that I doubt he even knew what was happening. It was the first time I was alone with Alexandra, and I asked her to apologize." Chris shoved his finger in Kat's direction, speaking through his teeth now. "I gave her a chance, but she *laughed* at me, said she had nothing to be sorry for, but I'd heard her that night when she'd said that they should put poison in one of Gramps's drinks. It was a clean way to go, she said, and that was so like her. Never mess up that pretty face, never break a nail. So I made her true, ugly face come out."

Bile stung the back of Kat's throat as she recalled the woman's mutilated features.

"I washed myself in the rain like I did with Duffy," Chris said, "then I went back to Gramps. Captain Ashton found us after that. Then everyone made like he was the killer." Chris chanced a smile at Kat. "But I knew you wouldn't let the captain get hurt. You'd protect him until I could finish what I needed to."

Chris had really thought everything out. No one ever gave him enough credit, she'd told him before.

Everyone sure as hell would now.

"Tell me about Eloise," she whispered.

He continued staring at her with that hopeful smile, rushing to please her with an explanation. "After Larry fell asleep, I followed you out to the bathroom. When you started back, I held my hand over Aunt Eloise's mouth and took her away. The rain was noisy, and she wasn't very strong. She ended up apologizing to me, though." Chris paused, his words getting sharper. "But I didn't believe her—because she was always *crying* and *manipulating* everyone with her tears. She did that to Gramps a lot, being happy to see him one second, and sad the next. Then you came to look for her. And I thought you saw me, too. And when you came back to the shelter, I thought you'd call me out."

She thought about how rattled he'd been at her return, but, in truth, *everyone* had been. "How did you sneak back into the group, Chris?"

His face reddened. "I managed."

Kat waited.

He could obviously tell she wasn't happy with his answer, and he bristled. "With all the craziness, I blended back into the group, okay? Everyone was outside getting wet. I had a dark shirt to hide the blood and I used the rain to wash the rest of it from my hands."

"Okay," she said, lowering her voice to a whisper. "Just sit down and tell me what's next, all right?"

"Nestor's next."

She stiffened. The knife, she thought, keeping it in her sights. I need that knife to stop Chris, to protect him from himself this time.

The birds around kept calling to each other and the sun shone even brighter. The forest was coming alive, but, inside Kat, all the innocence had withered away.

"Chris," she said, throat stinging. She lowered her head, finally losing her bravado.

Bounding over to her in obvious relief, Chris clung to her. Just as he'd always done. "Why're you sad for them? Everything's okay."

She wanted to throw him off her. Wanted to get back the kid she'd adored. "It's not just them. I'm sad for you, too."

"Why?"

"Because when you get caught—"

He held her tighter. "I *won't*."

She detected the metallic remnant scent of blood on his neck, even through her stuffed-up nose. Or maybe she was imagining it. Her stomach seized.

"Are you going to talk to Gramps about this?" he asked, sounding cautious.

How could she *not* tell Duke? Chris was talking like he'd taken the car out for a joyride.

"Shouldn't I?" She held him to her, looking over his shoulder and eyeing the knife that was only a foot away.

Then, out of the corner of her eye, she saw something white and stealthy creeping out of the bushes.

Will. And he was holding a kitchen knife.

No, go back. Get away before Chris senses a threat, before you disturb this peace we've got going.

But he kept limping toward them, no matter how much Kat tried to signal with her eyes.

Chris drew back from her a little, his brows knitted together. "When you talk to Gramps—"

The snap of a twig echoed like a gunshot.

Going stiff, Chris flew around, eyes wide and feral. A killer again.

He dove toward the knife.

But Kat had already done the same thing.

They stared at each other, her hand covering his on the grip. Even though she'd gotten there too late, she shook her head, telling him to back off, showing him how much it tore her apart to be his enemy.

She could see his heart breaking like a wave crashing and dying to foam as he realized that she'd use that knife against him.

Kat? he seemed to be asking in his eyes. I thought you might understand. I thought you loved Duke, too.

And she did—just not in the way either of them wanted her to.

The spell was shattered when Will lunged for Chris. Dodging, the teen yanked the knife out of the mud, yelling and kicking Kat away from him, rolling over the ground.

Kat struggled to her feet. Will had cornered Chris, but the teen was too quick. Flash-fast, his blade darted up, jamming into Will's shoulder. As Will reared back, howling, the teen pulled out his own weapon, stumbling backward then turning to run.

He broke through the bushes, never even looking back at the friend he'd destroyed.

Chapter 15

Back at the caves, the unexpected waited for them.

"A ship!" Nestor the not-so-innocent said as soon as Kat helped a bleeding Will into the shelter. The last remaining Delacroix was pointing at the beach, where there really *was* a black dot on the horizon. "Look, there's a ship out there!"

For a beautiful instant, Kat's shock over what she'd been through was forgotten. *Rescue,* she thought as she and Will peered at the ocean together.

An end to all this.

But it didn't take more than a split second for reality to pull back over them.

As Kat shot Nestor a lethal glare, she eased Will to the ground. She began searching for the first aid kit, although she knew there was no antibacterial ointment left to dress his shoulder wound.

Dr. Hopkins was standing next to her bed buddy, arms crossed over her chest. The hand bandages were gone. "We're here to surrender, if that's what you want to call it."

Nestor held out his palms, like he was expecting the rope again. He didn't realize it still bound the body of Louis.

"I knew," Nestor said, "that we'd see each other on the ship anyway, so Janelle and I came back for a truce."

"Why'd you do it, *Janelle?*" Kat asked, battling a cough. "You took a big chance for a piece of ass."

Much to Kat's shock, Dr. Hopkins glanced at Nestor with something pretty damned close to affection. Kat shook her head but didn't comment. She felt the same way about Will, didn't she? But the difference was that Dr. Hopkins had trusted Nestor enough to rescue him, not tie him up.

Trying to make up for that, Kat staunched Will's bleeding, then tenderly settled him amongst the life jackets. "Janelle ended up saving your life, Nestor, so I'm going to cut to the chase because getting on your case again doesn't matter right now."

The sound of someone throwing up outside the shelter caught her attention. Duke? Is that where he'd been? Just outside?

With dread, Kat hurried toward the sound, picking up a wooden club along the way for insurance. "Will, just tell them about Chris. Then we've got to get a signal fire going."

"Wait—" Will started, but she was already gone.

So much to take care of. And Chris was out there, waiting, willing to strike at whoever got in his way.

Holding back a wave of biting sorrow, Kat found Duke on his hands and knees vomiting dark blood. His whole body was shuddering. She glanced at him for a second, taking him in. Then she backtracked and grabbed a cup of rainwater.

Just stay strong, Kat.

"Here," she said as he crashed to the ground. She got him comfortable and led the cup to his lips as best as she could with her hand injuries.

While he washed out his mouth and cleaned himself up, Kat's chest shook with coughs. She couldn't stop staring. Duke's eyes—once so warm and cheery— were like sunken holes. His skin looked like a faded newspaper left soaking in the gutter. His hands trembled, and he dropped the cup. He'd disintegrated so fast.

"So," Duke rasped. His smile shook, but it was a noble effort. He talked slowly. "Why don't…we go out on the town tonight? Me in my tux…you in a lovely dress?"

He was lucid today, if romantic, like they were back on a San Diego beach, the sunset coating the waves as they chatted and laughed together. That was before Duffy had broken her illusions about what Duke really wanted from her, before Duke had told her how he felt.

"We've got a lot to talk about," she said softly. "And I don't know how to start."

"Well, if it's a...profession of how much you adore me...I understand. No woman...could resist me in this state."

He seemed so keenly embarrassed to have Kat seeing him at his most ruined. Obviously, he had no idea about the bombshell she was about to drop on him. She even had the terrible feeling that he was expecting her to answer his own previous declaration of love.

But the old Duke steamrolled over the tension, clearly noticing how she felt. "We've gone through...hell these past couple of days...haven't we? And I just want you to know...Kat, I'm so damned proud of you."

Her heart fell.

"I'm dead serious," he added. "More than...anyone, you've stood up and faced...what's going on. You...can do anything...not that I didn't know it before—"

A bout of gagging interrupted him, and Kat rubbed his back, affectionately stroked his face. Seeing the return of the man she'd adored saddened her.

Meanwhile, the others came out of the shelter, armed with everything they had: a couple of steak knives and wooden clubs. They also carried all the dry items they had.

"Fire," Will said with a tight mouth. "And we've got the mirror to signal, too."

He looked so pale as he stumbled along, his load pressing against the knife wound. Kat wanted to carry him herself.

"The mirror from the cosmetic bag?" she asked.

Will held it up, limping away, clearly making a studied effort not to see her with Duke.

She helped the frail man to his feet, then shouldered the burden of his weight as they got behind Dr. Hopkins, who said, "We balanced the need for signals against the threat of Chris. The signals won out."

"Chris?" Duke wheezed.

Kat and Duke had already fallen behind, giving them privacy. She took a big breath, stopped their progress for a moment as she carefully stroked his face.

"Chris is the killer."

With a gape, then a cry, Duke stumbled, and Kat fought to hold him, dropping her club. He absorbed the news, denying it, saying anything to convince her she was wrong.

But they just had no time for this. No time.

She tried to drag a decrepit Duke along as she told him about catching Chris with Louis then listening to all his confessions. As she finished they reached the beach, where Nestor and Dr. Hopkins were already setting up. A pale Will rested on the sand, club all but forgotten as he applied more pressure to his wound. She settled Duke next to him and dropped down her own exhausted body, coughing.

Watching Nestor collect tinder, Kat wondered if guarding him against Chris was even in the best interests of karma. He was no prime example of humanity, with his plots against Duke. She even resented that he'd put them in this danger.

Peering around, she shuddered, feeling Chris's

eyes on them from…somewhere. Behind a tree, back at the shelter.

Hiding and biding his time.

Keeping an eye on Duke, Kat worked on catching the sun's rays in the mirror, hoping to light the scrub. It caught, and after blowing it alive, she transferred it to a stick, to the stack of wood.

"Duke?" she asked, wishing he'd unball himself, show her he was willing to survive in spite of everything.

"Yes." His voice was soft. He stared at the ocean and held his thigh where Chris had stabbed him.

Her heart bled from his loss. "Chris never meant to hurt you. That was his last wish."

Will grunted from where he was now using the mirror to SOS the approaching ship. "Yeah, I'll bet Chris has the best intentions every time he sticks a blade into someone."

Duke's face melted into an expression of pure sadness. "Chris didn't stab me. *I* put that knife in my leg."

Kat's vision exploded, everything breaking into a million pieces that could never, ever fit together again. In a haze, she rose to her feet, playing Duke's words through her mind because she must have misunderstood.

But Duke merely shriveled inward, looking like he was willing himself to finally die.

"What did you say?" Kat took a tentative step closer. "What the *hell* did you just say?"

He didn't answer. A chunk of realization crashed together in her mind. "Was Chris lying to protect you while you protected him with an alibi? Or—"

"Yes."

The fire crackled behind her, echoing her mounting fury. Ridiculously, she said, "Do you realize that Will took the fall because of what you did?"

Everyone else was starting to gather near, just as confused as Kat was.

"*Will*," Duke spat. Oddly, he sounded much stronger now. "The first thing you think of is *Will*."

Her body warmed at the truth, even while she braced against Duke's betrayal. In his face, she was seeing a pattern.

Fear opened a cold hole in her chest. Chris had been right never to look at their faces.

Duke battled to sit up, then lost. He reached a hand toward Kat, but she took an emphatic step back, unwilling to help him anymore.

Stunned, he lowered his hand, his next words ragged. "Understand...Chris is the most sensitive child you'll ever meet. He feels...profoundly...when someone hurts him or when he does it to someone in return."

Anger, horror, disbelief made her blanch.

Nestor growled, then flew at Duke, teeth bared. Dr. Hopkins fought to hold him back.

"He's just an old man," she yelled.

Nestor wasn't having any of that as he resisted. Will rushed over to help.

"Chris *murdered* my family!" Nestor screamed.

Now the fire was roaring, heat licking at Kat as she held *herself* back. But what kind of threat was Duke now? She wanted to hear him confess...hear *all* of the ways he'd betrayed them.

At Nestor's outburst, Duke had reddened. "I can take care of Chris, Nestor. I always have."

The livid grandson went at Duke again, but Dr. Hopkins muttered something to him that sounded like "money." With cursing difficulty, he broke away from the doctor and Will and began pacing in the sand.

But Kat didn't stay back. No, she got to all fours, wanting Duke to look her in the eye, intimidating him.

"What do you mean you'll *take care of* Chris?"

Duke furrowed his forehead in pain, or maybe it was fruitless rage, or maybe…both. Brain tumor, she thought. And no meds to control the effects of it.

"I've…tried my best," Duke finally said, phrasing everything with disjointed deliberation. A sigh slipped out of him. "I wanted to…protect him, as much as he did me. And I did…for years and years. You have to understand…he's not a bad boy. If I tell you about him…I think you'll understand. You'll see why we can't…tell anyone what happened on this…island."

"What the—" Nestor began before Will held a finger up at the younger man, warning him to listen.

Kat's love and admiration built for him again. He was still a captain to the end.

"Chris was scarred." Duke sent them all a pleading gaze. "When he was little, he had a…nanny who started abusing him, without anyone's knowledge…for years. While Chris was alone…at home with her, she would…deprive him…of meals. Taunt him. Take pleasure in telling him 'no, you can't have this.' She did things that didn't leave marks on the outside…in a lot of instances. Sexual…physical…but she knew how to avoid getting caught."

Kat blocked out the thought of it. Bullied. Beyond bullied.

But then she dredged up the images of the victims' patterned faces. Those chased away any potential sympathy for the devil that'd taken Chris over.

Duke focused on Kat, sensing her momentary identification with his beloved grandson. "I admit…I coddled him. I felt guilty…for not seeing what was happening. My son and his wife…did the same thing. We gave Chris the world to make up for…what happened."

Nestor had picked up a stone. Staring at his grandfather, he weighed it, his gaze cold. "Coddled? Understatement. You made Chris believe that the world was his to own. You raised his dad and mom that same way, and that spread to the whole family. But, mostly, it was Chris, especially after Ephram and Christina died in that fire." Here, his voice cracked. "But we *all* felt for Chris and wanted to help him."

At the mention of the fire, Duke started retching, dark blood leaking out of his mouth. It was like the comment had wrenched him open… An ugly realization took hold of Kat.

"Chris didn't…?" she asked.

The old man spat up a little more, pain haunting his muddled eyes as he wiped at his mouth.

All she could hear was her own labored breathing. Chris's parents. The son and daughter-in-law Duke wouldn't talk about.

An impotent anger filtered over Duke's aged face.

"When Chris was ten, he had…a cat. He…" Duke grimaced. "He tied it up…'experimented.' To see if it could…take as much pain as he'd…taken from his nanny."

Nestor fell to his knees, mouth agape in horror.

A chill tore over Kat's skin. She glanced around at the trees, the bushes. Eyes seemed to be peeking out of all of them. *Never turn your back on the enemy.*

She inched closer to the old man. "More, Duke."

He'd rolled to his back, glaring at the sky, looking like he was placing blame on something other than himself or Chris. "I tried to make Ephram and Christina…understand…why he'd done it. I really did. I couldn't watch him…suffer alone. Not when I could've…stopped what happened to him with that nanny. I should've seen…what he was going through. I owed Chris so…much. But then they sent him away…to some 'behavior camp.' He couldn't stand to be away from me…so he took it out on his parents."

"*He* set their house on fire with them in it," Nestor said, palming the rock against the sand.

"I screamed, flailed around for answers…that weren't so easy to find. But I knew Chris had only done it…out of love for me. He couldn't stand…to stay away, to be told…not to see me again. How could I punish him…for that?"

Kat felt like she was dangling, about to lose her grip on what she knew of right and wrong. Twisted. She shouldn't be feeling sorry for Chris.

She hated being manipulated by this story, hated that Duke was justifying the killings. Was his judgment so bent from his disease? Or was Duke making sure that Chris could be redeemed just as he had—a man who'd messed up his own life with all the drinking and hell-raising?

Duke's carousing had contributed to his stomach cancer—a little reward he hadn't banked on. Did Duke want to give Chris the chance to avoid an ultimate punishment for *his* sins? Even though it was too late to redeem the magnitude of Chris's much worse crimes?

"We never knew." Nestor flew to his feet again, shaking the rock excitedly. "No one ever told us."

"Why should you know?" Duke groaned back, clutching his stomach. Slowly, he said, "You never visited us. And he had the best of therapy. Why do you think…the records of minors are sealed any-way…*Nestor?* So they can have a fresh start. Chris required that…and I gave it to him."

"Just like you gave him everything." Nestor's biting words abraded the air. "Like the chance to murder my family. What's it going to take for you to stop defending him? Maybe the only thing that'll work is when, one day, he goes ape-shit on *you*. Then you'll understand, Gramps. But…hell no." Nestor spiked his rock toward the approaching boat. "No way. Before that happens, I'm taking him to the cops so he can't hurt anyone else."

It was like someone had pulled a lever in Duke. He'd fully switched to the moody stranger by now, an angry man Kat didn't want to know. A man who seemed to be drawing strength from the dark pits of his soul.

"And don't cry *therapy* again," Nestor grated out. "It

didn't work before, and I'll be damned if that's all the punishment Chris gets *now*."

"He's a good boy…deep down—"

Nestor's eyes bulged. "*How* deep? There's no avoiding this. There's no covering it up. Nothing's going to bring back my family! You felt the same way after Ephram and Christina died. Losing your loved ones messed you up, Gramps. You hid from it, pretending none of it happened, but look at us now. Just look at what happened because you ignored what was really going on. If Grandma hadn't gotten sick and died, she'd—"

Duke covered his ears, writhing on the ground. Kat just watched him, crumbling. This was a man who'd lied to her, who'd known about Chris's violent tendencies.

Out of the corner of her eye she found Will watching her with stunned sympathy.

I was wrong, she thought. A bad judge of character, especially when it came to trusting Duke over you. Even if Will had trained her to mistrust him and she hadn't been strong enough to overcome those doubts.

Drained by the hatred, Kat sank back on her haunches. "Chris isn't going to stop. That's the bottom line."

Slowly, the old, beaten man raised his head, fuzzy eyes locking in on her like the sights on a gun.

She stared right back, refusing to be bullied.

Somehow, he'd thought she would understand, just like Chris had. Why? Because Kat needed his money so badly? Because he believed her affection, her *silence*, could be bought?

Her rage returned, burning out of control.

At the power of her returned glare, Duke's eyes went misty. There he was again. The man she thought had been her friend. But he was dead to her now. Unforgivably dead.

"You know Chris...suffered greatly for his...parents' deaths," Duke said, making one last obvious effort. "You know he...couldn't sleep...that even as a ten-year-old...he was suicidal." He grabbed his head and shook it. "All he wanted to do...was keep me safe. Can't you *grasp* that?"

"*You*," Kat said, rising to a stand, her breath coming harsh and fast, "are the last person to be making any damned judgments."

"How do you—" With a grunt of pain, Duke pressed his palms to his head again.

Caught between compassion and disgust, Kat turned to the group, told them what Chris had said about Duke's brain tumor, his lost medication and what effect that might be having on his mind.

"Dementia," Dr. Hopkins murmured from her quiet spot next to Nestor. "Altered perception and judgment. Maybe it was enough to turn Duke's defense of Chris into a more active shield of the kid's crimes."

Kat leveled a glance at Duke, who seemed ashamed to know that she'd been privy to the truth of his weakness. Had he withheld *this* information because he'd wanted her to think that he was in control, still strong?

Just as she was about to ask him, she stopped. The answer was obvious. Duke had wanted her to think that he'd be around long enough for them to be together—

even for just a few more weeks than he *really* had. He'd wanted to know that she felt something for him before his time was up.

Damn him, he'd just wanted to know. Like he'd wanted to know that his family loved him, too.

Manipulator. Puppet-master.

"I *am* sorry to hear about what's happening to you, Duke." Kat blew out a harsh breath. "But it went too far. You actively helped Chris with the murders, didn't you? Look at me, damn you! When you stabbed yourself, you knew that he had already killed Duffy."

Nursing his wound, Will staggered nearer, so wan he looked like he might collapse. Still, he raised his club and watched Kat for his cue to attack. The doctor stared at Duke in sheer horror. Nestor picked up a bigger rock.

Temper stoked, Kat hovered over the mentor she'd been so fond of. The mentor who'd used her.

"Chris would've needed help," she barked, "especially when it came to covering where he was. I don't know exactly what you did, but I know he would've had a hard time convincing everyone he was in the cave during Eloise's murder. Did you lie to everyone, telling them that he was there the whole time? *What did you do?*"

Duke's eyes went darker, as if a blurriness overtook them, an out-of-focus dimness like black smoke. "Yeah. I arranged…Chris's blankets so it…looked like there was a…body in them. And when Kat…started yelling and…everyone went outside…I put them back to normal. I distracted…the doctor, Larry and Louis when…

everyone ran out there. Things were…jumbled, no one was paying…attention to anything but Kat's…screams. All Chris had to do was…slide to the back of the group…as wet as the rest of us…were getting."

Kat fisted her hands, her whisper ragged with a disappointment so profound that it drained out something deep inside her. "You really *did* help him?"

Eyes watery, Duke nodded. Kat's skin drew back over her bones in cold terror.

"Actually…I was watching Chris," he said softly.

"Jesus," Will said, cocking the club.

God, Duke, she thought numbly. Good God.

A rock missed Duke's head by inches. "You deserve to die!" screeched Nestor, reduced to sobs.

Kat's hand whipped out to catch Duke by the withered throat. "Did you instruct him? *Tell me, you bastard.*"

"Yes."

Reflexively, she squeezed. Duke gagged.

"*You* were the one who realized that Will would take the heat for stabbing you. *You're* the one who demanded apologies from the victims. *You* gave him details about *The Twilight Zone.*"

"But he was…the one who thought of that." The flames from their signal fire were spearing, reflected through the darkness of Duke's eyes as he rasped out an answer. "He's the one…who saw the faces. Back on the boat…Chris told me what he'd heard…about the plotting. At that time…I knew things needed to be…set to rights, but…it was this island that gave us…the chance to do it. I wanted to…die knowing that they'd been punished. I explained…everything to Chris, and the solution…calmed him, because we both knew that this way…the family could never plot against him…once I was gone—he'd be protected. Then we carried…it out—ensuring our safety."

In tearing flashes, she imagined it all: Duke finding Duffy with Chris and demanding apologies, then guiding Chris through the kill, the artistic slicing. Chris watching Duke as the old man signaled for quiet, then stabbed his thigh. Duke standing over Chris as his pupil murdered and desecrated Alexandra.

Something evil had given him the strength to shadow Chris…something beyond mere sickness.

Kat pushed Duke away, and he coughed, holding his throat.

"And why didn't you go with Chris for Eloise?"

"My own daughter." Tears fell onto Duke's pale cheeks. "That…I couldn't bear to watch. But…he took care of what needed…to be accomplished. She would've done…the same to me, you know. She…most of all, was punished…for treating me so badly."

"And Louis?"

Duke reached up, touched a tear, seemed to take more sadness from it. "I was there, too."

Pale chills down her spine, a zing of violation.

She remembered that moment: Chris peering at the bushes—she'd thought he was just *thinking* about Duke and had been calmed.

Chris really *had* been calmed by Duke's presence because…

He had been there.

God…God…

"Duke, you baited everyone on this trip." She darted to him, grabbed the frayed collar of his tiki shirt, shaking him. "The Delacroixs, to try and see how much they loved you. Will, with the temptation of money. Even me. Why me?"

His gaze softened. "Because I wanted you."

Flames in Duke's eyes. A man who'd been taken over.

Disillusioned and broken, she walked away from Duke and, seeing the mirror she'd used to build the fire, she picked it up and heaved it against a rock. It shattered. In the shards, she imagined all her idiotic hopes, her naiveté. Her faith.

As if reminded of the mirror, Janelle scrambled over to it, picked up two pieces, then flashed them toward the distant boat. But she kept them in her sights.

"Gramps," Nestor said, crawling over, looking lost, confused, even after the explanations of all the ugliness. "Tell me it's just your head. Please? God, tell me you wouldn't have encouraged Chris this time if you weren't so sick."

Duke looked at the sky again, searching for an answer. But Janelle had already said it: He'd hidden Chris's crimes before, but it'd taken this extra perception-mangling push to make him do more than just damage control.

Still, the seeds had been planted long ago. Dementia or not, he was just as guilty as Chris.

Kat let out a primal yell and punched the sand, wishing it was Duke instead. Her hands throbbed, her head pounded.

"*Guys*." It was Dr. Hopkins. Frenzied, she was pointing toward a cliff, mirrors still in her hands.

Chris was there, watching them. As he held the knife by his side, the sun glinted off the blade.

Kat's stomach tumbled.

"We've got to kill him before he kills us, especially because he'll want Duke back," Nestor screeched.

With a choke of rage, Duke shifted violently. Will weakly stretched the club out, holding it in front of Duke's face. Nestor took up the slack, holding his grandfather down.

Kat's pulse picked up speed. Kill Chris. A boy. A misfit, just like her, who'd gone more than wrong.

Her heart resigned to what needed to be done, she glanced at Duke.

She'd tried so hard to be close to Duke. It hurt to admit that she'd been fooled, deluded.

"Nestor's right," Will said, slumping on the sand, hand to his shoulder wound. "If we leave Chris alive, we'll regret it."

Dr. Hopkins shook her head. "Just look at our fire, would you? There's black smoke going up and a ship coming our way. A plane should be here soon and they'll see our signs. If we've got the materials, I say we restrain him. It worked for the other supposed killers."

At the reminder, Will shot a lowered glance at Kat, and she knew she was still going to answer for her misjudgment of him later. And she wouldn't care, because "later" would mean they were both alive.

I'll kill Chris if I have to, she thought, the decision bitter, foreign…disturbingly necessary.

Will held her stare, then nodded. There was something in his eyes…respect because he saw that she was ready to face the danger?

"Kat!"

She glanced at Dr. Hopkins, who was staring at the cliff where Chris had been standing.

He was gone.

Kat pushed away all emotion, all the rage that was still dragging her down. She had to.

"Doctor, we need to find some restraints right away if you want to use them, or else we'll have no choice but to do the worst," she declared, ice-cold and frosted for a fight.

They rapidly prepared with stoic determination: After restraining Duke, Dr. Hopkins and Nestor cut strips of canvas from a couple of handy jackets in anticipation of binding Chris. In the meantime, Kat positioned all their debris around the older man, half hoping to block the immediate sight of him from Chris, just in case the boy got close enough to see his grandfather a captive. Even though Chris had most likely spied them violently arguing here on the beach, the sight of a restrained Duke would probably act as a trigger to the teen's ire and that would only compound their problems.

Then they armed themselves, even though Kat knew she'd have to be the one to confront Chris first.

All the while, she kept checking the boat. It was getting closer. Closer. But still much too far.

Skin prickling the back of her neck, she turned away from the water, fixing a glance on the cliff where Chris had disappeared. Next to her, Will grunted from his prone position on the sand. She looked down to find him struggling up as he went for his wooden club.

"What do you think you're doing?" she asked.

Pale and obviously drained, he fell forward before he got to the weapon, his arms trembling as he tried to hold himself up. God knew how much blood he'd lost.

"Listen," Kat said as she guided him back to a seated position. "This isn't your time to fight. You've got to stay here with Duke and take care of the fire. You've got to keep flashing those mirrors at the boat."

By this time, Janelle and Nestor had come over.

"I'm not—" Will started.

"Oh, yeah, you will, because we don't have time to argue." Kat glanced at the other two. "This is how it's happening—I'm intercepting Chris first. If anyone's gonna talk him down for restraining, it's me." She remembered his wounded expression when she'd gone for the knife back at that clearing and hoped he'd listen to her. "Maybe when he sees we're near to being rescued, he'll come to his senses."

Will opened his mouth but Kat interrupted.

"Not now, Will. I'm prepared if he doesn't listen." She touched the kitchen knife in her back pocket. "Nestor, you need to make yourself almost invisible— maybe go back by Duke. Chris will be headed here anyway to protect his granddad. If Chris gives me any trouble..." Kat blew out a breath. "That's when you guys freakin' know he's not ever going to be restrained and you get your asses near me to help. Got it?"

Nestor was already shaking his head. "You're sacrificing yourself—"

Janelle cut him off. "Just do it, Nes! We agreed restraint will work."

"You agreed to that, not me." Nestor's skin was rage-red.

No time for this! "Nestor, if Chris sees you and maybe even your girlfriend up close at first, he'll go ballistic. Game over. This way, at least we have a chance of keeping him calm. And Will's in no position to fight, so he stays here—"

She didn't have time to finish, because that's when they saw Chris.

He was a couple hundred yards away, sliding down an embankment, back to them.

"Make yourselves scarce before he turns around!" Kat whispered harshly to Janelle and Nestor.

Weapons in hand, they took off to a spot near Duke, barely making it before Chris landed and slowly swiveled around to face them. His arms curved by his sides, the knife flashing.

Kat's thundering blood canceled out everything else: a sudden cough, the rush of her movements as she grabbed some binding and stuffed it into her shorts at the waistband, Duke's gagged yells before Nestor and Janelle shut him up.

She picked up a small but heavy piece of wood. Good enough for some head knocking, if needed.

With one final glance back at the devastated Will,

Kat nodded. "Wish me luck." And she turned back around, striding forward as Chris began slinking toward her.

Chapter 16

Chris stalked toward Kat, slashing the knife through the air with each jerky step. Heart rate picking up, Kat prayed they could get him under control.

One hundred yards away.

"We were worried about you," she yelled.

Chris didn't answer, just kept advancing, eyes blank as he fixed on the camp behind her.

Fifty yards away.

Restraints? *Were* restraints going to work on this boy, who'd turned into a *thing?*

"Chris, you see the rescue boat?" She was trying hard to keep her voice level. "This could be all over—all the pain—if you'd just stop right now."

Forty yards away.

On edge, Kat reached behind her and laid her fingers on the kitchen knife in her back pocket. Her other hand tightened around the knob of heavy wood.

"Stop, Chris."

Jerking his empty gaze back to her, he faltered to a halt.

It'd been a warning shot. There'd been so many times in her life when she'd needed to fend off bullies with mere words that she was good at it. It didn't always work—you had to be ready to put up or shut up—but sometimes a miracle happened. Even when things looked bad, really bad.

Taking a step forward, Kat thought that maybe the front was working.

But he only gripped his knife harder and charged forward again, gaze burning into her.

Thirty yards away.

She gripped her knife, too. Ready.

"We can talk without the knife." Kat's throat was so dry she barely got the words out. "Remember how it used to be, Chris? You'd tell me about sharks or diving or whatever you were studying in school."

He halted again, then cocked his head. Something flickered in his eyes. Memory?

Her blood was a wild drumbeat. "Drop that knife, Chris."

He inspected the blade, like he was seeing himself in the shine of it. What was reflecting back at him? What kind of patterns did his own face make?

When he looked up again, his eyes were back to the shudder-inducing emptiness that made her start sliding out her knife.

"Where's Nestor?" he asked.

A tiny black bomb exploded in her stomach. "Chris, you don't want to come nearer to me."

"And where's Gramps?" His knuckles went white around the knife's grip.

"Duke's safe. Put the knife down and I'll take you to him." Yeah, if she could knock him out with the wood and restrain him.

Or maybe the knife was her best option now.

"You're lying," Chris screeched abruptly. Then he calmed a little, his voice still agitated. "He's still by the fire. Did you kill him?"

"I told you, no. Put your knife down and everything will be okay, Chris. Come on."

His face scrunched, his hand quaking and whisking the blade against his leg.

"I'm sorry, Kat, but you need to give him to me. This is justice. It's the way the world should work."

Hell, no, she thought.

A beat passed, one in which neither of them flinched. Then, suddenly, his eyes widened, and he darted forward, clearly intending to bypass Kat to get to Duke.

Maybe she should've let him get by her, then allowed the entire group to gang up on him. But a burst of adrenaline destroyed all common sense, and she whipped out her own knife while raising her other hand to bring the block of wood down on the back of his skull.

But she missed.

With a nauseating thud, she caught his cheek instead.

The contact brought him to the ground, his knife flying out of his grip. Huddling into himself, he touched his face. It came away dampened by blood.

Slowly, he raised a shattered gaze to her.

All Kat could do was brandish her weapons at him. He wouldn't get to her, no, never again.

He obviously sensed that, his face tightening into a betrayed scowl.

"I'm gonna kill him first," he rasped. "Captain Ashton. I'm going to carve him up like—"

Rage exploded in her chest, making her cry out as she dropped the wooden block and raised her knife.

Not again. She wouldn't have Will taken away again—

Sucking in a horrified breath, he exploded out of the sand and took off toward the stand of trees to their right. Without thinking, she sprinted after him, not knowing what she was going to do when she caught up—only knowing that he couldn't get away this time.

Janelle and Nestor, she thought, arms pumping as she gave chase, where are you? Hurry!

Her lungs squeezed together, rattling, and every bone seemed to be chafing the underside of her sore skin. Her head pounded in time to her heart, making her dizzy. But she was too determined. Too frightened to fail.

Janelle…Nestor…?

Kat closed the gap, straining with each stride. Even with the damp ground, he was fast, but she was, too, honed by surfing and diving. She was still an athlete, injured or not.

She pulled to within two feet away. *Last chance*.

With a burst of strength, she rocketed to Chris's side, then angled her body to slide into him.

Bam! He spilled to his knees, tumbling over the ground, coating his body with mud.

The trees cleared a little to reveal a drop off to a cove of water below. As that low cliff loomed in front of her, Kat tried to skid to a stop, but she had too much momentum. She tripped, lost her knife and ate mud. But in a flash she was on her knees. Tracking Chris, her back to the cliff's edge, she fought a cough that was jiggering her lungs and reminding her of her weakened condition.

He was holding his ribs, hunched over, panting, mud caked over him. A look of wounded puzzlement marred a face that had once seemed so innocent.

"Do you hate me, Kat?" he asked desperately.

She was blindsided by the genuineness of the question. Damn her.

Barely able to get the words past her wheezing, she said, "I don't hate *you*, I hate what you've *done*. I'm trying really hard to remember the old Chris. That's the guy I want with me right now."

"I can be the same person." His lower lip trembled. "I'm still the same Chris."

God, she wanted so badly to believe him. It was painfully tempting to give in to him and pretend that none of this had ever happened. All she wanted was to go back to normal.

But the Kat who'd seen the cut faces, the Kat who'd had to outrun fear through the trees and the darkness couldn't put faith in any of the boy's words. She'd made so many terrible decisions about trust in the past that she just didn't believe in her instinctive judgment anymore. And for damned good reason. Shaken back to reality, she thought of Will for a second.

Careful, she thought. One wrong word...

"You can still be the Chris I used to know," she said, voice thick, "if you give up and let me restrain you until the rescuers get here."

At first, the boy looked puzzled. But then he realized Kat wasn't going to give in to him, just as Duke had predicted. His fists bunched. A muscle started to tick in his tightened jaw.

When he exploded, the last of Kat's hope died.

But she reacted out of gut instinct, crouching over, hands in front of her, head lowered. When he came, she took him low, intending to lever his legs out from under him.

But that deceptive, wiry strength of his threw her off balance. He bowled her over, and they both rolled backward.

Before she could feel the earth disappear from under her feet, they were in the air, flying. Then, with a smack, liquid enveloped them and Kat's mouth filled with the salty rush. Downward, through the blue, and they soon hit sand. About five feet of water pressed down on her.

For a blessed moment, her ocean welcomed her back. Its blue serenity wrapping around her, it kissed her skin with sharp passion and comfort. But then, just as quickly, the fear, the darkness, rushed over her.

The danger.

That's when Chris pinned her with his body, hands squeezing her neck.

Escape...pushing at him. Get...me...out...

Shoving up one palm through the water, she caught Chris in the face, pushing him away, then surged upward to break the surface. She choked and gasped, her body screaming with the agony of open wounds burned by salt.

Air...air...

She heaved it in like there was nothing else that would fill her up. But when Chris crashed up out of the water, too, she knew she would have to act fast.

Sucking in a lungful, she swung back her arm at him.

But Chris used the arm as leverage, bobbing upward and driving down on her shoulders to force her under. She'd anticipated the move and countered by quickly catching him in the chin with her elbow. Using her momentum, she turned the rest of the way, coming to brace her feet against his chest then pushed away to escape. But he grabbed her hair, yanking her back under with him.

She had no idea how much air was still in her lungs, but it wasn't much. Not when bubbles were escaping her mouth with each combat movement.

Live, she thought, do *anything* to live.

His arms flailed, trying to get a grip on her. She wiggled around, using the water she loved, twirling through it like a slippery mermaid.

Inches away from the surface, and he caught her ankle just as she wrenched free. A sphere of treasured oxygen blurbed out of her. Kat watched it pop to the waterline, where the sun wavered out of reach.

He pulled her shoulders down, planting his shoes on her shoulders now to staple her to the sand.

Kat grabbed at his legs, scratched at them.

But it wasn't doing any good.

Out of control, she opened her mouth to scream, her body craving a breath it wouldn't get. As she stared at the surface, water invaded her mouth, her throat…

And then she went cold, the fear winning out, the wet sky crying for her. The memory she'd bravely fought for so long claiming her and triumphing in this final battle.

She was nine years old again, held under by the pulsing fingers of that tide. Waves combed over a surface that seemed a million miles away. But any second, her dad would be here. He'd grab her from the water and rush her to the shore and save her.

Any second now…

Time ticked by, each instant forever etched in every shimmer of sunlight through water—water that had once seemed like a second skin…a skin now being torn off. Water had been her temple, her everything, but now it was crumbling around her, into her, and singing in victory. Finally beating her.

Dad, where are you? she thought. Why aren't you here to help me?

But then she saw him. His dark eyes, his short hair, his browned skin. He was standing above her, his arms reaching down to save her in painfully slow motion.

And just as Kat anticipated being lifted to safety, he stopped, stared.

It wasn't her dad anymore. It was an image of Duke.

And he was watching her die, eyes blurred from the fever that had warped him.

Darkness crept over the edges of her vision, water and Chris's hands, his feet heavy against her body...she could no longer tell... Killing her...taking everything away...

She flinched, grasping the feet on her shoulders and stamping her to the sand.

He and Duke had robbed her of everything. Life. Trust. Her ocean.

This is *mine,* Kat thought. I've battled it, damn you. I've beaten it so many times before. You can't take it away, because I've worked too hard for it.

With a final burst of fury, she ripped the ankles off her shoulders and pushed her palm upward until it connected with something soft that made Chris ball into himself and drift away from her.

Time sped back into itself, becoming the fast motions of a demented second. She shot to the surface, taking in air, kicking out with her legs to keep Chris at bay.

Breathe, kick. Breathe, kick, kick.

Her lungs were burning, but she wouldn't stop. Not even when he surfaced, too.

Breathe, kick, kick, kick.

When her mind cleared, she lunged at him, twined her arm around his neck, wrapped her legs around his middle and squeezed with all the strength she had left. Chris gagged and fought, but she was so notched with adrenaline that she burned almost superhuman now.

She squeezed more, taking a deep breath, and Chris fell below the water.

Survive, Kat thought as her ocean slipped over her again, warm and welcoming. I'm going to survive whether it kills Chris or not.

But then, as sanity returned, she realized what she was doing.

Chris's breath was a stream of rising bubbles, his arms gone limp.

She unwrapped her legs, pulled him up, and tugged him toward the shore with an arm around his collarbone.

She could move her arm a little higher…one more big squeeze around his neck…and he'd be gone.

But that was the island talking, the crazy impulsive drive to live, the mentality of someone who'd been scared witless during her time on this scrap of killing land. Putting an end to Chris wouldn't erase the murders. It wouldn't make less victims. It'd just make more killers.

Even though every street-nerve was telling her to take Chris down, the part of her that wanted to escape the island to a better life wouldn't allow it.

You've got value, Duke had told her in his clearer moments. And no matter what he was now, she believed the words.

She dragged Chris to shore a woman who'd taken back her ocean. A woman determined to take herself back, too.

It wasn't until Kat returned that she found out Janelle and Nestor had failed her.

"We thought we should stay with Duke and defend Will," Nestor had said when he and Janelle had met Kat on her way back. "It was a split-second decision."

Kat couldn't argue right now. She'd spent the last of her energy collecting the few strips of material that she'd lost during the battle with Chris and restraining the passed-out boy. But she hadn't been able to search for her knife—getting her quarry back to the fire was top priority. Luckily, all her screams had attracted Janelle and Nestor so they could relieve her of Chris-duty before she even got out of the woods, but it was too little, too late.

As they took the limp teen from her, it was all Kat could do to traipse back to the camp and collapse near Will. She'd rail at Nestor and Janelle later, after…

God. She couldn't even find it within herself to check where the boat was anymore.

Will had cuddled her head in his lap and stroked her wet hair, avoiding any questions for the time being. He knew what she needed. Peace. Just for now.

"I knew you'd do it," was all he said as they waited for their rescue.

As if to make up for deserting Kat, Dr. Hopkins had taken Chris away from the fire to separate him from Duke when the teen awakened. She crouched near him, holding a kitchen knife near his throat. But Kat wondered if she had guts enough to use it.

Meanwhile, Nestor was kept from both Duke and Chris, so as not to enrage matters. He'd taken up the mirror-flashing tasks, useful for once.

Soon, Kat felt well enough to sit up. Noticing that the fire could use some attention, she went to it, picking up the last of their dried wood, and fed the flames. It put her in direct eyesight of Duke, who made a feeble motion with his bound hands indicating that he needed a drink.

Coughing, she prepared a coconut with one sharp edge of the broken mirror and undid his gag. After he finished, he shook his head, refusing to take the canvas bit back into his mouth. Kat relented because she figured Chris was out of hearing range and couldn't be influenced by Duke anyway.

"Please," he said, "just let Chris go. Look at him. He's as peaceful…as a lamb."

"He wasn't a half hour ago." Kat coughed some more, shivering, sapped.

Again, Duke's eyes turned dark. The mean, diseased Duke. "You," he bit out. "Dammit…you break my heart."

She steeled herself, knowing that this wasn't the same man she'd first met. Or was it? Had his tumor only brought out the worst, most manipulative parts of him? How much had she *really* known about him, anyway?

A project, Duffy had said. You're just a project.

"And you damn well break my heart, too, Duke." She set the coconut on the ground.

"I'm not the one…who made a slut of myself in front of everyone with the captain."

She held up a finger in his face, shutting him up. "*You* were all hot to see if Will and I would get back together, some sick thing you had in mind—"

Duke closed his eyes, anguished. "I never wanted him to have you, Kat. I'm the one…who loved you. Would do anything for you."

Anything. She couldn't listen to him anymore. His *anything* involved murder and bribery, things she hadn't ever imagined being a part of.

She couldn't forgive him.

She glanced over at Will, who was reclining listlessly against a few life jackets. He was watching them. She smiled, but he remained stone-faced.

Was he afraid that she would discard him and ultimately give in to Duke? If that was the case, they didn't know each other very well at all.

With a crumbling blow, she wondered if they ever would.

When she looked back at the older man, she realized that he was still hoping she'd come around. And why not? This was Edward Harrington III, a powerhouse who was used to getting what he wanted. It must've been killing him to know she was the one thing he wasn't entitled to.

Maybe, if he'd stayed the man she thought he was, things would've turned out differently. She could've remained fond of the integrity she thought he'd possessed, the support he'd always given her, the love he'd shown his grandson. But all of that had been false.

All of that had washed away with the tide.

Duke's eyes got a little lighter, the hazel from their days of sunsets and surf.

"Kat...forgive me," he said thinly. "It's hard to...realize that there's only one person in the world...who loves me unconditionally. And that person...is being taken away."

"You both earned it."

"Do you know what *your* love…could've earned?"

Here it was. The manipulation she'd expected. But she could take it, no problem. She'd taken so much worse.

Kat pressed her palms together. They still stung from the salt water. "Just shut up, Duke."

Okay. Truth be told, she was afraid that, if he didn't, her very human greed might rear up again. She might see the money falling from the sky, covering her in luxury. Maybe she wouldn't be able to withstand the temptation of saying three emotionally meaningless, yet oh-so-gold words to him.

I. Love. You.

But then she realized that she'd seen greed in its worst form, and there wasn't enough freakin' money in the world. And one look at a vulnerable Will only confirmed that.

"You could've…had it all." Duke sighed, the sound of a white flag whispering in a breeze. Slowly—he seemed to be losing energy by the moment—he said, "But I understand. You've…always been too truthful and stubborn…for your own good. Yet I see you struggling…you need the money. Don't deny it. So think about this…Chris needs a defender…when we get back—"

"*Never.*" Brusquely, Kat got to her knees, looming. "I would never lie about what you and Chris did, so don't you even make an offer."

Silence. His gaze was hopeless. She'd crushed something in him.

All he'd wanted was to hear some words, Kat thought. From me…from his family.

But he'd sure as hell guaranteed that wouldn't happen.

Gradually, a tone of betrayal seethed over him, claiming him, taking the place of the brokenhearted old man. He moaned, closed his eyes…

Another headache.

Kat reached for the gag, knowing that he would react to the pain with meaningless gestures. But she was too late.

He opened those dark, clouded eyes.

"I take everything back," he said, voice low and ragged as he jerked to avoid the gag. "I feel…nothing for you, Katsu. You're just…a goddamned *mutt* who doesn't know any better—"

She backed away in horror, frozen by his slur.

"—a confused suck-up who…never gives anything back. And…after all the places…I wanted to take you…after all I did for you…"

Even though Duke was nothing to her now, her heart had stopped beating at the word *mutt* and most of his words after that weren't heard. A man who'd often said he'd valued her, who'd seen the wonderful things she was capable of and had raised her dreams above all the limitations she'd set for herself after she'd left Will…that this man could so completely try to remove all of that… It left her without air.

But she breathed anyway. He couldn't rob her of survival.

A tremble had started in her throat, but now she

knew she wasn't going to cry, not for a murderer. She wasn't going to fall down and weep because she was just now realizing that she'd been trying to force this unworthy man into the place of her father, someone who would see past all her barriers and just love her.

It was like hearing about her dad's death again and knowing that every chance to get him back had failed.

Will raised his voice, but it was still weak. Only the undercurrent of a threat revealed strength. "Don't ever talk to her like that."

Duke turned toward Will, avoiding the gag Kat was trying to put into his mouth. "How about you…Captain Ashton? I've heard you…have a yen for upward…mobility. What would it take to buy you? Five percent of…billions?"

Kat's five percent. Now he was toying with them, seeing if he could wedge them apart. With surprising strength, Duke bit her when she tried to gag him again.

"What would it take," he said, growing more agitated, "to have you…save Chris, Captain? Fifty percent? No one back on…the mainland would have to know…what happened here—"

Too late for a gag. Kat looked over at Will to see him hesitate in an answer that should've been instant. She saw it in his eyes. He craved that money.

There, in the eternal tide of one moment, was the beginning of it: all Will's fantasies coming true. Reclaiming his family's name. Feeling like a true man because he'd become *somebody*.

God, it was happening again. Kat was drowning in suspicions, lost in his hesitation. Her power—her ocean—was slipping away, its flow cut by this one, all-important pause.

A replay of that night, his shock and regret at the pregnancy, all the things he'd denied later.

All the things she'd seen go through his naked gaze. She recognized them so well because she'd felt them, too.

The fear was back. The doubts. The underwater threat that had almost killed her earlier.

She glanced away, unable to watch, unable to swim in the depths of suspicion that were covering her and pinning her under. Even if he really did love her, he'd never gotten over his thirst for redeeming himself—his hunger for the money that promised to save him.

"Cram your offer," she heard him say to Duke in a rough, embattled voice. "And don't ask again."

It should've lifted her up, relieved her, but when she looked at him again, she was crushed, unguarded in the wake of the silent truth.

Now, in his eyes, all she found was hurt, because he knew exactly what she was thinking. That she'd gone right back to suspecting him of the worst.

"Kat…?" He sounded like he'd lost everything.

With sudden clarity, she realized that Will hadn't been the reason they'd broken up in the first place. It'd been *her.* She'd been the producer *and* victim of doubts, creating and succumbing to them, running away from them as she invited them along.

But that also meant that *she* had the power to save herself again. She wasn't at the mercy of his hesitations, real or imagined.

Not anymore.

She *could* finally take herself back.

During Will's pause, Duke had grown increasingly frustrated. A vein was pulsing in his temple.

"Duke, calm down," she said. "Don't—"

"Please!" He raged against his bonds. "Help Chris! He's…a good boy! Please let me—"

He choked to a stop, eyes bugging out, face the color of embers.

"Duke?" She flung the blanket off him. "Duke!"

Will began to crawl over.

Kat's first instinct was to start CPR, but then she hesitated. Duffy, Alexandra, Eloise, Louis. It was like they were keeping Kat's hands tied…

But who was she to watch him die? How could she just sit here…?

Remembering herself, she pressed her palms to his chest.

But it was already over. His breathing whistled in his throat, his face a mask of surprise and denial. Tears gathered in his hazel eyes as he gazed at Kat.

His mouth wrenched as he tried to talk.

She bent down in time to hear him speak.

But the words dissipated like spray, misting away before she could grasp them.

No matter how hard she tried to fight it, sadness attacked her, breaking her down to the girl she'd been before she came to the island. The girl who'd sincerely adored this man who'd wanted to help her. The girl who'd been played for such a fool.

Looking at him, she saw her father, the man who

hadn't even been able to afford a funeral for her to weep at. The man she'd lost touch with—the man she'd just plain lost.

As Duke's eyes sheened over with stillness, Kat didn't say a word. No *I love you*. No deathbed forgiveness. She hoped he was seeing all the faces she herself would picture during all the midnight hours to come: all the death masks that would haunt her.

Numb, she joined Will, who'd moved by the fire. She felt cold with every loss suffered on this island.

Over the flames, Will gazed at her. She saw his heart in his eyes, destroyed by the reawakened doubts both of them were having about each other.

Swallowed by grief, Kat was afraid to jump into him again, afraid she might drown in the alien liquid-blue of doubt.

And, soon, when the rescue helicopter roared overhead, Kat tried to be happy. But one thing kept her moored.

The suspicion that she and Will were floating on an ocean that she wasn't sure she could beat this time.

Epilogue

On board the Coast Guard cutter, Kat closed her eyes against the pale walls of the sick bay and rested her head against her pillow, giving in to the meds that were supposed to make her feel better. An IV poked out of her arm—the better to fight pneumonia with, the health service technician had told her.

But what was going to chase away those faces—the masks, the patterns—from her mind?

Pushing the images away, she opened her eyes again, turning her head to the side and training her gaze on the curtain that separated her from the rest of the room. She told herself everything would be okay: her roommate, Tracy, had already been contacted. Her best friend, the closest thing that Kat had to family, was waiting for her in San Diego, and she'd probably fuss over Kat endlessly.

Yeah, everything was fine now, she kept telling herself. Nestor was in isolation, and the ship's commanding officer had promised that he, himself, would see that the last Delacroix would be delivered ashore to face the music for his attempted shark-cage murder of Chris. Dr. Janelle Hopkins had been separated from everyone else, too, seeing as the CO considered her association with Nestor suspect. And, of course, Chris was under strict watch.

Yet present circumstances weren't what was really bothering Kat. Part of her feared that Chris and Duke might somehow get away with murder, that their crimes would be kept under wraps because of the Harrington legacy.

But she was going to do everything in her power to make sure that didn't happen. For the sake of everyone who'd died. For the sake of anyone who might get hurt by Chris in the future.

A cough welled up in her chest, as tight as her heart felt whenever she started to think about what was weighing her down the most.

Will.

She lay there some more, trying to imagine the ship slicing its way though the ocean back home, to a place where terror wouldn't hide behind the dark of a storm only to be lit by jags of lightning.

Just as she was forcing away the unsettling memories again, she heard the separating curtain open with the scrape of metal rings against the bar. With a start, she faced the intruder.

Her heart clutched, adrenaline racing as she took in Will's pale skin, the shaded red beneath his eyes, the sling that assuaged his wounded arm and shoulder. She'd been told that they'd patched him up and he'd been instructed to rest until they arrived in port.

He'd never been great at following orders, though.

"Hi," he said quietly.

Kat chanced a smile, too overcome to speak.

Almost shyly, he gestured to a chair at the end of her bed. She nodded, and he collapsed into it, just like he'd spent his last ounce of energy making his way over to her.

For a moment, he didn't say anything, just fixed his gaze on her. A soft, apologetic gaze.

"You doing okay?" he asked.

"Mmm." She worked up some saliva to talk. "Better."

"Good. I'm..." He trailed off, swallowing hard.

All the agony of the last time they'd talked, on the beach before Search and Rescue detected them, came rushing back. A lump jammed in her throat, making her eyes sting.

"You hear what the CO said?" Will continued, glancing at the floor instead of her, making small talk to ease their discomfort with each other.

"No." A whisper. It hurt.

"Freak storm." A slight smile touched his lips as he continued his assessment of the floor. "That's what started all this. They're researching what happened, and I know they're chomping at the bit to ask me a million questions—"

"Will?"

He finally looked at her, light illuminating the blue-green of his eyes.

A deep haven colored by the fear of what was keeping them apart. But there was something like hope there also. Wasn't there?

He's waiting for you, she thought. Waiting for you to test his temperature to see if it's okay to go all the way in.

But all her safety alarms went off, buzzing with the questions she'd always had about Will, suspicions, barriers.

Dammit, wasn't she strong enough to survive anything now? What was stopping her from taking this one little chance when it was nothing compared to all the others she'd endured?

The tightness in her throat ached. Making the first move wasn't "nothing." That's what was so scary. Taking another risk on Will was everything right now, especially after she'd lost so much.

Hadn't she made just as many mistakes, hesitations as Will? Hadn't *she* paused after Duke had offered her money to confess her love?

Yeah, she had. God, yeah. Neither of them was perfect.

At the foot of her bed, Will's eyes shone under a glassy surface, steeped with emotion. And Kat took a deep, deep breath, finally ready to plunge in.

To dive toward him, ready for whatever the unknown would bring.

* * * * *

Run, Ally! Don't be fooled by him. He's evil. Don't let him touch you!

But as the forbidding figure came through the mists toward her, Ally knew she couldn't run. His features burned with dark malevolence, and his physical domination of everything around him seemed to hold her like a net.

She'd heard the tales. She knew all about the Wolverton legend and the ghost that haunted The Willows, an elegant old mansion lost by Micha Wolverton nearly a hundred years ago. According to folklore, the estate was stolen from the Wolvertons, and Micha was killed, trying to reclaim it. His dying vow was to be reunited with the spirit of his beloved wife, who'd taken her life for reasons no one would speak of, except in whispers.

But Ally had never put much stock in the fantasy. She didn't believe in ghosts.

Until now—

She still didn't understand what was happening. The figure had materialized out of the mist that lay thick on the damp cemetery soil. A cool breeze and silvery moonlight had played against the ancient stone of the crypts surrounding her, until they joined the mist, causing his body to thicken and solidify right before her eyes. That was when she realized she'd seen this man before. Or thought she had, at least.

His face was familiar. . . so familiar, yet she couldn't put it together. Not with him looming so near. She stepped back as he approached.

"Don't be afraid," he said. His voice wasn't what she expected. It didn't sound as if it were coming from beyond the grave. It was deep and sensual. Commanding.

"Who are you?" she managed.

"You should know. You summoned me."

"No, I didn't." She had no idea what he was talking about. Two minutes ago, she'd been crouching behind a moss-covered crypt, spying on the mansion that had once been The Willows, but was now Club Casablanca. And then this—

If he was Micha, he might be angry that she was trespassing on his property. "I'll go," she said. "I won't come back. I promise."

"You're not going anywhere."

Words snagged in her throat. "Wh-why not? What do you want?"

"If I wanted something, Ally, I'd take it. This is about need."

His words resonated as he moved within inches of her. She tried to back away, but her feet were useless. "And you need something from me?"

"Good guess." His tone burned with irony. "I need lips, soft and surrendered, a body limp with desire."

"My lips, my bod—?"

"Only yours."

"Why? Why me?" This couldn't be Micha. He didn't want any woman but Rose. He'd died trying to get back to her.

"Because you want that, too," he said.

Wanted what? A ghost of her own? She'd always found the legend impossibly romantic, but how could he have known that? How could he know anything about her? Besides, she'd sworn off inappropriate men, and what could be more inappropriate than a ghost? She shook her head again, still not willing to admit the truth. But her heart wouldn't play along. It clattered inside her chest. The mere thought of his kiss, his touch, terrified her. This wildness, it was fear, wasn't it?

When his fingertips touched her cheek, she flinched, expecting his flesh to be cold, lifeless. It was anything but that. His skin was smooth and hot, gentle, yet demanding. And while his dark brown eyes were filled with mystery and wonder, there was a sensitivity about them that threatened to disarm her if she looked too deeply.

"These lips are mine," he said, as if stating a universal fact that she was helpless to avoid. In truth, it was just that. She couldn't stop him.

And she didn't want to.

Find out how the story unfolds in...
DECADENT
by
New York Times *bestselling author*
Suzanne Forster.
On sale November 2006.

Harlequin Blaze—*Your ultimate*
destination for red-hot reads.
With six titles every month, you'll never guess
what you'll discover under the covers...

nocturne™

HER BLOOD WAS POISON TO HIM...

MICHELE HAUF

FROM THE DARK

Michael is a man with a secret. He's a vampire
struggling to fight the darkness of his nature.
It looks like a losing battle—until he meets
Jane, the only woman who can understand his
conflicted nature. And the only woman who can
destroy him—through love.

On sale November 2006.

nocturne™

Save $1.⁰⁰ off

your purchase of any Silhouette® Nocturne™ novel.

Receive $1.00 off
any Silhouette® Nocturne™ novel.

Available wherever books are sold, including most bookstores, supermarkets, drugstores and discount stores.

Coupon expires December 1, 2006. Redeemable at participating retail outlets in the U.S. only. Limit one coupon per customer.

RETAILER: Harlequin Enterprises Ltd. will pay the face value of this coupon plus 8¢ if submitted by the customer for this specified product only. Any other use constitutes fraud. Coupon is nonassignable. Void if taxed, prohibited or restricted by law. Void if copied. Consumer must pay for any government taxes. Mail to Harlequin Enterprises Ltd., P.O. Box 880478, El Paso, TX 88588-0478, U.S.A. Cash value 1/100 cents. Limit one coupon per customer. Valid in the U.S. only.

5 65373 00076 2   (8100) 0 11265

SNCOUPUS

Save $1.⁰⁰ off

your purchase of any
Silhouette® Nocturne™ novel.

Receive $1.00 off

any Silhouette® Nocturne™ novel.

**Available wherever books are sold, including most
bookstores, supermarkets, drugstores and discount stores.**

Coupon expires December 1, 2006. Redeemable at participating
retail outlets in Canada only. Limit one coupon per customer.

RETAILER: Harlequin Enterprises Limited will pay the face value of this coupon
plus 10.25 cents if submitted by the customer for this specified product only. Any
other use constitutes fraud. Coupon is nonassignable. Void if taxed, prohibited or
restricted by law. Consumer must pay any government taxes. Mail to Harlequin
Enterprises Ltd., P.O. Box 3000, Saint John, New Brunswick E2L 4L3, Canada. Limit
one coupon per customer. Valid in Canada only.

52607136

SNCOUPCDN

TAKE 'EM FREE!

2 FREE ACTION-PACKED NOVELS PLUS 2 FREE GIFTS!

Strong. Sexy. Suspenseful.

SBOMB06

COMING NEXT MONTH

#113 VAMPAHOLIC—Harper Allen
Darkheart & Crosse

Carefree, cosmo-sipping triplet Kat Crosse hadn't been herself lately. Was she turning into a vampire as her father had before her? Vampire hunter Jack Rawls thought so, but couldn't bring himself to kill this beautiful woman…yet. Instead, Kat teamed up with Jack to stop the forces of darkness before they claimed her as their own.

#114 HIDDEN SANCTUARY—Sharron McClellan
The Madonna Key

Being able to locate the earth's hidden mineral energies had served oil field geologist Tru Palmer well in her career. But when her dowsing gift led her to a set of medieval tiles radiating an unknown force, Tru discovered her own mystical connection to a legacy of powerful women in France—a connection that just might get her killed.…

#115 A SERPENT IN TURQUOISE—Peggy Nicholson
The Bone Hunters

When fossil hunter Raine Ashaway teamed up with a renegade Texas archaeologist in search of lost Aztec gold, it was the chance of a lifetime. Myth linked the treasure to the fearsome Feathered Serpent—could this "god" be the undiscovered dinosaur long buzzed about by scientists? Raine was onto a big find—but with dark ritual and a ruthless killer dogging her steps, the bone hunter fast became the hunted.

#116 POSSESSED—Stephanie Doyle

For medium Cassandra Allen, channeling the dead was all in a day's work. But recently, one sinister voice from the beyond had begun to drown out all others. As a series of gruesome murders rocked her town, could Cass focus her powers to exonerate an innocent man—or would the evil spirit thwart her every attempt to find the real killer?

SBCNM1006